PREP SCHOOL
CONFIDENTIAL

PREP SCHOOL
CONFIDENTIAL

KARA TAYLOR

THOMAS DUNNE BOOKS

St. Martin's Griffin ☙ New York

THOMAS DUNNE BOOKS.
An imprint of St. Martin's Press.

PREP SCHOOL CONFIDENTIAL. Copyright © 2013 by St. Martin's Press, LLC. All rights reserved. Printed in the United States of America. For information, address St. Martin's Press, 175 Fifth Avenue, New York, N.Y. 10010.

www.thomasdunnebooks.com
www.stmartins.com

Design by Anna Gorovoy

Library of Congress Cataloging-in-Publication Data

Taylor, Kara.
  Prep school confidential / Kara Taylor. — First edition.
     pages cm
  ISBN 978-1-250-01759-8 (pbk.)
  ISBN 978-1-250-01760-4 (e-book)
  [1. Boarding schools—Fiction. 2. Schools—Fiction. 3. Murder—Fiction. 4. Conduct of life—Fiction. 5. Mystery and detective stories. 6. Youths' writings.] I. Title.
  PZ7.T21479Pre 2013
  [Fic]—dc23

                                                    2013003058

St. Martin's Griffin books may be purchased for educational, business, or promotional use. For information on bulk purchases, please contact Macmillan Corporate and Premium Sales Department at 1-800-221-7945 extension 5442 or write specialmarkets@macmillan.com.

First Edition: August 2013

10 9 8 7 6 5 4 3 2 1

For Charles Daskauskas

ACKNOWLEDGMENTS

Thank you to Anne Brewer and Brendan Deneen at Thomas Dunne Books, whose vision for this book made it come to life. Thanks for taking a chance on a writer who had barely graduated college. To Nicole Sohl and everyone else at St. Martin's Press—I appreciate all your time and enthusiasm.

To Suzie Townsend, the dream agent who became my actual agent . . . thank you for never giving up on me. And also for being my #1 fan (well, besides Brendan). I'm also indebted to Pouya Shabazian, Joanna Volpe, Danielle Barthel, and the rest of the amazing team at New Leaf Literary.

Dan Dubiecki, Lara Alameddine, and Carly Norris: you guys are amazing. Also Margaret Riley, Larry Salz, and Lucinda Moorhead.

This book never would have been completed without the support of my amazing friends Lindsey Culli, Kathy Bradey, Elizabeth Holloway, and Debra Driza. Thank you for always reading my work and talking me off cliffs when the time comes. To all of my other writer pals, you guys are the best cheerleaders anyone could ask for.

I'm lucky to have awesome friends who put up with me forgetting to return calls and occasionally refusing to leave the house. Kevin Thomas has been spectacularly patient with me for six years and counting. He's always there when I need to bounce ideas off someone, even if he's only read four books in his life . . . including mine.

I have to thank Ellen Hoffman and Joe Folks, who are living proof that teachers change lives.

And last but not least, my family. There are a lot of you, and you've all humored me if not encouraged this hobby of mine. Mom, although it's embarrassing, it's also cute when you tell anyone who will listen that I'm a writer. And last but not least, to my dad, who used to tell me I'd have a better chance of being struck by lightning than getting published.

PREP SCHOOL
CONFIDENTIAL

CHAPTER ONE

Any girl at St. Bernadette's Prep should know three things: Skirts need to be one inch above the knee only if a teacher is looking, a dab of nasal spray will make any zit less red, and the lock on Headmaster Bailey's office door can be picked with a credit card.

I know what you're thinking. Petty breaking and entering is *so* not Upper-East-Side–like behavior. But cutting chorus to make out with Martin Payne, a second-year senior, isn't Upper East Side, either, depending on whom you ask.

In my defense, the only reason Martin didn't graduate on time is that he had to take a year off for health problems. At St. Bernadette's, drug use is a "health problem," especially when your father is an alum who bought the fountain in the courtyard. And, yes, I can totally do better than Martin, as Ms. Cavanaugh pointed out when she caught me in the auditorium lighting booth with his hand up my sweater.

So, yeah. That happened. And Cavanaugh wouldn't have let me off the hook if I'd been kissing Christ reincarnated. I've been on her list since she tried to kick me out of chorus in ninth grade. Even when I'm in trouble, most teachers pretend to be mad for like five minutes and then chalk it up to my *witty charm* or *colorful personality*. Not Cavanaugh, though: My ability to talk myself out of most snafus really pisses her off.

Of course she wrote me up.

See, there's no detention at St. Bernadette's. Instead, at the end of the day, teachers write up reports of any *incidents* and send them up to Bailey, who decides what to do with the offenders the next morning.

I'm thinking Cavanaugh made a suggestion or two about what Bailey should do with me and Martin.

Normally, I wouldn't care about being called to Bailey's office. It happens so often, I'm considering buying up real estate there. Sometimes she and I have coffee while we chat about my latest escapades. Not a big deal.

Problem is, there's a chance that Bails will call my parents.

My parents are not on Team Martin Payne. In fact, my father hates the whole Payne family. According to him, they're everything that's wrong with old money. Not like my dad would know: He was the first on his side of the family to go to college. Harvard Law, in case you were wondering. As far as my parents are concerned, Martin has never had his hands near a non-PG part of my body, and I need to keep it that way.

Even if it means hanging out in a janitor's closet until everyone goes home so I can sneak into Bailey's office and steal the report before she reads it.

When I see the motion-activated lights in the hallway flicker off, I know everyone is gone for the day. I draw in a breath and count to sixty. Probably, I should cut my losses and go home. Not risk adding trespassing and theft to my list of offenses.

My mother's face fills my head. My mother, looking like a wounded deer who just found out her daughter got groped by a pothead.

I jiggle my foot, reapplying rosebud salve to my lips with my pinky. I've really, really got to get my hands on that report.

Oh, Martin. Totally not worth this. Why can't I stay away? I think it's partly because he wears Burt's Bees lip balm, and I'm a sucker for a guy with well-conditioned lips.

The headmaster's office is at the end of the corridor. Scratch that—it *is* the end of the corridor. Ceiling-high double oak doors swallow the entire wall, flanked by two plaques engraved with the names of previous headmasters. St. Bernadette's was built in 1912, and no one has ever thought to update the headmaster's office since then, locks included.

Wiggling my credit card—the one I don't use much—between the lock and bolt is almost too easy. I throw a glance over my shoulder, although I'm confident no one else is in the building. If I do get caught, I'll make up some lame excuse about how I needed to stay after for extra help in bio and my teacher forgot about me. And I forgot to, you know, leave.

Once I've wedged enough space between the lock and the bolt, I jiggle the handle until I can push the doors open. They groan under my touch as I open them into Bailey's office. I breathe in the smell of lavender and furniture polish.

My hands are clammy. I ignore the urge to wipe them on the front of my navy Ralph Lauren sweater—which is an almost exact replica of the St. Bernadette's uniform, except for the fact it highlights all the right places instead of the wrong ones and doesn't have that tacky crest over the pocket.

There's a metal basket for incident reports right next to the stainless-steel paperweight on Bailey's desk. Bails is no-nonsense—her desk doesn't have any portraits or signs of life to suggest she's an actual person outside of school. There're three degrees mounted on the wall behind the desk—from George-town, Dartmouth, and Columbia. I told Bails she should get a bonsai tree or something to improve the chi in here, but she ignored me.

I like Bailey. I mean, she's okay. So I feel shitty about rifling through the incident reports until I find mine. (Well, not shitty enough to stop me from peeking at who else got busted today. I don't know who Alice Lin is, but apparently she plagiarized her thematic essay on *Hamlet*.)

It's not too far from the top of the pile. *Dowling, Anne. Inappropriate sexual conduct on campus.*

What?! Since when is first base "inappropriate sexual conduct"? I read on, feeling my cheeks boil at the details Cavanaugh's included. This sounds like a bad erotica novel. I could probably get her fired for writing this kind of stuff about a student.

My cheeks are still warm as I fold my and Martin's reports, slip them into my purse, and lock the office door behind me. As I double-check to make sure the corridor is clear, my phone chimes.

Martin's number is on the screen. I never save him to my contacts, because Martin should only be a temporary fix when I get bored, and locking his number feels semipermanent. I sigh at his text message: *Meet me in the auditorium.*

So much for staying away.

Some guys are like barnacles. If you stick around for too long, they'll latch on to you and suck you dry. Martin is not. Sometimes he'll go weeks without calling or texting me, and I guess that makes him a little more appealing.

There's also his hair. He's tugging at the roots of his curls when I get inside the auditorium, which is typically the only thing he knows how to do with his hands when there's not a joint in them. Martin's mother is a Jamaican model. He got her silky hair, caramel skin, and height. He got his father's douchey personality.

"Annie." He slips his arms around my waist and pulls me to him. We're behind stage right's curtains. "I didn't think you'd have the lady parts to go through with it."

I push him away with one finger. "Shut up, Martin. I don't see you attempting any damage control here."

"That's because I don't have your biting wit and good looks to get me out of trouble." He tucks my hair behind my right ear and lets his hand linger by my collarbone. I slap it away and wrap my fingers instinctively around the Juicy Couture dachshund charm on my purse. It looks just like Abby, my eight-year-old dog. Yeah, it's a bit of a wacky accessory choice, but I can get away with it.

I think of the Christmas morning Daddy gave Abby to me and my mom. He'd tied a red-and-white-striped ribbon around her neck, but she ripped it off and shredded it before my mother and I got to see it on her.

I don't know why, but thinking of that Christmas makes me want to be around Martin even less. I turn toward the backstage door.

"So I guess we're not picking up where we left off this afternoon." Martin actually looks upset.

"Like you don't have four other girls on standby today," I say.

Martin pauses, as if he's remembered something. "You got mine too, right?"

I roll my eyes and thrust his report at him. "Here."

Martin eyes it. "What am I supposed to do with that?"

"Wallpaper your loft with it. I don't care." I turn to leave.

"Anne, wait. We have to destroy these." Martin looks paranoid. I'm torn between thinking it's because of the joint he smoked earlier and buying in to his paranoia.

We can't just throw the reports out for anyone to find and see the St. Bernadette's crest at the top. And if I hide them in my room somewhere, our cleaning lady might find them.

"What do you suggest we do, then?" I wave the reports in his face. "Burn them?"

Martin's eyes light up as if this is the greatest idea *ever*.

"You've got to be kidding." I shake my head.

"It's perfect. How else are we going to destroy them without a trace?"

"Um, a paper shredder?" My voice falters when Martin whips a lighter out of God knows where.

"Can you at least do that outside?" I hiss.

"Where someone can see us?" Martin shakes his head. "Loosen up, Annie. I disabled the smoke detectors in here months ago."

My breath lodges in my throat as Martin holds a flame to the edge of his report. The paper darkens and curls. The engulfed part of the paper dies just as quickly as he lit it, and he drops the chalky gray remains into the backstage trash can.

"Won't it smell like smoke in here?" I wave my hand over the trash.

"Until Monday?" Martin raises his eyebrows and hands me my report. And the lighter.

I totally know how stupid this is. But a tiny part of my brain remembers how perfectly Martin's incident report burned up before our eyes. Without a trace.

I grab the report from him. I can't get the lighter to light. Martin laughs at me and I give him the finger. On the fourth try, a flame springs up.

At first it's exhilarating, watching the hard-copy evidence of today's tomfoolery go up in smoke. Then, when I'm aware of how close the flame is to my hand, I shriek.

And drop the paper on the floor.

"What the shit, Anne?" Martin scrambles after the paper. "You were supposed to throw it into the garbage!"

"Omigodomigod OH MY GOD!" I'm flailing my arms as the horror scene unfolds before me. The flame catches on to the stage curtains. The *extremely flammable* stage curtains.

Martin grabs my hand, but my stare is fixed on the fire crawling up the curtain.

He yanks me by the elbow. "This is the part where we get the *hell* out of here."

We push our way out of the backstage door, onto East Eighty-ninth Street. Martin drags both hands down the sides of his face. "Shit."

I lick my lips. "We need to call someone."

"And get arrested? Hell no."

My thumb hovers over the 9 for 911. I dial and Martin curses again.

As the operator asks me what my emergency is, a thought crystallizes in my mind.

I am *so* not talking my way out of this one.

CHAPTER TWO

The police officer interviewing me seems completely baffled by the fact I just admitted to setting my school on fire. He said they were lucky enough to stop the blaze from spreading past the auditorium, and also that I should stay away from the firefighters because they don't take kindly to casual arsonists.

Which I'm not. It's only arson if it's on purpose: I Googled it while I was waiting for them. I've been trying to explain this to the cop, but he keeps interrupting me. We're on the front steps of the school, beneath the St. Bernadette's arch. The FDNY has set up a blockade on the sidewalk surrounding the school.

"So you're saying you *accidentally* lit the paper on fire?"

"No, I said I accidentally lit the *curtain* on fire. With the paper." I wrap my arms around myself as a breeze sends the smell of smoke my way. Dad would probably strangle me for talking to the police without a lawyer present. Namely, him.

"Look, it wasn't *completely* my fault," I huff.

The cop massages his chin. "Is that so?"

"It wasn't even my lighter. Smoking is disgus—" Two more sirens round the corner onto Eighty-ninth Street, even though the frickin' fire is out. Now I think the FDNY is purposely trying to embarrass me. There are eight million people in this city, and I'm pretty sure at least half are gawking from every angle of the street that isn't blocked off.

"Someone was with me," I say. "Martin Payne, my, uh . . . classmate. It was his idea."

I know it looks like I'm totally throwing Martin under the bus, but that slimy little weasel ran when I called 911. He *ran*. I never run from trouble. Trouble is like a dog that wants to rip your throat out: If you stare it down, you have a better chance of saving your ass.

The officer scribbles down Martin's name as two more cops escort someone past the blockade. The handful of granola I had for lunch threatens to come up when I see that it's Dean Barrett. As in the dean of students, and, by the way, *I'm totally fucked*.

Barrett doesn't even look at me as the police lead him to the auditorium door.

"Are you cold?"

I realize that the cop is talking to me, and I'm shaking. I nod a little, trying not to disturb the lump at the back of my throat. *Anne Dowling, you do* not *cry in situations like these. You figure out how to get out of them.*

"We're going to need you to come down to headquarters," my officer informs me after another one murmurs something to him that I can't make out. "You can call your parents, and we'll figure all this out."

"Wait—you mean now?" My toes curl with panic in my flats. "Am I arrested?"

"Well, no." The officer looks uncomfortable. "But you're a minor, and this is serious, so we'll need to ask you some more questions . . . properly."

"You mean you're going to interrogate me?" I squeak. "Don't I get to call a lawyer first or something?"

The cop lowers his voice. "I'm going to have to ask you to come with my partner and me. We'll drive you to the station."

I try not to pass out with mortification as the officer escorts me to one of the many cruisers lining the streets. When he's not looking, I dial my dad's cell. It rings until I get his voice mail.

The police station is twenty blocks from the school. I keep my head bowed over in the backseat of the cruiser the whole time, just in case. When I see a News Channel 4 van head toward St. Bernadette's, I dig around in my purse for my lip salve. Putting it on always makes me feel less stressed.

It seems the fire has caused quite a bit of traffic, because it takes almost a half hour to get to the station. I follow the cops inside, past a homeless guy handcuffed to a bench, who makes kissy noises and offers to share his cell with me. The cops sit me down on a bench across from him, and I catch a whiff of what I think is pee and McDonald's.

I clear my throat. "Is there, um . . . anywhere else?"

The younger officer ignores me and sits down behind his computer. A few clicks of his keyboard later, he says, "There's a water cooler at the front desk, if you're thirsty."

"How much trouble am I in?" I blurt.

The cop leans back in his chair and folds his hands behind his head. "I'll be straight with you. I won't be surprised if the school presses charges. . . . But you say it was an accident, and if this is your first offense—"

"Sir, you need to sign in!"

"Like hell I do! They're talking to a minor without an attorney or parent present!"

My insides frost over at my father's voice.

"Anne, let's go." Dad stops in his tracks in front of my bench. His pewter-colored tie is crooked, and his briefcase is half open. His expression is homicidal.

"Mr. Dowling." The officer stands up and extends a hand. "I'm Detective Holmes."

I can't help it—I giggle a little. I mean, really, a detective named Holmes? I wonder if Watson is nearby.

Dad glares at me and accepts Holmes's handshake. "I'll be representing my daughter from this point. If you have no proof of her involvement with the fire, I'll be taking her home now."

I wince, but Detective Holmes looks confused. "With all due respect, Mr. Dowling, your daughter confessed to being on school grounds unattended after hours and gave us the name of the classmate who helped start the fire."

Dad looks at me as if I'm dumber than the bacteria on the bottom of his shoes. He's never, *ever* looked at me like that before. When the older cop shuffles back into the room, I'm thinking there's no way this could possibly get worse.

"The Payne kid is at his parents' house," he says. "We're sending an officer to talk to him."

Or not.

It's dark by the time we get home from the precinct. Dad won't look at me. He speaks once on the elevator ride from the parking garage to our building.

"Put your phone away."

"But Dad, people are saying I burned the school down. I need to set the story straight."

"Away."

The doors open at the main level. Henry, the building doorman, beams his usual grin at us and asks my father if he won any big cases today. Dad snaps, "Excuse us," at him and presses the button that closes the doors in his face.

"I know you're pissed at me, but you don't need to take it out on him," I mutter.

"You're right. It's not his fault my daughter committed arson with a drug addict."

"It's only arson if you did it on purpose." The elevator doors open at our floor. I grab the sleeve of my father's suit. "It was an accident."

He doesn't yank his arm away from mine, but the look in his

eyes makes me want to crawl into a fetal position. "That's the best you can come up with?"

I trail behind him. "What's that supposed to mean?"

"You've been playing me and your mother like goddamn violins," Dad hisses. His lowered voice is for the neighbors' benefit, not mine. "We believed that every teacher who sent a note home about your behavior *had it in for you.* We believed that the vodka bottle under your bed came from your friends. So you'll forgive me if I'm having a little trouble believing that the fire was all Martin's fault."

I don't think it'll help my case to point out that I only said it was *partly* Martin's fault, so I keep my mouth shut and follow Dad inside.

I'm not surprised to see Mom draped across the chaise in the foyer, crying. She's always crying about something, like over people who don't send thank-you notes. Or, you know, her daughter setting fire to her very expensive prep school.

I'm not sure I blame her this time.

"Mom, please don't cry." I sit at the corner of the chaise and give her foot a quick pat.

"You are damn lucky the police aren't charging you with anything," Dad says.

By that, he means I'm damn lucky my father is one of the most highly sought-after attorneys in New York.

"The fire is all over the news," Mom sniffs. "On Channel Seven they even said two Saint Bernadette's students were involved."

"Christ." Dad tugs his tie off and throws it on top of the chaise's matching armchair. "They better not release her name, if they don't want a lawsuit."

"Hell-*o*, I'm still here." I sit up and level with my dad.

"Oh, I'm sorry. Did you need something from me?" He raises his eyebrows. "I would have thought keeping you out of prison would suffice for today."

"Daddy, come *on!*" I throw my head back, dragging out the *on.* "I'll write an apology letter to Bailey, we'll pay for a new auditorium, I'll do my community service, and everyone will forget this even happened!"

Dad slams his hand down on the end table, rattling a glass vase of carnations. "That is *not* how the real world works, Anne Margaret. You really think the headmaster will let you within three feet of St. Bernadette's now?"

Dad's words zip around in my head like pinballs. My brain can't make my lips form a simple question.

Is Bailey kicking me out of St. Bernadette's?

That would be impossible.

St. Bernadette's is *my* school. It's been my school since the sixth grade. I practically run that place! "I—I have to go back."

"Anne, go to your room, please. Do not call, text, or e-mail anyone." Dad pinches the area between his eyes with his thumb and index finger. "Your mother and I need to talk."

Dazed, I leave the foyer and head down the hall. The part of me that hasn't quite realized I'm in deep shit wants to get in touch with Martin. I need to know if the school called him and told him no, he won't be finishing his second senior year after all.

I want to barf as I sink into the down comforter on my bed—partly because thinking about Martin inspires that reaction and partly because I seriously can't stomach the thought of not going back to St. Bernadette's. Where will I go if they kick me out? Another prep school definitely won't let me in once they hear that I'm the pyromaniac from the Upper East Side.

If that happens, I'll have to go to *public school.* I'll be some lame prep-school expellee, just like in one of those awful movies that always end with some girl having a baby at the prom.

Or worse, I'll have to go to an all-girls school.

My phone chimes from my purse on the floor. I figure I should at least turn it off so my father doesn't hear it ringing and come bite my head off.

It's Chelsea calling. Dad said not to talk to anyone, but Chelsea isn't just anyone. She's been my best friend since our first day at St. Bernadette's. I flop back on my bed and answer.

"Oh my god, Annie, I've been calling you for the past three hours! Turn on the news!"

"Why, is my face on it?" I sigh dramatically.

"Very funny. There was a fire at school." There's a touch of hysteria in Chelsea's voice. "You said you were staying after, so I was so worried."

Guilt needles me. "Yeah . . . about that. Have you heard anything about, you know . . . whose fault it was?"

"No—fault? Someone started it on purpose?"

I pause, letting Chelsea's breathing fill the silence. She has really bad asthma, so when she gets riled up about something, she does this squeaky breathing thing. People used to make fun of her for it. I made sure that was short-lived.

"Anne . . . why aren't you saying anything?"

I don't know why. Chelsea's going to find out the fire was my fault eventually. Won't everyone?

"Um, Chels." I dig my nails into my throw pillow. "I probably won't be back in school on Monday. And probably the rest of the year."

Silence. "Wait, you mean you— Are you messing with me?"

"No." I sighed. "Just, if anyone asks, tell them it was an accident. And only part of the auditorium burned."

"Anne, if you're playing some sort of joke—"

"Chels. I've gotta go." There are footsteps in the hall, accompanied by Dad's shouting and Mom's teary responses. "I'll try to call you tomorrow."

I hang up and slide the phone under my pillows. I think I just handed my throne over to St. Bernadette's new Queen Bee.

When I wake up the next morning, I know something is seriously wrong, because I smell bacon. Mom banned bacon from our kitchen after we watched *Babe* one night and she had one of her mini-meltdowns about how nothing in life is fair.

The smell gets closer, then there's a knock on the door.

"Annie? Can I come in?"

"Sure, Mom." I sit up in bed, double-checking that my phone is concealed by the mass of pillows.

She opens the door all the way and then just hangs outside. She has a tray balanced on one arm, and it looks like there's fresh fruit and whole-wheat toast on it as well as the bacon and eggs. "Are you hungry?"

My mother made me breakfast, even though she and Dad wouldn't talk to me last night. The last time Mom made breakfast for me was when I had chicken pox in elementary school. She made banana chocolate-chip pancakes with a smiley face drawn on them in whipped cream.

I need to know what the catch is here and whether it's worth bacon as a peace offering. Mom rests the tray on my lap, sits on the edge of the bed, and looks around my room like she's surprised I no longer have a Hello Kitty poster on my wall.

"How did you sleep?" Mom watches me with bloodshot eyes, but she's not trying to make me feel guilty. She's actually concerned.

"Okay. Do you and Daddy hate me?"

"Oh, sweetheart, stop it," she says. "We're just . . . very disappointed."

I don't say it, but I think that's worse, actually. I take an apprehensive bite of the bacon.

"Anne, I have to tell you something." Mom puts her hand on the comforter over my knee, but she's leaning away from me at the same time. "Daddy and I talked last night about how to handle this . . . and we're not sure going to another school here in the city is the best option for you."

It's suddenly hard to swallow. "Then where am I supposed to go?"

"Your father knows someone who was able to get you into a

new school." Mom looks uncomfortable. "You start in a few days. It's a boarding school."

I almost gag. "You've got to be kidding me. *Boarding school*?"

So my parents are dealing with their embarrassment over the fire by sending me to some boarding school God knows where. What if it's in Siberia? Or even worse, New Jersey?!

"Annie, the Wheatley School is very prestigious. This will be great for you."

I perk up a bit. "Wheatley? Is that in England or something?" I see an image of myself wearing Burberry outside Buckingham Palace, just waiting for Prince William to notice me as he takes his morning walk. Some lady at Lord & Taylor did tell me once I look like Princess Kate.

Mom purses her lips. "Not that Wheatley. It's right outside of Boston."

I feel like I've hit my head.

"Boston?" I wail. "BOSTON?!"

"Oh, come on. You've been there before and liked it. Boston has a lot of history."

I push the breakfast tray aside and flop back onto my back. "Do you know what they call people from Boston, Mom? 'Massholes.' They're assholes, but they think they're special because they're from Massachusetts."

"Don't be crass, Anne," Mom snaps. "You don't have a choice in this. Your father already mailed out the security deposit and booked you a train for Sunday."

"What?!" My nose gets all prickly and stuffy like I'm about to cry. "You're just sending me away without letting me make this right?"

Mom's gray eyes are a little glassy now. "Honey, you'll thank us later. And I know you'll love Wheatley."

I sit up and bury my face on the shoulder of my mother's cardigan. "All my friends are here. Please don't make me go."

Mom decides to deal with my whining and pleading by pointing out Boston's best features, which, as far as I can tell, are limited to old men dressed in Revolutionary War uniforms roaming the streets and fewer people peeing in the middle of the subway. I want to shrink into a ball and hide in my night-stand drawer.

Mom leaves me with the now-cold eggs. I know my begging is futile for now; my parents are so embarrassed about the fire that they're sending me somewhere where people will forget about me. I really have no choice but to go to Massachusetts.

Staying there is another story.

CHAPTER
THREE

My father can't come with me and Mom to Boston, because he has to be in court Monday morning. His client is facing life in prison, and apparently that's more important than being there to send his only daughter off to Massachusetts for the next five months.

Five months. It's plenty of time for me to lay low, get good grades, and prove to my parents that I'm responsible enough to come back to New York next year. By then, the fire will be old news, and maybe Bailey will let me come back. This is nothing an Edible Arrangement and some A's can't fix. It has to work, because there's no way I'm spending my senior year at the Wheatley School.

I checked out their Web site. Not only are their uniforms an atrocious shade of *cranberry*, but all of the girls featured on the home page were wearing headbands. *Headbands*. The only place a headband belongs is on a second-grader. Or in a landfill.

The headbands aren't the worst part, though. What really sucks is that the Wheatley School is really, *really* frickin' small.

St. Bernadette's is sixth to twelfth grades, with about three hundred kids per grade. The Wheatley School only offers ninth to twelfth grades, and get this: *They only accept fifty kids each year.* That's practically *incestuous.* As if being the private-school expellee from New York wasn't bad enough (because let's face it, I'm not fooling anyone by starting at one of the most elite academies on the East Coast in the middle of January), I have to deal with a gaggle of headband-wearing girls who have been in every class together since freshman year.

It takes Mom and me almost fifteen minutes to find a cab from the train station. We're both quiet on the drive to Wheatley, and although I've convinced myself I don't care enough to be nervous, my stomach is producing acid at an alarming rate. A green road sign informs me that we're a mile away from the Wheatley School, and soon enough, I'm stepping into my customized, headband-wearing version of hell.

Hell is actually really pretty. The redbrick buildings circling a courtyard look like my father's pictures of his alma mater, which I guess makes sense, since Harvard has a partnership with the Wheatley School. I even read that some seniors are allowed to take classes there.

So the campus is kind of nice. I guess. The charm wears off when Mom and I find the student center, which has obviously been renovated recently. The lobby has high ceilings and a fish tank.

A directory leads us to a room labeled STUDENT SERVICES, where an older woman named Barbara is waiting for me with my ID card and schedule and all other sorts of important information. Honestly, I tune out the second she tells me my ID card is also my room key, but I'll need to find out the door access code from my roommate.

Roommate.

How did I not see that one coming? At all the boarding schools I've seen on TV, the kids had their own rooms and mini-coffeemakers. I even brought one. Now I'm supposed to share my room with someone who may or may not be a sociopath?

Mom's hand is on my shoulder. "Anne, honey, I've got to catch a cab."

"Oh. Right." My head hurts, like I've gone a couple of minutes without breathing. Mom is really leaving, and in three days, she and my father will be in Paris for their anniversary. And I won't be home, in our apartment, planning out enough shenanigans for the two weeks they'll be gone.

"We'll take great care of her." Barbara beams at my mother, who looks really, really sad. I'd like to think it's because she's leaving her only daughter five hours away from her, but something tells me it's also because I'm a humongous screwup.

Mom hugs me and tells me she loves me and reminds me to call once I get settled in. I squeeze her back, and then she's gone, leaving me with Barbara, who has this shit-eating grin on her face that says, "Aren't you so excited to be at this *important* school with all your *important* new classmates?"

Barbara tells me that I was supposed to meet someone named Dean Watts now, but she's busy having her baby early or whatever, so some kid named Brent Conroy is coming to give me a tour instead. I immediately picture some nasally Student Council president with khakis worn up to his belly button, because those are the types of boys I saw on the school's Web site. It takes every ounce of energy I have left not to sigh.

"I think you'll find the Wheatley School very welcoming," Barbara says with a smile, as if she can detect my growing sense of dread.

I nod, but the pit in my stomach grows as I hear the thwacking of shoes behind me. I turn around to see a blond girl in the doorway. She's pretty, but her face is kind of pinched and her hair colorist went a little nuts with the highlights. I'm surprised she's wearing a bright pink sweater and jeans and not a uniform, until I remember it's Sunday. She steps into the room.

"Hi. I'm Alexis Westbrook." She lingers on the second-to-last syllable, as if I should know who she is or something.

Barbara looks confused but not disappointed to see Alexis. "Where's Brent?"

"Oh, you know." Alexis flashes a grin that makes me wonder if she murdered him and stuffed his body into a closet. "If you wait for Brent, you'll be waiting 'til you're old and gray."

I don't like the singsongy way Alexis says this. And I definitely don't miss the sideways glance she shoots me.

"I'll be showing Anne around. Dr. Harrow wants to meet her first, though," Alexis says to Barbara, as if I'm not standing three feet away from them. She flips her long hair over her shoulder. She's not wearing a headband, but I still don't like her.

Alexis leads me outside and into a really old-looking building with refurbished cherrywood floors.

"So, I hear you're from New York? Which part?" Something in her voice tells me that she knows exactly where I'm from, down to the street address of the prep school I almost burned down.

"Manhattan," I say.

Alexis lets out a little *"ah"* and twists one of her pearl earrings. She's so sizing me up right now. Trying to figure out if I've got the New York attitude to go along with the black boots and tights.

That'll depend on whether or not she pulls that *talking about me like I'm not in the room* crap again.

I pretend to be engrossed in the portraits and plaques lining the hall walls so I don't have to make small talk with Alexis. Already, I see names I recognize on a NOTABLE ALUMNI plaque. Conroy. Westbrook. My curiosity gets the best of me.

"Arnold Westbrook. Is that your father?" I ask.

"Grandfather," Alexis says. *"Steven* Westbrook is my father."

Evidently, I'm supposed to know who Steven Westbrook is. I shrug. Alexis half-rolls her eyes when she thinks I'm not looking.

Mercifully, she stops in front of a door with VICE-PRINCIPAL engraved on a gold nameplate. Alexis raps on it twice and tucks her hair behind her ears. I catch her running her pinky over her two front teeth, too.

I understand why when the door opens. Dr. Harrow is *young*. Well, young-looking for someone old enough to have a PhD. He's tall with dark hair, a strong jaw, and ice-blue eyes—the type of eyes that could get you to admit to anything.

"Come on in, ladies." His voice is friendly, and he has sort of a Midwestern accent.

Dr. Harrow extends a strong-looking hand to me. "Pleasure to meet you, Ms. Dowling. I'm Dr. Harrow. Have a seat."

I ease into a leather chair facing his desk. Just *pleased to meet you*. Not, *pleased to meet you, we've hidden all the matches and restocked the fire extinguishers in preparation for your arrival*. So far, so good.

"The pleasure is mine." I turn up the charm a little bit. Anything to win over the administration and expedite getting the hell out of here on good behavior.

Dr. Harrow nods at the red folder Barbara gave me. THE WHEATLEY SCHOOL is embossed on the front. "I see you've already heard about the nuts and bolts of boarding school, but I personally wanted to welcome you. Dean Watts's replacement hasn't arrived yet, and Headmaster Goddard had a previous engagement, but they wanted me to tell you they're happy you're here, as well."

Sure they did.

Dr. Harrow is about to say something else when a rap on the door interrupts him. He nods for Alexis, who is standing in the corner, to open it.

"Ah, sorry I'm late." A boy is standing in the doorway. He doesn't look sorry at all. But he's *really* cute, so he has my attention.

"Mr. Conroy." Dr. Harrow bobs his head. "This is Anne Dowling. The student you were supposed to show around."

Disappointment surges through me. *Supposed to*. As in, not going to now.

"Brent Conroy." He shakes my hand and smiles. He's about my height, with short, wavy brown hair and brown eyes. His smile isn't perfect, but I can't look away. He's on the shorter side, for a guy, but with his shirtsleeves rolled up to his elbows, I can tell he's definitely athletic.

And he's *definitely* my type.

I give him a small Queen Elizabeth wave. One corner of his mouth curls up.

"Dr. Harrow, I apologize for not getting here on time," Brent says. "I'd be happy to show Anne around now."

Alexis stiffens beside me. She looked horrendously insulted by Brent's presence before, but now her eyes are practically crossing.

"That's not necessary," she snips. "No reason for Brent and I both to miss the Student Government Association fund-raiser."

So that's what this is—some sort of pissing contest between the school's male alpha and female alpha. Either they're both trying to mark me as their territory, or they really don't want to go to that fund-raiser. Even Dr. Harrow realizes how awkward this whole situation has become.

He clears his throat. "Ms. Westbrook, I feel terrible that I pulled you away from the fund-raiser . . . and I did give the SGA advisors advance warning that Brent wouldn't be able to attend today."

Alexis squeezes her bottom lip between her teeth and lets it go. Her nostrils flare. "Sure. As long as Anne doesn't mind taking a tour with Brent instead."

There's no way to respond to this without sounding like a mega-bitch, but I'm pretty much set with the eight or so minutes I've already had to spend with Alexis. I like to give everyone a chance, but something about this girl fills me with insta-dislike.

"I don't mind. It was great meeting you, Alexis." I square off with her and give my best winning smile, because even *I* don't want an enemy here yet. But something in the dagger glare

Alexis gives me before leaving the office in a huff tells me I was screwed the second she laid eyes on me.

Dr. Harrow walks Brent and me into the hallway. "Nice to meet you again, Anne. Hopefully we won't be seeing much of each other." Then he winks.

He disappears behind his door before I can figure out what the appropriate reaction to a vice-principal *winking* at me is. Brent must sense my confusion.

"Dr. Harrow, is, ah . . . in charge of discipline," he says.

"Got it." My face is hot.

"Not that a nice girl like you would end up in the VP's office anyway." Brent gives me a goofy smile, and it hits me. He totally knows I got kicked out of St. Bernadette's. Everyone here probably does.

"'Nice girl,' huh? And here I was worried there would be rumors of me burning down my last school before I even got here."

Brent is suddenly overcome with a coughing fit.

"It really wasn't even that big of a fire." I find myself rambling.

Brent looks like he's stifling a smile. I'm quiet for a minute as we walk down the hall in the opposite direction of the main entrance. I try not to be distracted by the spicy scent of Brent's cologne, because I'm not pathetic enough to be entranced by what is literally the first boy I've met at this school.

Brent leads me into the courtyard, which is sealed off by more ivy-covered brick buildings. Two guys in shorts and T-shirts reading WHEATLEY CREW walk toward us. They hold up their hands for Brent to slap. The whole transaction is wordless. Brent gestures to me. "Guys, this is Anne Dowling. From New York."

"Hi," I say.

The one with a floppy mass of black hair and tan skin nods at me, a smile taking over his whole face. "What's up? I'm Murali."

The other guy's eyes dart from Brent to me, as if he's looking for evidence about what Brent's take on me is. He finally extends a hand. Why are people so obsessed with handshaking here? "Hey. I'm Cole Redmond."

Cole is taller and buffer than Brent, and ten times preppier, from his blond crew cut to his Pumas.

The boys continue heading in the opposite direction. Brent tells me they're his rowing team buddies. Of course this school has a crew team. It's only the most WASP-y sport ever invented.

"Murali is in our British lit class," Brent tells me, and I'm almost too busy checking him out to notice he said *our*. Almost.

"How do you know I'm in British lit?" I narrow my eyes at him. "I haven't even looked at my schedule yet."

"I know lots of stuff. Including the lucky girl who gets you as a roommate."

I almost fall over right there. "Tell me. Please. Please."

"Isabella Fern," Brent says. "She's nice."

Nice tells me nothing. Dad's Aunt Mary is nice, but she still wears her dead husband's ashes in a locket, and her house smells like a pet store. "Can you tell me anything else about her?"

"She's really smart. Quiet. Keeps to herself." Brent shrugs. "I'm in AP physics with her."

The fact that Isabella is taking an advanced physics course her junior year tells me pretty much all I need to know.

But I'm not here to make friends.

CHAPTER
FOUR

Brent leaves me at Amherst, the upperclassmen girls' dorm, which looks like a cross between the college dorms I've seen on TV and the type of hotel you'd find in the mountains somewhere. I step onto a new-looking carpet and look down the hall. Most of the doors have whiteboards hanging on them, and glittery nameplates decorated with pictures probably cut out of *Cosmo* and *Seventeen*.

I sigh as I pass a door with a black script *Alexis* decal. Maybe there's more than one Alexis in the junior class.

My room—417—is at the end of the hall, across from the elevator. The only decoration on the door is a glow-in-the-dark star, the kind little kids put on their bedroom ceilings. For a second, I totally consider running back downstairs and camping out on the lounge couch until someone notices me. It feels wrong to just barge into Isabella's room, even if it is technically my room now, too.

I don't know how long I've been staring at the door before the elevator dings behind me. Two girls shuffle out. They're both head-to-toe J.Crew ads—pastel leather ballet flats, cashmere sweaters, pearl stud earrings.

Headbands with bows on the side.

Their conversation stalls when they spot me lingering outside Isabella's door. They exchange a look, and the strawberry-blond girl nods at the brunette, who speaks: "Hi. Are you locked out?"

I actually don't know, since I haven't even tried to open the door, but I smile and shake my head. "No . . . just thought I'd wait to meet my roommate. Out here."

"Oh." The brunette cocks her head, her green eyes a little disbelieving. "Well, we're in four-oh-three if you need anything. I'm April, and this is Kelsey." She nudges the blonde, who offers me a nervous smile and adjusts her square-frame glasses.

As they disappear behind their door, I realize they didn't ask who I am.

Who are you kidding, Anne? Everyone here already knows who you are.

I finally decide I need to get out of the hallway and avoid any further awkward interactions. When I swipe my ID through the door, the keypad lights up. Crap. I forgot Barbara mentioned there was an entry code.

"Are you trying to get in?" a small voice sounds from beside me. I give its owner a once-over. She's a few inches shorter than me, and she has deep brown eyes with long lashes. Her brown hair is in thick, spiral curls that could be disastrous in the wrong hands, but she has them neatly pulled back away from her face.

I think I've just met my roommate.

"Yeah," I say, feeling sheepish. "I don't know the code."

"It's four-three-two-one," Isabella says, looking even more sheepish than I feel. "My memory is awful."

"I'm Anne," I say as she punches in the code.

"I know." Isabella pushes the door open. "Sorry. That came

out kind of snotty. I meant that I knew you were coming. Some guy from Student Services brought your suitcases up."

I follow Isabella into the room. It's bigger than I expected, and afternoon sun floods through the window on the far wall. Isabella's side of the room is neat. Her twin bed has a blue-and-white-striped comforter and a gray body pillow. The desk at the foot of her bed is covered with markers, folders, and a MacBook. There's a string of plastic owl lights across the top, where she has all of her textbooks stacked against one another.

"Cool lights," I say.

"Thanks. We're technically not allowed to have them, but Darlene doesn't care." Isabella pauses. "Darlene is our RA. She's a grad student at Harvard, and as long as no one kills each other, she's pretty cool."

I tear my eyes away from Isabella's side of the room. Homesickness pokes at me as I take in the sterile-looking white bed and empty desk. I try not to think of Abby curled between the black-and-white pillows on my bed at home.

Isabella tells me she's going to the library for a little while, and I highly suspect it's to let me have some privacy while I unpack. For a fleeting moment, I think this whole boarding-school thing might not be so bad. Then I open my suitcase and see the black dress I bought at BCBG with Chelsea for Derrick Bradford's New Year's Eve party. Three hours before we were supposed to get ready, I started throwing my guts up and had to stay home. The dress still has its tags on.

At the time, missing the party hadn't seemed like such a big deal because I assumed there would be others. I'll never get to wear that dress now.

It takes me so long to unpack and make my bed that I barely notice when Isabella slips back into the room.

"Hey, dinner is in fifteen." She sits on the edge of her bed, putting on a pair of socks with mini-periodic-element tables on them. "You up for a break?"

I know I should eat something more than the spoonful of

yogurt I had for lunch, but I can't stomach the thought of going to face my classmates—all of them—for the first time. Even though I might see Brent again. Even though Isabella will probably let me eat without making awkward small talk.

I mean, the nerdy socks and *Star Trek* poster over her bed have *got* to go, but I kind of like Isabella.

"Um, I should probably finish unpacking and make my bed," I say. "Long day."

Isabella nods, like she gets that I'm not ready to be thrown to the wolves yet. "I'll bring you something."

She's gone before I can argue otherwise. I suck in a breath and hold it for a minute. I guess I'll set up my desk first if I'm going to adopt the whole studious thing this semester.

When my computer whirs to life, I have to sign into Wheatley-ResNet. The first thing I do is Google Steven Westbrook.

He's a Massachusetts senator. *Of course he is,* I think as I shut my laptop. I flop down on the bed—my bed—and stare at the *Where's Waldo?* poster on Isabella's wall for a while. I never find him.

My heartbeat stalls for a second as the lock on the door clicks. Isabella ducks inside the room, balancing two brown take-out boxes.

"I hope you like baked mac and cheese." She sets one box down on my desk. "It's Mexican night." Her face grows somber. "Never eat the food on Mexican night."

"Didn't you want to eat downstairs?" I ask, hoping I don't sound like I'd rather she be down there. Because I don't. At least I think. "I mean, you didn't have to rush back. I feel bad."

"Don't." Isabella is leaning back in her chair, already digging into her mac and cheese with a plastic fork. "I have a huge art-history exam tomorrow, so I wanted to get back early."

Isabella included a piping hot dinner roll and a brownie with my mac and cheese. It's difficult not to stuff the entire box down my throat, even though I make a mental note never to let my new roommate make nutritional choices for me again. As I eat, I thumb through my folder until I find my schedule.

"Are you in Robinson's art-history class?" I ask Isabella. "First period?"

Isabella nods and presses a napkin to her mouth. She rolls her chair toward me. "Can I see your schedule?"

I hand it to her and turn back to my dinner as she looks it over.

"We only have art history together," she says. "I was in your Latin three class, but I had to drop it." A dark look eclipses her cheery expression as she says it. "Anyway, it's a good class." Isabella gives me my schedule back. "Upton gives a ton of work, but she's a lenient grader."

I don't know how anyone can use the terms *good class* and *ton of work* in the same sentence, so I stay quiet. Isabella follows my lead, and we eat the rest of our dinners in silence. When she's done, she crawls onto her bed with her laptop. I lie on my side, facing my empty, whitewashed wall. I should probably hang up the photos I brought from home, but something about decorating my side of the room feels permanent.

I close my eyes and fight off the prickling in my nose. I'm not going to be a cliché and cry myself to sleep my first night at boarding school, but, God, I hate it here. Sure, the boys are cute, my roommate is nice, and the mac and cheese is really good . . . but it's not St. Bernadette's.

It's not New York.

Isabella settles into her bed next to me, plugging earphones into her laptop. I can hear heavy bass leaking out of them. I watch her for a few moments, her lips muttering along with the lyrics and her hand suspended over a bag of gummy worms.

She's singing along to a rap song—a really intense rap song about busting caps in snitches and shanking prison guards.

"Oh, sorry." She catches me staring and pulls out an earbud. "I need something to get my adrenaline going when I study."

I blink at her. Isabella turns back to her laptop, and I dig out the copy of *Marie Claire* I never finished reading on the train yesterday. I'm halfway through Tim Gunn's column when I hear violins and Isabella singing in a light falsetto.

I put my magazine down. "Is that . . . the *Les Misérables* soundtrack?"

Isabella gives me a blank stare and takes out her earbuds again. I repeat myself and she nods enthusiastically.

So my roommate is batshit crazy. I want to laugh, but hearing *Les Mis* makes me wish I were back in New York so badly I feel like I'm going to explode. "I love *Les Mis.*"

Isabella nods, her eyes wide, like she gets why. She turns up the volume on her laptop so "One Day More" is blasting, and she starts to sing all the male parts in full-on baritone and tenor. I'm holding in a laugh so big my body starts to shake, when she stands up on her bed and starts singing the female parts in a falsetto.

"Hey." She collapses on her bed, out of breath when the song is over. "I have the Twenty-fifth Anniversary Concert version on DVD. Wanna watch?"

"What about your exam?" I ask, but she's already pawing through the basket of DVDs next to her nightstand. When she finds it, she slips it into her laptop and slides to the floor, gesturing for me to follow. I grab my pillow and make a seat out of it next to her. We watch the first half in silence, passing the gummy worms back and forth between us.

"I would kill to see this on Broadway," she finally sighs. "You probably already have."

I nod. We're both full-on ugly crying by the time Éponine dies in Marius's arms. When a knock sounds at the door, I scramble to my feet. Isabella sniffles and answers it.

"Hi." Alexis pokes her head in the door, her voice sugary. "Can you guys lower that music a little? I mean, *I* don't care, but there are probably people trying to do homework. . . ."

Isabella gives Alexis a wordless thumbs-up, which she turns into the middle finger once she closes the door.

"Sorry," Isabella says. "She's, uh . . ."

"It's okay," I say. "I met her earlier."

An awkward silence envelops us. I can see that Isabella is struggling with how to approach this: On the surface, Alexis and I both look like the type of girls who would pick on girls like her just because we could.

I want Isabella to know I'm not like that.

"She seems like . . . a stuck-up bitch," I say.

Isabella looks at me in surprise and laughs. Then she curls her front lip up to imitate Alexis's slightly larger-than-normal front teeth, and we're both laughing.

"So, did you meet any of our other charming classmates today?" she asks.

I pull the elastic off my ponytail and let brown waves fall over the side of my face so I don't have to look at Isabella. "Um, Brent Conroy." My voice squeaks a little.

"Oh, man." She shakes her head as if to say, *Not you, too.*

"What?" I ask, a little crankily. "He showed me around. He's really nice."

"And *cute,*" Isabella says, like I purposely left that part out.

"Yeah, he's cute," I huff, and focus my gaze on the screen. "Anyway."

Isabella turns her attention back to the screen, a smile creeping across her lips. I feel my cheeks getting hotter by the millisecond. Alexis's comment about waiting a long time for Brent taunts me. There's definitely something Isabella's not telling me about Brent.

But whatever. I have more pressing matters to deal with.

Like starting classes tomorrow.

When I wake up to alarm sounds and a woman's cries of "DANGER! EVACUATE!" my first thought is that someone is playing a sick joke on me. Because the irony of my dorm building catching fire or flooding or being attacked by terrorists on my first day is just too much.

I throw my comforter off in a panic and look over at the unmoving shape of Isabella's body. I feel my mouth hang open slightly as I realize the alarm sounds are coming from her bed.

"Isabella." Nothing. "Isabella!"

She sits up with a start and reaches for the black square-framed glasses on her nightstand. She stares at me for a moment as if she can't quite remember who I am, then yawns and digs out a phone from under her pillow. The frantic alarm sounds stop.

"What the hell was that?" I ask.

"That . . . is the only thing loud enough to wake me up in the morning." She stretches. "Usually."

Yes. Isabella is certifiably nuts. But she also seems to know everything: like that the second-floor bathroom is always empty in the morning because all the swimmers live on that floor and they shower at the pool, and that you should never order an omelet from the dining-hall worker with the handlebar mustache because he takes forever and will make you late to class.

My plan to fly under everyone's radar is smashed to pieces when I get to my first class and realize there are only ten students in it.

My teachers pretend to be thrilled to have me, although it's obvious they've never had to deal with a student starting this late in the year. I definitely have to figure out who my father knows at this school, because I see no other reason why they would let me in.

I head back to Amherst after French lit to drop off the ten-pound stack of textbooks I accumulated over the morning. Luckily, Isabella is there, so we walk to the cafeteria together. While she waits on the hot-lunch line, I go for the salad bar. We meet up and choose a round table near the soda fountain.

"Please don't tell me that's supposed to be pizza." I point at the limp-looking pieces of pita bread on Isabella's plate. They're covered in red sauce and what looks like dog throw-up.

"Of course it is," she says. "It's hamburger pizza. You don't have hamburger pizza in New York?"

This is worse than I thought.

"Hey, you're in my French class, aren't you?"

I turn around to face a pretty girl with long dark hair. She looks vaguely familiar, and she's flanked by the J.Crew girls from our hall—April and Kelsey, although I can only tell them apart by Kelsey's glasses.

"I think so," I say.

"I'm Remy." The girl extends a hand and sits down across from Isabella and me. "Can we sit here?"

I look at Isabella, who nods, even though April and Kelsey have already slid into the other empty chairs. "You live on our floor," they say, almost in unison.

"Your bag is adorable," Remy says. "Did you get that at the Pru?"

I stare into her wide, blue Bambi eyes, because I have no idea what the Pru is. "Uh, no . . . I got it back in New York."

All three of the girls are smiling, a little too eagerly.

"Oh. Yeah. We heard you were from New York," Remy says with awe.

Is that code for *We heard what you did and we'd like to sit here to absorb some of your street cred*? Isabella pretends to be fascinated with her pizza, but it's obvious that these girls sitting with her is about as normal as Morgan Freeman sitting with her and narrating her every move. I mean, they haven't even acknowledged her presence.

As if taking cues from Remy, April and Kelsey proceed to compliment my nail-polish color and necklace. Half-listening, I find myself scanning the cafeteria lines for Brent. My stomach somersaults as I spot him making his way toward the soda fountain, followed by the two crew guys he introduced me to yesterday.

Brent's face lights up as his gaze falls on me. I run my tongue over my teeth, checking for stray lettuce pieces, as he waves and heads toward our table. I return his grin before I notice Remy waving to him from behind me.

I try not to be too mortified as Brent and his entourage settle in at our table as if they always sit here, although it's clear the table isn't made for eight people.

"Afternoon, ladies," Brent says, grabbing a chair from the table next to us and squeezing between Remy and Cole. "Who got the hamburger pizza?"

Isabella lifts her eyes guiltily and doesn't say anything as the other girls offer "ew"s and gagging noises.

"So, Anne, how's your first day going?" Brent asks.

It's then I notice that it's not just his eyes on me. Everyone at the table is watching me, waiting for my response.

And it's not just my table. When I pick my head up and scan the cafeteria, I realize that most of the eyes in the room are on me. No, not on me. On us.

I've inadvertently brought the popular table to me.

"Um, not bad. Typical first-day stuff," I offer.

"You're in our art-history class, right?" Cole asks.

"Of course she is." Murali pokes his straw through the top of his soda. "You spent the last five minutes failing to gather the balls to ask her if she needed help finding her next class, remember?"

Murali grins at me while Cole contemplates the fork in his hand as if he wants to stab Murali in the jugular with it. I smile in spite of myself, because they're both pretty cute. I'm itching to look over at Brent and see if he notices how red Cole's face is, but I play it cool and act like my salad is the most interesting thing at the table.

Everyone wants to compare afternoon classes with me. As they pass my schedule around the table, alternating between approving and disapproving guttural sounds (Remy and April have modern dance, for the required fitness credit, with me on

Tuesdays and Thursdays), I smell bitchiness behind me. It's a combination of celebrity perfume and the type of strawberry lip balm a nine-year-old would wear.

Isabella and I share a conspiratorial look as Alexis looms over our table, hand on her hip. The arrogant way she carries herself makes a little more sense to me now that I know she's a senator's daughter.

"Hey, Lex," Remy says, with a nervous glance in my direction. "This is Anne."

"We've met." Alexis's frosty gray eyes lock on mine. I've clearly stepped all over the toes of her Michael Kors flats—which are really cute, as much as I hate to admit it. If anyone notices, they're not showing it.

"I'm going to the SGA room," Alexis announces. She pronounces it "*rum*," and I have to stifle a laugh. "Valentine's Day rose orders are starting to come in, if anyone wants to help me get a head start."

No one makes any motion to get up or provides any excuses about not being able to help. Everyone is looking at me guiltily, and I realize I'm the reason they're staying.

I'm officially the Interesting New Thing, and no one wants to miss out on what I'll do next. So far, all I've done is eat some salad, but who knows when I'll dish out the real story of how I almost burned St. Bernadette's down?

Alexis scans the table as if she can't decide who she hates the most out of all of us. "Fine. Lizzie is meeting me there anyway."

I feel bad for Lizzie, whoever she is, as Alexis stalks off. And maybe it's just me, but it feels as if the table breathes a collective sigh of relief when she's gone.

"Okay, now I need to know what you did to her," Isabella asks as we leave the cafeteria. "You've only been here a day, so I have to admit I'm a little impressed."

"I really don't know," I lie. "Should I be scared?"

Isabella tugs on her scarf to tighten it as a wall of wind assaults us. She glances over her shoulder; at first, I think it's to shield her face from the incoming cold, but her silence says she's checking to see if anyone is listening to us.

"Of her? Yeah," she says. "But don't you get what just happened in there? That was totally an initiation."

"Into what?" I snort. "The Headband Club?"

"Exactly." Isabella turns and smirks at me. "Don't you get it? They've heard all about you. They're grooming you to be their new leader."

CHAPTER
FIVE

I don't know why the popular crowd seeking me out doesn't make me feel more at home. My parents and teachers always like to talk about my "natural leadership tendencies" (in other words, constantly leading Chelsea or my other friends into trouble), but I feel weird about people wanting to be my friend only because they think I'm some badass from New York.

At St. Bernadette's, it didn't matter where your money came from, since everyone's parents were attorneys or plastic surgeons or famous rock stars; you had to prove yourself to earn your status. The fact that Remy and Company won't even wait for me to prove myself makes me distrust them. I mean, someone other than Alexis has to have noticed that I don't exactly fit in here. I didn't think it was possible to be too preppy for a prep school, but these Boston kids are proving me wrong. All of the guys have the same side-swept-bangs haircut, and the girls dress as if the Jackie Kennedy look were part of the uniform. They all take themselves so seriously.

They're nothing like my friends at home, who could rock

Ray-Ban eyeglasses and wouldn't think twice about ditching school to grab frozen hot chocolates at Serendipity.

I guess I should be happy I'm not at the bottom of the totem pole here, but by Wednesday night, I tell Isabella she's going to have to hide all sharp objects from me if I have to go to the dining hall again.

It's obvious Brent and Remy's crowd wouldn't sit with or even talk to Isabella if it weren't for me. I also can't figure out who she hung out with before I showed up. She sometimes talks to Molly, a nervous-looking girl on the floor beneath us, but it doesn't seem like there are any groups missing a member, when I look around the cafeteria.

When we get to the dorm with our sandwiches from the campus Subway, Alexis and her minion, Lizzie, are parked on the two lounge couches, surrounded by stacks of pink and red construction paper and enough glitter to stock a gay rave in New York for a year. As president of the Resident Council, Alexis is in charge of decorating the dorm, as she loudly explained during calculus this afternoon.

"Hi, ladies." She looks up when she sees us, her coral mouth twisted into a sneer. "Sorry we kind of took over here."

Obviously what she really means is *Try to sit here with us and I'll end you,* but I return her syrupy smile. I feel Isabella stiffen beside me.

"No problem," I say. "We'll go to the third-floor lounge."

We have to stop off at the room so I can get my laptop, anyway. The fact I don't bring it to class completely baffles Isabella, who keeps her MacBook in a vinyl case plastered to her side all day.

There's a hot-pink Post-it note waiting for us on the door. Or waiting for me, since my name is scrawled in bubbly script at the top.

Anne,
Mini-coffeemakers aren't allowed. Please get rid of it before Darlene sees.

And at the bottom, there's a heart drawn in sparkly gel pen.

"You've got to be fucking kidding me."

It's the first time I've heard Isabella curse. She rips the note off the door and squashes it in one motion. "Welcome to Alexis's sticky-note club."

Maybe it's the thought of not being able to make chai lattes in the morning, or that stupid, mocking heart, but the note *really* pisses me off. Alexis is not only a bitch, but a passive-aggressive, Post-it-note-leaving bitch. She had a million opportunities to tell me about the coffeemaker today, but instead she left me a nasty little note for everyone to see.

Isabella seems even more livid than I am as we settle into a table in the empty upstairs lounge. "We're not getting rid of that coffeemaker. Darlene wouldn't care, if she knew. And I don't want to go back to drinking the rat pee from the cafeteria."

This gets a small smile out of me, even though there's a pit in the bottom of my stomach. A hot-pink, Post-it-note-sized pit. "Are you sure? I don't want to get us in trouble."

"Trust me. If she pushes it, I'll tell Darlene about how Alexis has an illegal power strip in her room just so she can plug in all of her hair-torture devices. Seriously, I'm so *sick* of her crap."

This new layer of venom to Isabella's voice shocks me a little. "So why do you hate her so much?"

"Do I need a reason? She's just . . . she's the worst of any of them."

We let her words hang in the air between us for a minute. I think about Isabella's Old Navy weekend wardrobe and her dinged-up computer. It hits me what she really meant when she said any of *them*.

She doesn't consider herself one of them. And I'm betting that whatever Isabella's father does, he's not a senator.

CHAPTER
SIX

Friday is the only day this week Brent isn't late to English. The seat next to me is still open when he walks in. I pretend to be immersed in scrolling through the e-mails on my phone as he slides in next to me. When I don't look up, he pokes my side.

"Oh, hey." I put my phone down. "No grand entrance today?"

"I like to mix it up. Keep things interesting." He wiggles his eyebrows at me.

I don't say anything, because it sounds like something I'd say, and I don't like when people take my lines.

Fowler, our instructor, tells us to turn to Book 4 of *Paradise Lost*. I'm rifling through the tissue-paper-thin pages of my literature anthology when Brent nudges me again.

He leans into me so he doesn't have to whisper. "I have to ask you something after class."

"Why can't you ask me now?"

Fowler looks at me and repeats for us to turn to Book 4. Loudly.

I'm not going to let Brent see how much I'm dying for class to be over now. I'm not going to be distracted by the incredibly realistic doodle of Fowler in Brent's notebook—complete with nose hairs and an oversized bow tie—even though I'm pretty sure he's only drawing it to make me laugh.

Fowler has this thing where he insists on doing all of the reading himself and randomly calling on people to see who's listening. I guess I'm on his shit list today, because I'm the first person he locks eyes with. "Ms. Dowling. What is your reading of these lines?"

I glance down and quickly reread the passage he's talking about. Jackpot: One of the people who had this textbook before me highlighted it.

> . . . *do they only stand*
> *By ignorance? Is that their happy state,*
> *The proof of their obedience and their faith?*

Then, scrawled in the margins: *Ignorance is blind faith. The fall = a metaphor for subverting authority.*

I clear my throat, look up so it doesn't seem like I'm reading from notes, and say as much. The atmosphere in the room stiffens, and I wonder what it is I've said that's wrong.

A wry smile spreads across Fowler's lips. "That is a very astute observation, Ms. Dowling. If only it were about the passage to which I was referring."

Brent nudges me and points to the right passage, but Fowler has already moved on to someone else. I silently curse whoever highlighted the passage, because apparently Fowler doesn't even care about it.

To make myself feel better, I flip to the inside cover in the book. There are a list of names scrawled beneath the THIS BOOK BELONGS TO sticker. I match the handwritten notes in *Paradise Lost* to one of them: Matthew Weaver.

"Don't feel too bad," Brent tells me after class. "Fowler humiliates everyone at least once a semester. And I thought what you said was pretty smart."

I wrap my scarf around my neck and follow Brent out of the building. "Yeah, well, I didn't even come up with it. Matthew Weaver did."

Brent raises an eyebrow at me. "Hah. Funny. Where'd you hear about Matt Weaver?"

"My textbook. Why, you know him?"

Brent opens his mouth, then closes it. After a beat, he says, "Matt Weaver went here more than thirty years ago. He disappeared during his junior year. They never found his body."

The textbook in my arms suddenly feels different. "How is anyone even sure he's dead?"

Brent shrugs. "There's a ton of rumors about what happened to him. People like to mess around with the freshmen and say he got lost in the forest and eaten by wolves."

"That's ridiculous. There are no wolves in Wheatley, right?" Brent is silent. *"Right?"*

"Right." Brent laughs. "A lot of people say Matt was tripping on acid or something and died of hypothermia. A woman who lived across from there said she saw a young guy go into the forest the night he disappeared."

A chill passes through me. We're on the path that loops around the outer edge of the forest instead of zigzagging through campus. "And they never found his body?"

"Nope," Brent says. "Hey, about that thing I was going to ask you . . . There's a party in my dorm this weekend. You should come."

I'm trying to picture what a party at a Massachusetts prep school entails. I picture a bunch of people in Boston College T-shirts playing beer pong and talking about elections and baseball and other crap I don't care about.

"I don't know," I say. "Can Isabella come?"

Brent hesitates. I don't think it's meant to be mean. Probably he just doesn't get why, of everyone I've met here, I prefer to hang out with a nerd like Isabella.

"She's actually really cool," I tell him.

"Yeah, sure she can come." Brent looks like he's going to say something else, but he smiles. "Especially if it gets you there."

Okay, so, going to a party and risking getting in trouble two weeks after getting kicked out of St. Bernadette's probably isn't in my best interest. But I never was good at staying away from boys who look really good in ties.

Remy practically tackles me as she opens the door to her room Saturday night. "Does this mean you're coming?"

She and Alexis are roommates, but luckily, the harpy is off stealing souls elsewhere tonight. Kelsey and April wave at me from Remy's bed, where they're sitting cross-legged.

Remy gives me the rundown of how the whole sneaking-out-of-the-dorm thing works. Weekend curfew is midnight, and there's a resident advisor on duty downstairs from then until the morning. The only other way out of the dorm is the door at the bottom of the laundry-room stairwell, which locks from the outside. As long as we leave a paper clip wedged into the door, we should be able to sneak in and out after checking in with the RA.

I stop in my room on the way out to say good night to Isabella, who's sitting on her bed with a book she's not reading open on her lap. She looks up at me, gnawing on her thumbnail.

"You okay?" I cock my head at her. She's been acting like she's on another planet all day. I couldn't convince her to come to the party. I'm a little paranoid she's upset I'm ditching her for the first night this week, even though that doesn't make sense, because she's been doing just fine on her own all year.

"Just a little tired." She closes her book and yawns. It's a slow and methodical one, as if even she doesn't believe she's tired. "I'll probably get an early night."

"I promise not to be loud and obnoxious when I get back," I say.

"You know I could sleep through a nuclear holocaust." Isabella grins at me.

When I find Remy, Kelsey, and April waiting for me in the hall like a pack of loyal Pomeranians, I'm reminded just how far away from home I really am.

I almost tell them I'm not going to the party. I'd much rather be watching reruns of *House Hunters* and making fun of Alexis with Isabella. But the thought that maybe Isabella needs a break from me propels me down the hallway to where the girls are waiting.

A tall boy with sand-colored hair meets us at the back door of the boys' dorm. Remy introduces him as Phil, and he smiles at me, his tongue poking through the small gap between his front teeth. He looks like a Phil.

Phil leads us upstairs, which is an exact replica of Amherst, except there are two doors to each room. We stop in front of 201A, which is leaking the type of whiny alternative music people only listen to at American Eagle.

"The crew team guys live in suites," April explains.

"They have their own bathrooms." Remy sighs.

"Wait, they get special rooms because they play a sport?" I ask. "Why, so their menstrual cycles sync up or something?"

"I like her," Phil says to Remy, sliding his ID into the door. She's still laughing at what I said, and I can't help but hate how pretty she is with her perfect top row of teeth showing. There's no way every guy in this school isn't in love with her.

Not that I'm threatened or anything.

The living room is about the size of my room at home, and it smells oddly okay—and by okay, I mean okay for four teenage guys living with minimal adult supervision. There are two straight-backed couches like the ones in the lounges here, and a TV with video game boxes stacked on each side.

Cole and Murali open the door, their eyes immediately falling to the sea of female legs in tight black skirts. I opted for something less obvious—a gray lace skirt over black tights. I still feel all three pairs of male eyes make their way over to me.

"Welcome, ladies." Murali bows. "May I offer you some wine?"

"It's not even from a box this time," Phil says, as if this is a major accomplishment. "Sebastian brought a whole case home from his vacation last summer."

Sebastian is a tall boy with a doofy grin on his face and really dark eyebrows. His black hair is styled too high in a way that turns my douche-sensors on.

"And who is the new lovely lady?" His voice lilts with a subtle accent. French, probably.

"This is Anne," Cole says. Reluctantly. "Anne, this is Sebastian."

The boy sticks out a hand with really long fingers. Everything about this kid—his eyebrows, nose, hands—look too big for his body, despite his height. "Pleased to meet you, *belle dame*."

I offer him a polite smile. *"Enchanté de vous connaître."*

Sebastian's face turns pink, but he smiles. Cole and Murali raise their eyebrows.

"What?" I say. "Six years of French."

"Ah, the language of love, no?" Maybe it's just me, but now Sebastian's accent seems more exaggerated. When someone calls him over, he bows to me and kisses my hand. I don't know whether to gag or laugh, so the tickle in the back of my throat is a mix of both.

"Sebastian's father is a French diplomat," Cole says when he's gone. "He's lived in the U.S. since he was five. The accent is how he picks up girls. Or tries to, at least."

"Thanks for the warning," I say, with a smirk to let him know I didn't need it.

Cole passes around plastic cups of wine as I'm introduced to a few more guys from the crew team and two athletic-looking blond girls named Jill and Brooke whom I recognize from some of my classes.

Brent isn't here yet, so I join the game of Never Have I Ever around the coffee table. I've always thought it was a lame game, but at least it helps me get some more information on my classmates. I'm halfway through my third glass of wine when someone says Remy is related to John Adams.

I'm laughing my head off, when everyone starts staring at me, and I realize, no, they're not joking. I mumble an excuse about needing the bathroom.

When I get back, Kelsey latches on to my arm and starts slurring about someone named Justin, who said he would be here tonight but isn't because he's hooking up with some freshman skank. I'm reminded of the fact that I still haven't seen Brent, and scan the room for him.

My heart catches in my throat as I see him in the corner of the room, talking to the volleyball girls. I'm torn between feeling butterflies that he's here and wanting to ignore him for not coming to find me, when he's the only reason I came in the first place.

I decide on ignoring. Five seconds later, Kelsey blasts a hole right through my brilliant plan to make him think I don't care he's here by yelling, "HEY! BRENT!"

He looks over. His expression quickly morphs from indifference to amusement.

"Really smooth," I say to Kelsey as Brent makes a *Hold on a second* sign to the volleyball girls and heads toward us.

"You made it." Brent leans against the wall next to me, his shoulder almost touching mine. "Now I need to avoid Cole until he forgets I owe him money."

"You *bet* on whether I'd show up?" I eye him over my shoulder. We're both kind of looking ahead and not at each other. But I'm glad he's here.

"Brent, why didn't you tell me about Justin and the ninth-grade skank?" Kelsey blurts, grasping both of us for support.

"Because you're drunk, Kels, so whoever did tell you is an idiot." Brent gently sets Kelsey up against the wall and turns to me. "This is Sloppy. Have you met the other dwarves? Pukey and Dopey?"

I survey the living room. April is lying on the couch with her head in Cole's lap. Remy is telling everyone who will listen that Phil hasn't changed his socks in two weeks since he's convinced the Patriots won't make it to the Super Bowl if he does and isn't that *disgusting*?

"Interesting party," I say.

Brent laughs. "You have no idea what spending all your time with the same people for three years will do to you."

"I'm getting an idea," I say, watching as Murali and one of the crew guys drag Phil across the kitchen floor by his socks.

"How long have you been here?" Brent sips his beer, meeting my eyes for the first time tonight. He has really nice eyelashes for a guy, I notice. I also notice that Kelsey is gone, and it's just me and him.

I shrug. "Hour or so. You?"

" 'Bout a half hour. Nice of you to say hi."

"What?" I turn my whole body toward him. "I didn't even see you come in. You could have said hi to *me*."

"I'm too nervous to say hi to hot girls." His pupils are slightly larger than normal.

"You're full of crap." I smack him in the chest. His T-shirt is really soft, so I let my hand linger there. He steps in closer to me, as if he doesn't want me to stop touching him.

"You don't have a drink," he says. "Want one?"

"I had one already. And then another one." I tilt my head to the side, letting my hair fall across the sliver of bare shoulder created by my silky black top. It's the most manipulative move ever, because any guy with a normal testosterone level would reach out and brush the hair away, but Brent seems relatively immune.

"And you don't want another because you'll turn into that?" Brent nods toward Remy, who's crawled onto the lap of one of the crew guys and stolen his neon green sunglasses.

"My parents sent me up here so I could reform my bad-girl ways," I say. "I'm giving it a shot."

"Well, if you ever need help from the resident good boy, I live here. In this room." Brent points to the floor. The miniscule gesture sways him. I put my arm on his shoulder to steady him. The buzzed leading the buzzed.

No one is looking at us. This is that crucial moment where we either sneak off together or rejoin the party. If we go back to hanging out with everyone else, our chances of getting each other alone again pretty much suck.

"Hey, Brent!" Cole yells from across the room. He holds up a Ping-Pong ball. "Partners?"

"Ooh. Crap. Forgot I promised him." Brent pokes me in the side again, and just like that, I'm ditched.

I don't think I've ever hated beer pong more in my life.

I play a few more games of Never Have I Ever before I glance at the screen of my phone. It's 1:09 A.M. already and I've just about had enough. From the looks of it, Pukey and Sloppy look like they have, too. April is slumped over the side of the couch with her hand over her mouth, and Kelsey is crying to Cole, who is massaging her back with one hand and trying to make a shot in beer pong with the other.

"I think it's time to go," I say to April, helping her sit up.

"Really?" She peers up at me. "Did my mom call and say so?"

"Yes. She also said you're in big trouble if you throw up on the way back to the dorm."

Remy makes it very clear she will end my life if I try to make her leave, but Brent stops the beer pong game for long enough to help me pry Kelsey away from Cole.

"Have Kelsey text me when you guys get back to the dorm safely, okay?" he says.

"I think he likes you," Kelsey says when we get outside. April is trailing behind us at the pace of a baby sloth, and I'm half-considering carrying her so we don't get caught.

"He would have given me his phone number and told *me* to

text him if he liked me," I say crankily. "But he told me to have *you* text him."

"Brent's, like, super private with that stuff," Kelsey says. "I think he hates boarding school."

"Who hates boarding school? I love boarding school," April informs us.

I don't have time to obsess over Brent's mixed signals when we get to our floor and I realize I left my ID card in the room. My buzz is rapidly wearing off, I'm getting a blister from my boots, and I really, really want to go to bed. I knock on the door, even though I know it's no use. Light off. Isabella passed out. Anne screwed.

"Knock louder!" Kelsey's voice is a dull roar. I'm pretty sure she was going for a whisper. I shush her, panic creeping into my chest.

"What if Darlene hears and comes out?" I ask. "Her light is on!"

"Just say you got up to go to the bathroom and forgot your key," Kelsey says.

"Dressed like this?" I hiss. "She thinks we've been asleep for the past three hours! I can't get in trouble my first effing weekend here!"

Kelsey's eyes well up again. I ignore her and call Isabella, but it goes straight to voice mail.

"I have to sleep in your room," I tell Kelsey.

"Fine," she sniffs. "Only if you promise not to yell at me again."

For frick's sake. I cross my heart for her and follow her into her room, where April is sprawled on the carpet.

"You can sleep in her bed," Kelsey says. "She can't fall onto the floor and get a concussion if she's already lying on it."

So reassuring. I crawl into April's bed anyway, though. She has microfiber fleece sheets, which quickly get rid of the chill in my body. Kelsey is snoring lightly within minutes. I say a quick prayer for my parents, hungry people, and that April doesn't throw up everywhere, because the only one I'll clean up puke for is my dog.

Of all the nights for Isabella's phone to die.

When I wake up, I check to make sure April and Kelsey are still breathing. It's light-ish outside, so Isabella should be awake and getting ready for the Wetland Conservation Club outing that she's been talking about all week.

That's right. The Wheatley School has a *Wetland Conservation Club.*

I grab the furry blue bathrobe hanging from the back of Kelsey and April's door and slip it on as a precaution. I look like an overgrown Sesame Street character, but the last thing I need is to run into Alexis when I'm wearing the same clothes I had on last night.

"Isabella." I knock loudly this time. "Isabella!"

The light is still off. I call her phone, but again, straight to voice mail. Isabella must have overslept: There's no way she'd be able to get up without her phone alarm.

I can stand here pounding on the door and wake up the whole dorm, or I can bite the bullet and tell Darlene I'm locked out. At least I can use the *I went to the bathroom and forgot my key* excuse now.

Isabella isn't in the bathroom, even though my gut knew before I checked that it would be useless. I knock on Darlene's door and gnaw the inside of my lip while I wait for her to open it.

"What's up, Anne?" There's a phone cradled between her neck and her shoulder, and her expression and voice say she really wants to get rid of me. What's she so anxious about this early in the morning?

"I'm locked out," I say. "And Isabella won't wake up."

"You're gonna have to wait a couple of minutes," she says. "I'm kind of dealing with something right now."

She retreats into her room. It's a suite, like the guys have, and I notice there's someone sitting on Darlene's living room couch. It's Emma, the RA from downstairs. She's on the phone, too, gnawing at her nails.

And that's when I realize something must be wrong. I'm practically trembling with curiosity by the time Darlene comes back out, key in hand. I follow her in silence as she opens the door to my room.

But Isabella isn't there. Her bed is untouched.

"Where is she?" I ask aloud.

"Didn't you see her this morning?" Darlene asks.

Shit. "Um. Not exactly. I stayed in April and Kelsey's room last night."

Darlene pushes her superblunt bangs up her forehead. "It's okay. She probably went for coffee or something."

"Her wallet is on her nightstand, though," I point out.

Darlene's face drains of color as she processes this. "Anne, when was the last time you saw Isabella?"

"Last night, at ten," I admit. "I was . . . hanging out with some other girls until late."

"*Fuck.*" Darlene pulls out her cell phone, and I'm so taken aback I plop down on my bed.

"What's wrong?" A panicked sensation is flooding my body.

"A body was found in the woods this morning," Darlene says, her voice tightening. "I've been trying to find out more for the past hour."

"No, no, no." My hands fly to my mouth. "It can't be her."

"I don't know. Just be quiet. I have to call Dr. Harrow and let him know."

It can't be her. It can't be her. Please don't let it be her!

Maybe I forget to breathe. Maybe deep down, I know it's her, and I can't handle it, because I black out.

The last thing I see before I do is the police officer in my doorway.

"It's *not* your fault." Remy squeezes my knee. We're on a couch. The lounge couch. We're in the lounge.

I can't remember the last five minutes. Or maybe it's been longer. Did I say it was my fault? I must have. And it's true, right? Because I left Isabella alone to go to that stupid party last night, and now she's dead.

"Anne, it's not your fault. Look at me."

I do. Remy's eyes are glassy. There are a couple of other girls hanging around the lounge, sniffing, wet streaks on their faces. They're crying for a girl they wouldn't have given the time of day to last night.

I'm not crying, which makes me think there's something wrong with me. I should be crying. My roommate died this morning.

Someone hands me a paper cup of water. It's a male hand. Brent sits on my other side and begins to rub my back. Sparks shoot to my stomach as I remember my hand on his chest last night. Him leaning into me. His touch now is totally different, though. I'm reminded of the way my mom rubs my back when I'm sick.

And suddenly I'm in kindergarten again and my mom just dropped me off, and I really, really want her back. I start to cry.

"Hey, girls, can we have a minute?" Remy says to the on-lookers. I can't look at them as they disperse.

"Rem," Brent says, his voice warning. We both look up.

There's a police officer in the doorway. I know he's looking for me before he opens his mouth and asks if there's an Anne in the room. I raise my hand stupidly, like I'm sitting in class and no one's died today or anything.

Brent and Remy get up to leave, and my hand instinctively curls around Remy's. She squeezes it back. "We'll be right out-side."

The officer clears his throat. "Anne, I'm Detective Phelan. I know you've had a difficult morning, but if you're okay to answer them, I have some questions about Isabella."

"What happened to her?" I ask. Just like that. Like he didn't just say he was the one with questions.

"The investigation is ongoing." Detective Phelan scratches his neck.

And that's when I know. Isabella's heart didn't stop. She didn't fall and hit her head on a rock.

"Someone killed her," I say. "That's what you won't tell me, right?"

The detective's radio goes off. He reaches for his belt and silences it. "Yes. We're treating this as a homicide."

Homicide. The word is like a punch to my stomach. Homicides happen in New York City, where there are drug dealers and gangs. They don't happen at fancy prep schools in Massachusetts, where everything is brick and covered in ivy and safe.

"Anne, do you have any idea why Isabella might have been in the woods last night?"

"I don't know," I answer honestly. "I only moved in a week ago. I really didn't know her at all."

Officer Phelan nods. "When did you last see her?"

I tell him how my friends and I went to the boys' dorm and didn't get back until after one.

"So, you don't know if Isabella ever went to sleep last night?" Officer Phelan repeats.

I nod. The look on his face says this little detail seriously complicates things.

"Okay." He sighs. "Someone will contact you for an official statement soon, but in the meantime, I'm going to have to ask you not to talk to anyone about what we discussed. Especially not reporters."

There are girls I've never seen before lurking outside the lounge when Officer Phelan leads me outside. I suddenly can't stand the thought of them looking at me, of anyone looking at me, even though that's who I am: the girl everyone looks at.

Everyone looks away and scatters back to their rooms when they see the detective. They all look terrified, and I can't shake this feeling that it's me they're scared of. Like they're inside my head and can hear me replaying the last conversation I had with Bailey before the fire.

Trouble has a way of showing up wherever you are, Anne.

CHAPTER
SEVEN

The story is all over the news. The administration is mega-pissed because they didn't get to notify everyone's parents first. They have all the RAs round us up like cattle and tell us any student who talks to the media or the police without obtaining permission from Dr. Harrow or Dean Tierney will be subject to disciplinary action.

Everyone seems more freaked out by *that* than the fact a student was murdered.

I know the police don't have a clue who did it, because since the story hit the news, I've been sitting at my laptop, reading every article I can find. They're all ridiculously short, and none even mention Isabella by name.

A 16-year-old female Wheatley School student was found dead in the woods adjacent to the Charles River. Police are ruling the death a homicide, but there are no suspects yet.

There's nothing else. Even by the next morning. This is a country that can track down a terrorist by a fingernail, yet no one in a town this small knows anything about who could have killed Isabella right in the school's backyard.

Or they do, and they're just not saying anything. All because of some stupid old headmaster who thinks the sizable checks to the school will stop coming in once all the mommies and daddies find out their future presidents and congressmen have been talking to the police.

It makes me want to throw something.

I almost do on the breakfast line, when I hear some nasally sophomore complain to her friend that the administration should have given everyone the day off. I want to throw her against the wall, even though I've never physically hurt anyone in my life.

"If you're going to be an insensitive bitch, you might want to check to see who's behind you," I snap at her.

I've lost the minuscule appetite I came here with, so I storm off the line before the girl has the chance to respond. Like she even would. In my haste, I knock shoulders with someone who has a much bigger and harder shoulder than mine.

I let out a sharp cry of pain without meaning to.

"I'm sorry," the guy says in this really strained, low voice. He's in my Latin class; I don't know his name, but he's huge and he wears Clark Kent glasses and he always knows the answer to Upton's questions. His eyes move to the girl I verbally bitch-slapped and then back to me. He heard everything.

He's not apologizing for bumping into me. He's just sorry— either for what the girl said or for Isabella or maybe even me.

And I can't handle anyone feeling sorry for me. Not after I left her for the party.

I'm out of the dining hall so fast it probably looks like I actually have somewhere to go.

I get to history early because the only thing that sounds worse to me than showing up for class is going back to the dorm and watching the police go through Isabella's stuff. My professor is waiting for me with a note instructing me to go to Dr. Harrow's office. I hope it's because the police found something, even though deep down I know I'm in for a *Please don't start pulling your hair out and eating it because your roommate died* speech.

Dr. Harrow looks like he's aged about five years since I saw him a week ago. He stumbles out of his chair when I knock on the door. "Anne. Come in."

My brain is lighting up with *Danger! Danger! He knows about the party!* I tell myself that Dr. Harrow is young and gentle and probably not the type of person who will expel me for sneaking out Saturday night.

He tells me everything I expected him to tell me. That nothing like this has ever happened at the Wheatley School before; the faculty is very shocked and saddened; it's especially tragic this had to happen my first week here. He gives me the building and phone number for Student Support Services. It's all so . . . expected. That's why he throws me when he says, "Anne, forgive me if this is too forward, but did you and Isabella get along?"

"What? Of course we did." I shift in my chair. "I mean, I've only known her since Sunday."

Knew. Knew her.

"Did she . . . confide in you about anything?" Dr. Harrow presses on. "Or did she say anything at all that might have suggested she was in trouble or worried about something?"

"No," I say. "She seemed a little off on Saturday, but she only told me she wasn't feeling well."

"And she didn't say anything about going anywhere or meeting anyone Saturday night?"

I shake my head. "Shouldn't the police be asking me this?"

"Anne, you should know that the administration and staff are cooperating fully with the police, despite any rumors you might hear to the contrary." Dr. Harrow leans back in his chair. "Since you lived with Isabella, the police think you might be able to help them."

Something about his voice tells me he doesn't agree with the police, but he goes on. "The headmaster has given them permission to contact you again. For an official statement."

"Okay. But they should probably talk to people who knew her better than I did."

"Of course they will." There are grayish brown bags under Dr. Harrow's eyes, which are a brilliant blue. I believe him. "But right now, you're the closest the police are to finding out where Isabella may have gone Saturday night."

As I collect my bag and let him walk me to the door, I get the feeling he probably wasn't supposed to tell me that.

But there's something else bothering me. Something that doesn't make sense about what Dr. Harrow said. *Nothing like this has ever happened at the Wheatley School before.*

I think of what Brent told me last week, about Matthew Weaver. A missing student who is probably dead hardly counts as nothing. Have they really forgotten about him?

And will everyone forget about Isabella just as easily?

The only reason I go to dinner that night is because Remy and Company won't get out of my room unless I agree to. And I can't keep watching them eye Isabella's side of the room like she's going to jump out of the closet any minute and yell that this is all a big joke.

Even though I wish it were.

The dining hall is the quietest I've ever heard it when we walk in. Everyone is talking in hushed voices, and the looks on their faces say they're all talking about the same thing. A few pairs of eyes linger on me as we find the most private table possible.

Cole and Murali spot us from a table not far away. They pick up their trays and move toward us, leaving Alexis completely alone at the table. My gag reflex goes off as she rolls her eyes and follows them.

Murali squeezes my shoulder and Cole nods to me. Alexis, of course, ignores me and sets her tray down on the table a little too hard. A male RA walks by us, depositing a white sheet of paper on the table.

"We have an assembly after dinner. Goddard is going to talk to us," Alexis announces without even looking at it.

No one questions it, because it's just the sort of thing Alexis would know about and we wouldn't. Apparently the headmaster showing his face is a Really Really Big Deal, though. Everyone suddenly looks antsy in a way that makes me seriously wonder what this Goddard guy has done to strike such fear in their preppy little hearts.

I reach for the white paper. *Mandatory assembly in Blackwood Hall at 7:30 this evening. Attendance will be taken.*

"Do you think they know who did it?" Kelsey asks.

"It was probably some drug dealer," Alexis says. "Why else would she be in the forest in the middle of the night?"

I set down my fork. "Did you get that idea from your ass, Alexis? Because I know you didn't get it from the news."

Murali looks like he wants to give me a high five. Everyone else looks at Alexis. Her cheeks flush as deep as her sweater, and she's about to open her mouth when someone loudly shoves a chair between me and Remy.

"Scoot over," Brent says to her. Wet curls poke out from beneath his knit hat.

"You okay?" Remy purses her lips at Brent. She pushes her bowl of sliced strawberries toward him, but Brent ignores it and turns to me. "Have you heard from that detective again?"

"Not since I talked to him yesterday."

Alexis's voice is clipped. "You talked to the cops?"

"Of course I did," I say. "Isabella was my roommate."

"They told us not to." Alexis stares at me like I belong in a school where the main subjects are shoe-tying and counting change. It's the same way she looked at me my first day, and then again when I walked into her Calculus class.

If I didn't have more obvious things to worry about, I would take this bitch down.

"I talked to my dad today," Cole cuts in. That gets everyone quiet.

"He's the attorney general of Massachusetts," Alexis says without looking at me, even though I'm obviously the only person at the table who didn't know this.

Remy shushes her. "What'd he say? Does he know anything?"

"He wouldn't tell me much. He said the police commissioner is going to release more information tomorrow . . . but they're saying this probably wasn't random. Whoever killed Isabella probably knew her."

A hush falls over the table. April opens her mouth as if to say something, but Alexis gives her a hard look. April picks up her fork and turns it over in her hands.

No one is looking at one another.

I know the man who's stepped out onto the auditorium stage is the headmaster, based on the sheer fact everyone looks like they're about to wet their pants. Bailey has the same effect on people, until you do something totally ridiculous, like program your best friend's cheating ex's laptop with a virus that blasts "I'm a Slave 4 U" on loop during theology class. Then she'll crack and laugh at your moxie while sharing peanut M&M's with you in her office.

Headmaster Goddard doesn't seem like the M&M-sharing type.

The auditorium is so quiet I can hear my heartbeat.

"The Wheatley School and community lost a valuable member this weekend," he begins. "Isabella Fernandez was a hardworking, generous, and kind-hearted student and friend. We ask you to respect her memory by avoiding the temptation to speak with any members of the media you may see in the surrounding area.

"I understand many of you have questions regarding the senseless nature in which this promising young woman's life was taken away. Unfortunately, the faculty does not have the answers to your questions at the current time. Rest assured that the staff, administration, and Suffolk Police are confident in your safety on campus. Security will be increased in light of the pending investigation. However, this incident should serve as a tragic reminder that *leaving* the dormitories after proscribed curfew hours is a serious infraction."

Is he trying to say that this was Isabella's fault? What an asshole.

Goddard clears his throat. "Any student with pertinent"—he pauses on the word—"information that may aid the investigation is reminded to see me, Dr. Harrow, or Dean Tierney, Dean Watts's replacement. Thank you for your respectful attention. Memorial service information will be available in the coming days."

Goddard exits, and Harrow steps onto the stage. The climate in the auditorium immediately relaxes. Harrow clears his throat and taps the top of the microphone. He tells us how sorry he is that we've lost a classmate in such a brutal and senseless manner, but I tune out once he starts playing rumor patrol. I've been reading enough news articles to know the facts:

1. Isabella's throat was cut.
2. She had no personal items on her except her Wheatley Student ID.
3. No one in the teachers' cottages across from the forest heard or saw anything.

My roommate is dead, I realize, as if for the first time. I turn my head and survey the sea of bodies behind me. Almost everyone is watching Harrow with unsettled looks on their faces; some have their eyes cast downward, whispering to the people next to them. How could no one have seen Isabella the night she was killed? By sheer probability alone, someone must have run into her.

My roommate is dead. And someone here knows more than they're telling.

CHAPTER
EIGHT

I really wish I could take back whining about not being able to wear my new BCBG dress, because it's the only thing in my closet appropriate enough for Isabella's wake. The sleeves are long and the skirt comes up to my mid-thigh, but with black tights and a sweater, I almost look like I know what I'm doing.

I was six at the only funeral I've ever been to. Grandpa Harold died. Enough people came to fill up St. Patrick's Cathedral, and when my mom wasn't listening, my father said all of them probably just wanted to make sure he was dead. I don't really remember much other than that St. Patrick's was the most beautiful thing I'd ever seen, so I spent the whole service pretending I was Esmeralda and inside Notre Dame.

After getting dressed, I French-braid my hair and sit on the edge of my bed. My stomach hurts and I just want to go home. I know my parents would let me, considering the circumstances, but there's no check big enough from Kenneth Dowling to convince any school in New York to accept mid-semester the arsonist from the Upper East Side.

I can't switch schools again without totally screwing up my

transcript and whatever chances I have left of getting into a decent college. I have to stick it out, even though the coolest person I met here is laying in a casket instead of tormenting me with corny songs she made up to remember dates for her history test, like she should be right now.

Remy, April, and Kelsey are waiting for me downstairs. They're all in gray wool skirts and ruffly black blouses, their hair held back by headbands. I look so out of place in my heels, and I feel even more out of place because I'm not related to a president and I've never been to Nantucket. I can't even figure out the train system here by myself, which is the only reason I'm not going to the wake alone.

We meet Brent and Cole by the bell tower between the dorms. The service is being held in Somerville, which is about a fifteen-minute "T" ride outside Wheatley. (I now know that the T is the Massachusetts term for the subway, thanks to an embarrassing dinner conversation where I thought everyone was talking about golf.)

It's too cold to talk as we walk to the station and wait for the train. There are a couple of people from our class waiting on the platform, their eyes on the ground, on their cell phones. *They don't want to make eye contact with us,* I realize. It annoys me, because we all have something in common right now—our classmate died—and it really wouldn't freaking kill anyone to act like it.

There aren't many free seats open on the train. I sit between Remy and April, watching as Brent offers the last open seat to a girl who flushes like she's both nervous and enthralled that he actually spoke to her.

When she sits down, I get a good look at her round and freckly face. She's Molly, the girl I saw Isabella talk to after class sometimes. Without thinking, I get up and squeeze through the standing bodies, nearly causing a super-embarrassing scene when the train lurches forward and my heels threaten to give out beneath me.

"Excuse me," I say to the boy sitting next to her. "Do you mind if I sit next to Molly for a sec?"

The boy looks from Molly to me and shrugs before leaving me his seat.

"How do you know my name?" Molly asks. Her voice isn't accusatory. Just curious.

"Isabella told me you guys were kind of friends," I say.

"We weren't close or anything." Molly casts her eyes down and flicks a piece of lint from her skirt. "But she was a townie, too, so—"

"A townie?"

Molly's cheeks redden. "It's what everyone calls kids from the suburbs who go to the school on full scholarship. Isabella's family lives in Somerville."

"Oh." I'm not surprised or anything, since I knew Isabella didn't really fit in with the rich kids. It's just weird that I'm learning all of this stuff about her now. Would she ever have told me herself?

"I'm Anne, by the way," I say.

Molly bobs her head. "I know. Isabella liked you a lot."

Now I'm surprised. I mean, I really liked Isabella, and we had a lot of fun together, but in the back of my mind I had this feeling that she was only . . . tolerating me. Like she was stuck with this princess-y new roommate from New York City, so she might as well make the best of it.

A little part of me wishes that had been the case, so I could feel less sad right now.

"I just can't believe this happened to her," I say.

"Mm," Molly replies. When I look over at her, she's studying her hands.

Almost as if that *Mm* was her way of not agreeing with me.

There are newscasters outside the funeral home, along with police officers telling them to back the hell off. The police com-

missioner released the full details of Isabella's murder in a statement on Wednesday, and so far, the school and police have been
able to keep the reporters off campus.

Isabella's wake is nothing like Grandpa Harold's funeral. Everyone looks like they can't quite believe they're here, as if
they're walking through a dream. Or nightmare. I take a prayer
card with shaking hands and gather the nerve to look at Isabella's casket.

It's closed, with pink and yellow roses covering the top. To
the side is an enlarged school portrait of Isabella, surrounded by
smaller family photos. I study them as I wait in line to pay my
respects. In most of the baby pictures, Isabella is with a boy.

I feel as if I'm going to pass out as I reach the front of the line.
I kneel on the cushioned riser like I saw everyone else do and
close my eyes. I don't think I can do this. I don't even belong
here, really. I only knew Isabella for a week.

I squeeze my eyes shut tighter. *Thanks*, I say in my head.
*Thanks for sharing your gummy worms and helping me find
my classes and being nice to me when I really needed it.* And
then, almost as an afterthought: *They're going to find whoever
did this to you. I promise.*

When I stand up, I notice a guy staring at me. He definitely
doesn't go to the Wheatley School. His dark brown, almost
black hair covers his ears and the back of his neck. His eyes are
dark with bags underneath, and he has a five-o'clock shadow.

But he still sets off a string of thoughts in my head that are
totally inappropriate to be having in a funeral home.

He looks away when he sees me watching. He's standing
with a redheaded woman who has her back to me, and a frail-
looking man in a wheelchair.

These are Isabella's parents. I don't need the photos by the
casket to tell me this. The face of the man in the wheelchair is
enough; he looks like his whole world just fell apart.

My gaze moves to someone—an older man—standing just
beyond Isabella's family. He catches my attention because he's

by himself, his hands in his pockets, looking over at Isabella's casket in this voyeuristic way that completely creeps me out.

He has a thick gray beard and mustache, and his dress shirt is too tight over his round midsection. His eyes lock with mine for a moment, then he turns and pushes his way through the crowd.

I lose him in an eyeblink, because the funeral home is packed. Most of the junior class is here, along with a bunch of teachers, Dr. Harrow, and a woman whom I assume is Dean Tierney, because she's too old to be Dr. Harrow's wife and too important-looking to be a teacher. She's one of the only people here not wearing black; instead, she's got on an ugly tweed jacket.

I put the dean and the creepy guy out of my mind for now and circle around to the younger guy who was watching me.

I wait for him to finish accepting an awkward hug from a balding man before I step forward. His dark eyebrows knit together when he sees me.

"Um, hi," I say. "Are you Isabella's brother?"

He nods but keeps a distance between us that says he's not sure who the hell I am or why I'm talking to him. "Anthony. Were you friends with her?"

"I was her roommate."

Anthony's hands go into the pockets of his suit jacket, which looks sort of lopsided and wrong on him. "I didn't know she got a roommate."

"I only knew her a week," I say guiltily, like that doesn't give me the right to be here or something. "I'm sorry for your loss. She was really sweet to me."

I expect Anthony to thank me, but instead he lets out a short laugh and lets his eyes flick to the ceiling before holding my gaze. "Yeah. She was really sweet."

I can't tell if he's being sarcastic or not, but the way he's staring at me now freaks me out a little. His eyes are the color of steel, like Isabella's. I'm about to pronounce our conversation dead when he says, "So you're new at the school or something?"

I nod. "I'm from New York."

"So that explains the funny accent." Anthony's mouth curls into the smallest smile.

I ignore this. "Did you go to the Wheatley School, too?"

Anthony shakes his head. "I'm not *gifted* like my sister. I go to public school."

"Oh. I thought you might be in college. You look a lot older than her."

"She was my twin." He's staring at me again. "You're the only one of her friends who's even said anything to me or my family, you know."

"They're all freaked out, I think." I pause, not sure why I'm telling him this. But I've been dying to talk to someone about it. "The administration is being weird. We have to go to them first with anything we know and get permission to talk to the police."

Anthony's tanned face deepens a shade. "You gotta be shitting me. It's like they're practically throwing it in everyone's face that they're covering for someone."

"You think they know something they're not telling the police?"

"I *know* they are." Anthony's voice is hard. "Iz used to say how she couldn't sneeze at that school without someone noticing. And they expect my family to believe that no one saw or heard a thing the night she was killed?"

I'm suddenly too warm in my sweater. Everything he's said makes sense. There's so much more I want to ask him, but I know we can't keep talking here. Not when Anthony's supposed to be here to grieve.

Not when I don't know who's listening to us.

I'm about to let Anthony go back to his family when he says, "Hey. You never told me your name."

"It's Anne." I flush, all the way to my toes. God, I'm being ridiculous. He's not my type at all. I think I even saw dirt underneath his fingernails when he brushed the hair out of his eyes before.

I find Remy and everyone else in a corner, huddled together and looking super uncomfortable.

"Hey, did you see that creepy old guy hanging out in the corner?" I ask. I give them the man's description.

"Oh, that's Professor Andreev," Cole says. "Our physics teacher."

"He looked kind of sketchy," I say.

"Brent thinks he's a Soviet spy." Remy rolls her eyes. "Don't get him started, or he'll tell you his whole conspiracy theory."

Brent and I fall behind everyone else as we make our way to the funeral home's exit.

"You know, Isabella was doing independent research with Andreev last year," he says. "I know he's creepy, but he's won all these awards and grants and used to work in a lab. He could get anyone in to MIT."

Was that where Isabella wanted to go to college? MIT? It makes me sad that I never found out.

Wet, slushy snow is coming down outside. There's a line to get inside the funeral home now. The sound of yelling startles us; I look over at the line, expecting to see someone duking it out with a reporter.

Instead, I see that everyone has cleared a space around Anthony and a slightly older guy who looks really pissed off. My pulse quickens as Anthony gets in his face and snarls, "You got some goddamn nerve showing up here."

The guy's voice is angry, taunting. It also sounds a lot like Anthony's. "You really wanna lay a hand on me here, Anthony? You trying to kill your father, too?"

Anthony's fist flies out and connects with the guy's jaw. A few people cry out in surprise and rush to him as he doubles over. Within seconds, I'm being herded away and listening to Kelsey whine, "Oh my God, oh my God," as if the whole scene is going to leave her needing therapy.

"That was bizarre," Brent says, but I'm looking backward to see what happened to Anthony. I can't see him in the crowd that's gathered outside the funeral home now. The reporters are going to have a field day with that one.

"Who was that guy?" Remy asks, her voice shushed.

"Isabella's brother," I say.

I'm still so shocked at what happened that I barely hear Cole when he says, "Sounds like the guy he punched out thinks he might have killed her."

CHAPTER
NINE

What I should be doing after Isabella's funeral: moving on with my life as if everything were normal, and trying to focus on getting the hell out of Massachusetts.

What I should not be doing: having trouble getting my mind off her extremely attractive brother and staying up until 4:00 A.M. reading news stories about her murder.

Every story ends the same way. Who would want to kill a brilliant, quiet girl attending the prestigious Wheatley School on a full scholarship?

I know I'm looking for something that's not there: answers.

I feel an overwhelming sense of despair when I get to Issues in Contemporary History the next morning and see the desks arranged in a circle, because I was really looking forward to catching up on sleep. I've always liked history, but the title is seriously the most interesting thing about this class. Even the professor looks like he wants to fall asleep as my classmates spout out rehearsed little speeches about *cultural hegemony*.

They all take themselves so seriously, as if they're not raising their hands every thirty seconds, someone will tell the Ivy League admissions board on them.

I choose a seat at the edge of the semicircle, aware of the probing eyes watching me. From across the room, Alexis nudges Lizzie and mutters something to her. Annoyance flares in me, then curiosity.

Alexis wasn't at Isabella's wake yesterday. She obviously wasn't friends with Isabella, but neither were most of the people in the junior class. I mean, all I'm saying is that even if I didn't like her that much, I'd still go to my classmate's wake. Especially if she lived on my floor and I interacted with her every day.

I keep an eye on Alexis as Professor Matthews writes the topic for discussion on the board. Isabella's feelings toward Alexis were no secret, but I'm starting to think maybe there was more to Isabella's hatred than a few bitchy sticky notes. If Alexis really just saw Isabella as some loser townie who wasn't worth her time, she would have put on a fake smile and gone to the wake like everyone else. Because that's what Alexis is: an over-exfoliated, pearl-earring-wearing fake who only cares about looking like the perfect senator's daughter. And the perfect senator's daughter does not risk looking like an insensitive bitch by being the only person not to show up to a classmate's memorial service.

Unless she was purposely avoiding it.

"Mr. Crowley, why don't you start us off?"

I turn my attention back to the discussion, both relieved that Matthews didn't call on me and terrified because I have no idea what we're talking about.

Mr. Crowley, whose first name I think is Dan, straightens his tie and glances at his notes. "Uh, well, I agree with Davis's position on a postcolonial perspective, but I think his limited view of history compounds the very problem of marginalization he seems to be critiquing. . . ."

I can't help but look at Alexis again; this time it's not my fault, because she's being super obnoxious and rolling her eyes at everything Dan says. She even leans over to Lizzie and writes something in her notebook. They smirk at each other after Lizzie reads what it says. It's so rude I could explode.

So when Dan is done speaking, I raise my hand. Matthews nods to me, and everyone looks up from taking notes. I haven't spoken in this class yet. "I have to agree with Dan. I found the tone of Davis's article especially"—I lock eyes with Alexis and wait until everyone is sure I'm staring at her—"condescending."

She glares back at me, her cheeks flooding with color. She puts her pen down and folds her arms across her chest as Matthews prattles on about how Dan and I raise excellent points he hadn't considered before. Now that I've gone and publicly thrown the gauntlet down, everyone is watching Alexis with curiosity.

At least it'll stop her from making fun of everyone for the next forty minutes. It's totally worth the death stare Alexis is giving me now.

She literally looks mad enough to kill me.

The teachers don't talk about Isabella's murder much. At least, they don't say anything that wasn't already said in the "official" statement addressing the situation we all got in our e-mail.

The administration is shocked and saddened by Isabella's death.

Still, the Wheatley School is ranked number 2 on the *U.S. News and World Report* list of safest prep-school campuses.

But maybe we shouldn't go anywhere alone until her killer is found.

Remy, April, and Kelsey embrace that last part as an excuse to follow me everywhere. When we get to the dining hall for dinner, they come with me to the bathroom, even though the only reason I went in there in the first place was to get away from them.

I lock myself in a stall and respond to the text message I got from Chelsea earlier:

I'm okay. Things are super freaky here, and I'm dying to come home. Call u in a few hours. xoxo

I see Kelsey and April's feet lingering in front of the bathroom mirror as Remy slips into the stall next to mine.

"I heard a lot of people are going home this weekend," April says. "They're scared to stay in the dorms after what happened."

Kelsey is quiet. I watch her feet shift uncomfortably.

"You were screaming in your sleep last night again." April's voice is hushed.

"Sorry," Kelsey says. "It's just . . . you're not scared or anything?"

"I don't know. They told us not to be."

"April, do you think that . . ." Kelsey whispers as Remy's toilet flushes. My heart races as April speaks again.

"Kels, that's crazy," April hisses. "She could never—"

"What's crazy?" I ask. Remy and I open our stall doors at the same time.

April and Kelsey share a look. They glance at Remy, and April lets out a nervous laugh.

"It's nothing. Really." She shrugs.

"We should get back to the table," Remy says, throwing a look at April. "We left our bags there, and the guys probably got up to get food."

None of them make eye contact with me as we leave the bathroom. There's obviously something they won't say in front of me . . . and now I'm dying to know what—or whom—they're so afraid of.

My ID card is missing when we get back to the dorm. It's not in my bag, which makes absolutely no sense, because I keep it tucked in the ID sleeve of my wallet all the time.

"I just had it at the dining hall," I say to the RA at the front desk. Even though an ID is needed to get into the dorm, since Isabella's murder, there's always someone at the desk to double-check them.

"Maybe you dropped it there," Remy suggests. "We could go back and check. . . ."

We all look out the dorm window, at the tiny flakes falling from the night sky. I know what everyone is thinking: It's frickin' cold, and no one really wants to take the walk back with me.

"It'll be there in the morning." I sigh.

I get Darlene to let me into my room, still frustrated. How could I have lost my ID? I slipped it right back into my wallet after the dining-hall lady swiped it to let me in.

Darlene leaves and I flip the light on. My body goes stiff when I see what's on my desk.

My ID card.

CHAPTER
TEN

I make sure whoever was in here didn't take anything from me or Isabella before I curl into a ball on my bed and try to stop hyperventilating.

Someone was in my room. Someone stole my ID card right out of my wallet and used it to *break in to my room.*

What's even worse is the thought that I could have easily run into whomever it was. If I used my card to get into the dining hall, the person had to have stolen it while I was in the bathroom.

And the person—*she*—was able to get past the RA downstairs *and* knew the door entry code.

She lives here.

I immediately knock on Darlene's door. She sighs a little when she sees me, as if to say *What now?* I don't really blame her, since my knocking on her door ended with a dead body last time.

My throat is tight by the time I'm done telling Darlene what happened.

"Anne, it's okay. Are you sure you didn't just leave your ID there by mistake?"

"No. I had it with me at the dining hall."

"And there's nothing missing from your room?"

"Not that I can tell." I sniff. "But I don't know if they took anything of Isabella's."

"Anne, are you sure you didn't forget to show your card at the dining hall? You're probably just really stressed after all that's happened," Darlene says. "I can change your entry code, if that makes you feel better."

It doesn't. And it doesn't change the fact that someone went through my bag and left my ID card on my desk, as if to taunt me. They could have kept my card, but instead, they just left it on the desk.

To leave the message that they were there.

I don't sleep at all that night. The next morning, I skip breakfast and go straight to Dr. Harrow's office. He's not there.

"Excuse me, but when will Dr. Harrow be in?" I ask the secretary in the office across the hall.

"Not until later." She doesn't even look up at me. "You can leave your name in the book over there."

"But this is really important," I plead. "Someone broke in to my room."

The woman picks her head up. Apparently this isn't something she hears often. "I suggest you tell your RA."

"I *did*. She didn't do anything. I need to see Dr. Harrow."

"Is there a problem?" A woman pokes her head out of the door behind the secretary's desk. Her dyed red hair is in a bun, and she looks like she's in her midforties. I recognize her from Isabella's wake, mostly because she's wearing the same tweed jacket.

DEAN JACQUELINE TIERNEY, the plaque on her door says.

"Someone broke in to my dorm room," I blurt.

The dean gives me a once-over. She doesn't bother to introduce herself or ask who I am. Obviously she already knows, but still. I don't trust her.

"We've never had a break-in in our dormitories before," she says.

Yeah, that anyone *reported*, probably. "Well, someone was in my room. They stole my ID card."

Dean Tierney blinks and gives me a small smile, as if this is the biggest crock of shit she's heard in a while. "Was anything taken?"

I swallow. "No. But someone was definitely in there. Can I talk to Dr. Harrow?"

"Dr. Harrow is away," she says. "I'll alert him to the issue when he returns. If you'd like a new room, please go to Student Services. I'm sure they will accommodate you."

I stand there, stunned, as the dean disappears into her office again. After everything that's happened this week, Tierney is still so concerned with staying a *U.S. News and World Report* Safest Prep School that she's not going to report the break-in? I don't want a new room. Student Services offered me one right after Isabella was killed. The only open rooms are triples in the freshmen dorms, which honestly makes being murdered in my sleep look not so bad.

I wait until I'm out of the administration building to give in to a few tears. Obviously I can't go to class now, and I don't want to go back to my room. I could go to the police, but what would I say? *Hey, I have absolutely no evidence, and they didn't take anything, but someone was in my room.*

I wipe my eyes with my gloves and take a deep breath. *Keep it together, Anne. You can't go home. You need to get through this.*

I use my phone to search for places in Boston that sell pepper spray. Whoever was in my room might have killed Isabella.

They might have been looking for something, and if they didn't find it, they might try to come back.

But if they do, I'll be ready.

It's Saturday morning. My father is having a hissy fit on the other end of the phone because I didn't mention that the girl who got killed was my roommate, and that's apparently something the school sends parents e-mails about.

"Did it just *slip* your mind?" His voice crackles. He's calling from an international phone.

"Daddy, chill out. I told you I knew her. You and Mom would only freak out and come up here if I told you she was my roommate, and that wouldn't help anyone or change anything—"

"Do you even understand what you've done?" I can practically hear the veins in his neck throbbing, threatening to burst all over his Marc Jacobs tie. "The school said you gave a statement to the police. *Without legal counsel present.*"

"How could you expect me not to talk to the police when I was the last person to see her alive—"

My throat closes midsentence. Oh. It hits me again, like a punch to the stomach: I was *the last person to see Isabella alive.*

My father is silent on the other end. I grab the rosebud salve from my nightstand and start slathering it on my lips.

His voice is calmer now, like he's talking to a client. "Anne, if you had anything to do with this, I need to know *now.*"

I feel as if I've been slapped. "What—are you serious? You think I would—"

"Of course not. But if you even saw or did anything that could give them a reason to get you involved—"

"I *didn't.*" Hot, angry tears pool in my eyes. This is all just so messed up. I'm five hours from home, my roommate is dead, and my own father thinks I had something to do with it. All because I couldn't stay away from a stupid boy.

I let myself have a brief fantasy of pushing Martin Payne

down the stairs for getting me into this mess. Even though I know if I wasn't so damn stupid that day, I wouldn't have been in the auditorium with him after school to begin with.

But I'm not going to be stupid again, and I'm sure as hell not going to sit back and let everyone here whisper and point fingers at me.

"Anne, we're going to handle this. Do *not* tell your mother we spoke about this; it'll kill her. I'm going to say there was an emergency at work and book the first flight out of Paris—"

"No! I mean, please don't cut your vacation short, Daddy."

"But—"

Knocking at my door makes me scramble out of bed in a panic. Was someone out there listening the whole time? "Daddy, I gotta go I love you *please* don't come up here bye!"

I hang up before he can protest, and I run a hand through my hair. I'm still in the yoga pants and tank top I slept in.

Darlene is hanging in the hall, as if she's afraid to get too close to the room. It's a good thing, because I never did get rid of my coffeemaker.

"Hey, Anne. Um, someone is here to pack up some of Isabella's belongings. I hope you don't mind."

"Oh. Of course not," I say, although it's a little weird, because Detective Phelan and some other guy were here a few days ago. They took Isabella's computer and some laundry and other personal items.

Darlene shuffles away, and I can practically feel every part of my body turn red as I spot Anthony on the other side of my door, his hands in the pockets of his leather jacket. He takes one out to give me a halfhearted wave that shows he feels as awkward as I do.

"Sorry to surprise you," he says as I let him in the room. He's carrying two small cardboard boxes that aren't nearly big enough to hold all of Isabella's stuff.

"It's fine." I cross my arms over my tank top. "Are your parents coming?"

Anthony shakes his head. His hair looks a little cleaner than the last time I saw him, and he shaved. The thought that it's maybe because he knew he was going to see me sends a jolt of electricity to my toes. "My mom is a PA at MassGen. She works nights, so it's hard for her to get here. And my dad is really sick, as you probably noticed. MS."

I nod, even though Anthony isn't looking at me. His eyes are on Isabella's side of the room. His body is tense as he glances from her bed to her desk, like he's staring at the room of a stranger.

I sit on my bed and pull my knees up to my chest. I'm suddenly aware of the fact that there's a really attractive guy in my room who also might be a little unstable, and no, I am not wearing a bra.

Butterflies swarm in my stomach as I watch his eyes rest on my chest. He totally notices the bra thing, because his cheeks and neck flush.

"So, er, do you want help with . . ." I point to the boxes at Anthony's feet.

"Huh? Oh." His gaze drops from me to the floor.

"I mean, if you want me to leave so you can have some privacy, I understand too—"

"No. Stay. If you want."

I do. I don't really understand why, but I want to be wherever Anthony is right now. Maybe it's because he's the only person who's not afraid to talk about Isabella.

And he could be the perfect person to help me.

We pack up the things the police didn't collect as evidence—Isabella's DVDs, a plastic box holding nail polish and handmade braided bracelets. We work in silence for a while, until Anthony finds a file folder on her desk. "Hey, do you think I should throw all this out? It's just graded papers and other crap."

I shrug and he hands it to me. I rifle through its contents; it looks like Isabella saved everything she did since September. Her work from Latin is at the front of the pile. She got an A on the first assignment.

"Find something interesting?" Anthony asks.

"I don't know," I murmur, flipping through the rest of the assignments. Why the heck did Isabella drop this class? The lowest she got on anything was an A–. The stack ends in mid-October.

"Anthony, did your sister mention a class she dropped?" I ask.

"No. We weren't close." He's studying me now. "Why?"

"Just curious." I need to know what Isabella replaced Latin with. When Anthony turns back to the box of DVDs next to Isabella's bed, I poke around her desk until I find her schedule.

Instead of Latin, Isabella's eighth period was . . . study hall? This can't be right. Isabella didn't need a study hall. Every free second Isabella wasn't in class *was* her study hall. It definitely doesn't make sense that she dropped a class she had straight A's in.

"What's that?" Anthony's voice behind me makes me jump.

"Isabella's schedule. Something's weird. She dropped a class she was getting A's in for study hall."

Anthony's face scrunches up as he considers this. Even if he wasn't close to his sister, he's thinking what I'm thinking: It doesn't sound like Isabella.

"She could have been trying to avoid someone in that class," I say. "If I can find out who, then—"

"You're serious, aren't you? The police can't get anyone to talk, but you think *you* can?"

"They're more likely to talk to me. I'm not a threat to them like the police are."

"I don't get it." There's an edge to Anthony's voice that makes my heart sink. "What's in it for you if the school loses its reputation over this? Why aren't you like everyone else who doesn't give a shit who killed my sister?"

There's a lump in my throat, but I refuse to let him see how much that stung. "So just because my parents can afford to send me here I must not care about your sister, or anyone but myself for that matter? How do you know I'm not here on scholarship, too?"

He gets up and points to a picture of me swimming with a dolphin. "I'm guessing that wasn't taken in Florida."

"No. Turks and Caicos. What does that have to do with anything?" I demand.

Anthony takes half a step toward me, his mouth twisted in a smirk as if I've just confirmed all of his assumptions about me. He's close enough that I can see the ghost of a scar over his full upper lip.

"I'd tell you not to get involved and let the police handle my sister's murder," he says. "But I can tell you're not gonna listen anyway."

"No, probably not."

"Look, I want to know who killed her, too. But if you're not careful about snooping around here, you might as well attach a target to your back."

"I'm not afraid of these people because their parents are senators or diplomats or whatever," I say.

"Yeah, well. Maybe you should be."

CHAPTER
ELEVEN

I was in an episode of *Law and Order* when I was seven. Mom and I were in line at the post office when a casting director approached us. They were shooting at the courthouse across the street, he said, and I was perfect for an extra role they were trying to fill. All I had to do was let some lady hold me while screaming about how no one could ever take her babies away from her. Even though she'd kidnapped me.

Anyway. In the episode, the lady was in some cult, so the detective went undercover pretending he wanted to join, and that's how he got the rest of the members to implicate her in a string of murders.

What I'm getting at is that's all I really know about how the police do their thing when no one will talk to them. So that's why I've decided that if I'm going to get any sort of useful information about what got Isabella killed, I need to do it from the inside.

I can't just float around on my own and hang out with the alpha crowd when I feel like it anymore. I need to become one of them.

But when I get to the dining hall Monday morning, Kelsey is the only one at the table. She's picking the blueberries out of a muffin and arranging them in rows on her napkin.

"What's wrong?" I take the seat next to her and sprinkle pepper on my egg whites.

"Nothing's wrong." Kelsey's hands fly to her face. "Why, are my eyes puffy?"

"No." I point to her napkin. "But that's the kind of behavior they institutionalize people for, you know."

Kelsey sighs. I follow her gaze across the room, where a guy is waiting on the waffle line. The top button of his shirt is undone and his hair is swept to the side. Gross.

"Is that Justin?" I ask.

"Sh! What if he hears us?" Kelsey hisses.

"He'd need to have our table bugged to hear us from over there. Besides, he hasn't looked over here once." I adjust my voice a bit, knowing I probably need to be gentler with Kelsey. "You're gorgeous. You can do better than a creep who preys on freshmen."

"He broke up with me so he could focus on college stuff," Kelsey sniffs. "But he texts me all the time saying he misses me and doesn't want to lose me."

Now I'm the one sighing. "Kels, he wants you to be his backburner girl. He wants to hook up with whoever he wants and know that you'll still be there when he's mature enough for a girlfriend again."

Her face screws up, and I'm praying she doesn't have a meltdown right here at the table, because people who cry in public make me super uncomfortable. But instead, she says, "Oh my God. You're right." She balls up her napkin of blueberries. "What am I supposed to do?"

I reach across Kelsey for her phone and scroll through the contacts until I find Justin's number. I hold it up and make her watch me delete it, her eyes wide with panic. "You go cold turkey. That way he knows he's busted, and he feels like a dumbass."

Kelsey looks dumbstruck for a minute as I hand back her phone. But by the time Remy and April find us, she's smiling to herself and eating her muffin like a normal person.

Both girls look surprised to see me at the table, but April's mouth hangs open when she sees Kelsey. "She's eating."

Kelsey shrugs. "Anne and I talked. I'm feeling a lot better now."

Remy and April gape at me, totally unaware that they're still standing with their trays. Their faces are frozen with awe, like I've performed a miracle.

"Wow." Remy sits next to me. "Just wow."

One week, I estimate. One more week of this, and I bet Kelsey will tell me anything.

Professor Upton is five foot one with a frizzy blond bob. Her face is forty while the rest of her is obviously sixty. She gives me an icy smile when I approach her before Latin class. "Yes, Ms. Dowling?"

"I was wondering if I could ask you a question," I say. "About Isabella Fernandez."

Upton pushes her glasses down the bridge of her nose. "I'm not certain I can answer it. But go on."

"Why did she drop this class?" I ask.

Professor Upton's jaw sets. She shuffles the papers in her hands and avoids my eyes. "I'm not entirely sure why you're interested in that, Ms. Dowling."

"I'm just curious." I bite my lip until my eyes well up, hoping it'll make me look like the traumatized roommate.

Upton studies my face. "This is a high-level class. Not everyone can keep up with the demanding level of work. Isabella was struggling," she adds, before turning away from me.

I stand there, gaping, before it sinks in that the conversation is over. *She's lying.*

I'm still trying to work out why Upton would lie, as I pick a new seat at the back of the room. If I'm going to figure out the real reason Isabella dropped this class, I'm going to need to scope everyone out.

"Can, uh, I sit here?" The voice is small but familiar. Molly settles into the seat next to me, slowly, as if it's radioactive.

I look up at her. She's playing with the thick, messy braid over her shoulder. How did I not realize she was in this class? Probably because she sits here in the back every day, which means she's asking my permission to sit in her usual seat.

"Of course," I say.

Molly fidgets as she waits for her laptop to boot up. She can't keep her hands off her braid or her glasses. I'm obviously making her really nervous, so I decide it's probably best to wait until after class to talk to her.

We're declining nouns today. Upton scratches out a chart of different cases on the chalkboard. She's my only teacher who refuses to use a projection machine, and her room is wall-to-wall with books that desperately need a Swiffer Duster.

But I guess such a depressing room is fitting for learning about a dead language. I copy down Upton's chart in my notebook, keeping one eye trained on the rest of the room. I barely know anyone in this class; Latin definitely attracts the nerdy types.

Upton turns and faces us. "We'll start with the genitive of *principus*." A few hands go up. "Mr. Andersen. Please."

"*Principus* and *principum*." The voice is a dull rumble from the table next to me. It's Giant Clark Kent—the kid who bumped into me the morning after the police found Isabella's body.

"*Optime*." Upton gives him a clipped smile and writes his answers on the board. He hangs his head, twirling the pen in his hands. Then, as if he can sense me watching, he looks up at me with a deer-in-the-headlights stare.

I offer him a small smile, but he looks away quickly.

I'm starting to wonder if having a social problem is a prerequisite for being in this class.

"Hey, Molly, do you have a sec?" I ask when Upton lets us go.

She doesn't look up as she slides her laptop into its case. "Um. I guess."

"Cool." I follow her out into the hall. We hang back and let everyone go past us. "I wanted to know if you knew why Isabella dropped that class."

Molly pales. "I don't."

"I'm not stupid, Molly. She must have told you something."

Molly yanks me inside an empty classroom, away from the stragglers in the hall. "So what if she did? I'm not stupid, either. I know what you're trying to do, and trust me. It's not going to work."

I stand there, massaging my elbow, not because she hurt me when she grabbed it but because I'm so shocked she did. "If you're too scared to go to the police, then—"

"You don't get it," Molly snaps, her voice low. "I'm not supposed to talk about what happened, or I'll lose my scholarship. Isabella should never have gotten me involved."

"You'd let your friend's killer walk free so you can keep your scholarship to this school?" I shake my head in disgust and step toward the door. "Let me know if it's worth it."

Molly grabs my arm again. This time, she's rolled up the sleeve of her sweater. Bile rises in my throat: There are discolored lines running across her wrist. Scars.

"It started with the girls at my old school calling me a dyke," she says. "I went home and did this after they broke in to my locker and hid my stuff around the school. Now go ahead and tell me going back to public school isn't so bad."

I don't know what to say to her.

"Upton lied to me about the work being too hard for Isabella. She was trying to get away from someone in our class, wasn't she?"

Molly hesitates, which is all the answer I need.

The classroom door squeaks open, startling us both. Upton pokes her head in. "Did you need something, ladies? There's no class in this room this period."

"We were just talking," I say brightly. "Sorry, Professor."

Her eyes don't leave us as we duck past her and back into the hall. I turn back once there's a considerable distance between her and Molly and me.

Upton is still watching us, and her face says that she heard everything.

CHAPTER TWELVE

The police have finally moved the crime-scene tape separating the forest from the edge of campus. I hate the idea of going to look, like some morbidly curious gawker, but after class, I find myself taking the back way to the dorms.

The sound of dead leaves crackling under my boots is the only noise on the path that leads from the athletic fields to the forest. The quiet here drives me crazy; it's not the type of quiet that you hear in New York City once you get used to all the noise. It's just silence, broken up every hour by the clanging of the bell tower in the middle of campus.

I don't know if I'll ever get used to that.

I pause at the edge of the forest, anxiety settling in my chest. Why did I come here? To give myself nightmares? Because the endless expanse of trees with bare limbs twisting into the sky like gnarled arms is creepy enough without picturing Isabella's body lying cold in a pile of leaves.

The sound of my phone chirping startles me. I have an e-mail from antfern314@gmail.com.

anne,
I need to talk to you about Isabella. I don't know if you'll read
this in time. I didn't know how else to get in touch with you.
I'll be at Alex's Auto Body in Somerville from 3–7 today. If
you take the red line to Davis Station, it's right across the
street.
anthony

The auto body shop is so loud that I'm asking the guy in over-
alls out front for the fifth time if Anthony is here before I see
him in the side garage. He's wearing a grease-stained Pearl Jam
T-shirt and has his hair pushed back with a navy bandana. His
perpetually pissed-off expression softens a little when he sees
me and waves me over.

"So you're a mechanic," I say, trying to ignore the smell of
gasoline and motor oil hanging in the air.

"Part-time." His gaze travels up and down me. "Nice uniform."

"I know you didn't have me take the subway out here so you
could make fun of me."

"I wasn't making fun of you. And it's not called the subway
here, Derek Jeter." He smirks. "Now I'm making fun of you."

A thought crosses my mind: Why didn't Anthony just give
me his number and tell me to call him? Did he ask me here because he wanted to see me again?

He ushers me to an office the size of a closet at the back of a
garage. Under different circumstances, I might be excited to be
sneaking off into a small space with such a hot guy. But this one
is kind of a jerk; he's dirty, and he's my dead roommate's brother.

He's also the type of guy who punches people at memorial
services.

"Before you say anything," I begin as he closes the office
door, "I have to ask you something."

Anthony folds his arms across his T-shirt. They're not big,

like someone who works out a lot, but toned, like he's always using them. "You want to know why I punched out my cousin at the wake."

"How did you—"

"I saw you outside the funeral home when it happened. And I could tell you were about to explode trying not to ask me about it the other day."

I let the silence settle around us for a moment before I ask: "So why'd you do it?"

Anthony sits on the desk. We're at eye level now. "My cousin Paul's side of the family loves to run their mouths. They've been saying for years that going to that school was going to mess Isabella up. All those drugs and privileged brats." His expression hardens. "When we found out she was dead, Paul said Iz never would have had to leave public school if it weren't for me."

I think of Molly and the pink scars on her wrists. It sends a shiver through me. "She *had* to leave public school?"

"No. She'd been working her ass off to get into the Wheatley School since the fifth grade. But that's not how everyone remembers it." Anthony lets out an annoyed noise. "My parents wanted to get her away from me. I was in some fights in middle school. They were afraid of their little genius being known as the girl with the fuck-up brother."

Something clicks in my brain. "You didn't like her much, did you?"

Anthony shrugs and shifts in his seat. "We didn't get along."

I remember the horrible sound of Anthony's fist connecting with his cousin's face, and I wonder if there's anyone with a pulse Anthony *does* get along with. And then there's this unsettling feeling in the pit of my stomach, like I need to put as much distance between him and me as possible. He's obviously got a violent side, and as much as I don't want it to be true . . . what if he killed Isabella? It could have been an accident. Maybe they were arguing, and he lost his temper. . . .

I shake the thoughts out of my head for now. "So, why did you ask me here?"

Anthony blinks, as if he'd forgotten I'd come for a reason. "Oh. Yeah. You know how you helped me sort through the crap in Isabella's desk? You don't remember seeing a flash drive, do you? A purple one?"

"No. Maybe the police took it."

Anthony shakes his head and slides off the desk so he's standing. "It wasn't on the list of items they gave us. And I checked her room at home."

"What's on the flash drive?"

"I don't know for sure. But she came home for a weekend last June and almost had an aneurism because she thought she lost it. I only remember 'cause I made a comment about her having national security secrets on the thing, and she screamed at me that it wasn't a joke. It's weird no one's found it."

My toes curl in my flats as I try to process this. I'm suddenly nauseous. Whoever was in my room could have stolen the flash drive. "Did she say anything else about it?"

Anthony's face clouds over. "Just that if her teacher found out she almost lost it, she'd be dead."

I almost forget to breathe for a moment. "Did Isabella tell you the teacher's name?"

"I can't remember it. But it was something weird, European maybe—"

"Andreev." The name tumbles out of my mouth. Anthony's expression lights up. "Yeah, that's it. You know him?"

"He was at the wake," I say. "He's older, maybe sixties. Kind of overweight, big glasses."

"That's weird," Anthony says. "Most of her teachers came up to talk to my parents, but I don't remember him."

It is weird. Sounds like he was avoiding them.

One thing is clear though: I need to find that flash drive.

I'm so busy combing through Isabella's desk that I forget I promised Remy and the girls I'd go to the library with them before dinner. The knock at the door nearly gives me a stroke, because the last thing I need right now is to be caught snooping through my dead roommate's stuff.

I ignore my father's voice in my head. There's no way anyone here thinks I could have hurt Isabella. My dad is a defense attorney, and defense attorneys are paranoid. I'm not going to let him make me paranoid, too.

I consider bailing on Remy because I'd rather stay here and see what I can dig up on Andreev, but her overeager smile reminds me that I really have to commit to landing my new spot at the top of the food chain. So I return her smile and pretend I'm so, so psyched to be studying with the Headband Club.

Besides, I'm obviously not finding the flash drive tonight.

Since Isabella preferred to do homework at her desk and I followed suit, this is the first time I've been to the library. I hope it's not obvious how far my eyes are popping out of my head as I take it all in: the chandeliers hanging from the million-foot-high domed ceiling, the rows of polished mahogany tables. Everything and everyone is silent and bathed in an amber glow, as if this is a magical place where the seeds of excellence blossom in young minds.

I'm pretty sure this is the first place they bring parents who are skeptical of the thirty-five-thousand-dollar-a-year price tag.

I half-listen to April and Remy bicker back and forth about what chapters their teacher said would be covered on the biology test. Kelsey shoots me an appreciative smile when I look over at her.

Okay, so maybe I don't feel totally out of place with Remy, April, and Kelsey, like I do when I'm sitting in class listening to everyone talk about the political fund-raisers and galas their parents drag them to. From what I can gather, almost everyone here has super-powerful parents. For once in my life, I'm kind of an outsider.

I wonder if this is what Isabella felt like as a townie. Her murder might be last week's news to everyone else around here, but I can't stop thinking about her and her dorky socks and goofy laugh. Could someone really have hated her enough to kill her?

Someone taps my shoulder. When I turn, no one's there. Brent slides into the empty seat on the other side of me.

Remy looks up at Brent, her forehead creasing. "Are you okay? I thought you were going to look at skis with Cole at the mall."

"Change of plans," Brent says. "That all right with you, Mom?"

Remy rolls her eyes and turns her attention back to Kelsey, but I catch her glance from Brent to me, her heart-shaped lips pinched together.

Brent pulls out a newspaper, and while I wait for my laptop to boot up, I check out the front page. In the corner is a tiny box with this headline: STILL NO SUSPECTS IN CASE OF SLAIN STUDENT.

One week, and that's what Isabella has been reduced to. A quarter-page headline with cheesy alliteration. I tug on the front page to get Brent's attention. "Can I see this for a sec?"

He hands the front section to me and I peek at what he's reading: RED SOX EYEING ROOKIE PITCHER. How studious of him. For a second, I wonder if he's only here because I am. I ignore how close he's sitting to me and turn back to the newspaper.

Police say they are following a number of tips in the murder of Isabella Fernandez, 17. Fernandez's body was found early last Sunday with significant neck lacerations. In a televised statement last night, Police Commissioner Frank Allan confirmed that no arrests have been made, and detectives have not yet identified any persons of interest. Fernandez was a student at the prestigious Wheatley School, where faculty and students remain baffled by the brutal murder of a young woman one friend called "quiet and well liked." Dean of students James Harrow remarked, "The Wheatley School is dedicated to working with investigators in order to provide the community with answers to this senseless crime. Security has been increased on campus merely as a precaution; we do not believe there are any threats to our other students or staff." Investigators say there is currently no evidence a student was involved in the homicide.

I resist the urge to crumple the paper into a ball. What a crock of shit. The administration isn't dedicated to anything except covering their asses and doing PR damage control. I fold the paper and push it back to Brent, a little too roughly.

He looks up at me and then down at the front page. "I know you're not annoyed over the rising price of gas."

"This article about Isabella is bullshit," I whisper back. "Harrow is acting like a little puppet for Goddard. I bet they paid off whoever runs that newspaper to say that there's no evidence anyone here was involved. The media is the scum of the earth."

I'm suddenly aware that Kelsey, who's sitting close enough to hear us, is staring at me awkwardly. Brent's eyes are smiling.

"Brent's dad owns that paper," Kelsey whispers to me.

"Oh." My face is about a million degrees. "Sorry. I mean, I'm sure your dad is a lovely man."

"I wouldn't know. Don't see him much." Brent's smile gets bigger as my face gets hotter. *Foot, meet mouth.* I pretend to be totally immersed in composing an e-mail until he looks away.

I discard the fake e-mail and do a search on Eugene Andreev. The first two hits are his faculty page on the school's Web site. I check it out, but there's not much there except contact information and a brief bio, which tells me he has a degree in physics from the University of Moscow and a doctorate from MIT. It doesn't say what he got that doctorate in. Probably some advanced science that only exists at MIT.

I copy down Andreev's office number and return to the search results. The only other hits are for some Russian actor.

There's got to be more out there on Andreev. I twist the silver ring on my thumb, thinking back to my literature class at St. Bernadette's. In one of the Russian books we read, there was this guy named Yevgeny who got typhus, and I remember Mr. Crane saying that *Yevgeny* is the Russian form of the name *Eugene*.

I quickly type in *Yevgeny Andreev*. Nothing, but the search engine asks me if I mean *Evgenie Andreev*. Sure, why not. I click, and feel a rush of adrenaline to my fingers when I get a ton of hits. Half of them are in Russian, but I can tell I've got the right Andreev.

A bunch of the links lead to articles Andreev wrote for scientific journals. I can't access most of them, because the Wheatley School doesn't have subscriptions to the journals. One string of words keeps popping up in the abstracts though: *antimatter catalyzed nuclear pulse propulsion.*

I copy and paste it into the search engine. There's an online encyclopedia entry for it. I scan the page quickly, knowing that I wouldn't understand any of this stuff anyway.

I freeze when I hit a phrase that makes my stomach fold over. Even I know this one:

nuclear bomb.

I can't sleep that night. I roll over to face Isabella's empty bed. *What were you mixed up in?*

What if Isabella discovered something in Andreev's research that got her killed? It took me thirty seconds to figure out the guy was a major creep at her wake. Brent's conspiracy theory might not be so crazy after all.

I've got to find out if Andreev has Isabella's flash drive. What if he killed her to get his hands on it?

I already checked Isabella's desk, but now that I know what might be on the flash drive, it makes sense that she wouldn't leave it where someone could find it easily. Problem is, that leaves about a billion places for me to look for it.

I start with her desk again, because Isabella was practical. If she wanted to hide the flash drive, she'd probably pick somewhere where it'd be easily accessible. Most of her stuff is packed up in boxes, waiting for Anthony to borrow a car to take them home or for his mother to get a weekend off work and pick them up herself.

I comb through her files of schoolwork, shaking each one gently to make sure the drive isn't tucked into one of the pockets. Fifteen minutes later, there's only one box left. This one is filled with her desk trinkets: her calendar, a box of thank-you cards, a framed picture of her ferret, Mr. Spock, and a painted clay box that looks like a middle-school art project. The initials I.A.F are etched on the bottom.

I open the box again; it's filled with paper clips, mismatched earring backs, and other crap. At the bottom is a Post-it note folded into a tiny square.

Lexington Hall 108.

I don't have any classes in Lexington Hall. I find the campus map Barbara gave me my first day and run my finger down the key. There's no Lexington Hall on it.

The fact that Isabella wrote down the address and saved it could mean nothing. Her missing flash drive and Andreev's research could also mean nothing, but I can't afford to think that way. Not when I don't have much else.

CHAPTER
THIRTEEN

Remy and the girls are selling Valentine's Day rose-grams at a table during breakfast, and Brent isn't here. He rarely eats breakfast in the dining hall, so I guess he's not a morning person. Or he's more like a does-whatever-the-hell-he-wants person and no one says anything because he's so damn cute.

The thought of eating with Cole, Murali, and Phil is only slightly more appealing than eating alone. They're nice guys, really. But there's only so much I can listen to as Murali diagnoses everything with a pulse (Brent: trust issues; Remy: ADHD; Kelsey: codependency) and Cole and Phil argue about their fantasy-baseball teams.

I find Cole on the omelet-station line, towering over a group of freshmen girls who still haven't learned that giggling like a bunch of morons is not the way to get a cute older boy's attention. He smiles when he sees me approaching.

"You ready for the art-history quiz?" he asks.

I press the heel of my hand to my forehead. "Crap."

I totally forgot. I was too busy snooping through Isabella's stuff. "Hey, Cole, is there a Lexington Hall here?" I ask without thinking.

Cole tugs at his tie. "There used to be. Who told you about Lexington Hall?"

"I heard someone mention it," I lie. I don't have a reason not to trust Cole, but at this school, I don't really need one. I definitely can't tell anyone about all my snooping around.

"That's funny," Cole said. "Cause Lexington Hall burned down when my grandparents were students here."

Now *this* makes me pause. Why did Isabella care about some building that burned down before she was even born? The easy answer is that Isabella cared about a lot of weird things, but my gut tells me I need to find out more.

"Hey, Cole." Alexis walks past us, giving a sweet little wave over her shoulder. Cole waves back, looking embarrassed.

"She hates me," I say brightly when Alexis is gone.

"Nah. Lex is just . . . I don't know." Cole lowers his voice and looks over his shoulder. "She sucks. None of us guys like her, but she and Remy used to be a package deal."

"Used to be?" I ask. "They seem pretty friendly. And they're roommates."

"It's because Rem is too nice," Cole says. "Me, her, and Alexis . . . we sort of grew up together in Concord. Our parents were friends."

The only thing I know about Concord is that the British got their asses handed to them there. In my head, I'm picturing a place like Westchester. Only lamer.

"Anyway, Remy and I made a lot of new friends when we started school here, and for a while we tolerated Lex, but . . ." Cole's voice trails off as we reach the front of the line.

I watch him load four pancakes onto his plate. "But what?"

"It's nothing really." Cole shrugs. "We just don't hang out with her much anymore."

I take a pancake for myself and follow Cole to the table.

Don't people realize that when they say "It's nothing," they're pretty much guaranteeing that it's something?

There's got to be another reason my new friends are avoiding Alexis. I sit between Cole and Murali and let them argue about what format Robinson said the art-history quiz is in. I watch Alexis sit at a table with Lizzie, and Brooke and Jill, the two blond, athletic girls from the party. She looks up and catches me staring.

Her eyes fill with fear before she looks away. No, not fear. Paranoia.

Holy shit, I realize. It was Alexis who was in my room. It had to be: Whoever stole my card has to live in Amherst to have gotten past the RA. And I didn't see Alexis at dinner that night, which would have given her plenty of time to grab my card while the guys were getting food and then get back to the dorm.

My pulse is beating so loudly in my ears I can barely hear Cole and Murali. *Alexis broke in to my room.*

What was she looking for?

I swallow, thinking of how Alexis missed Isabella's wake. Could she have hated her enough to kill her?

Professor Andreev is in his office during lunch. My plan is to talk to him just long enough to figure out how hard it'll be for me to break into his office when he's not there.

The door is closed, but through a narrow pane of glass I can see Andreev sitting at his desk, eyes fixed on his computer screen. I take the opportunity to examine the lock on his door. It's old—even older than the locks at St. Bernadette's. I should be able to wiggle this one open, but there's no telling what kind of locks he might have inside his office, especially if the flash drive is there. If I had killed someone to steal something from them, I'd definitely want to lock away whatever I'd taken.

It's not that hard to think like a criminal. But I guess if you want to get technical about it, I *am* a criminal.

I rehearse my lines in my head quickly before knocking on the door. Andreev looks up and ambles over, his body tilted forward slightly under the weight of his round gut. He blinks when he sees me.

"Can I help you?"

"Hi, Professor Andreev. I'm Anne Dowling. Isabella Fernandez's roommate."

Andreev's cloudy eyes fill with regret. "Ah, yes. Such a tragedy. She was the most brilliant student I've ever had. Come in, come in."

His office smells like sulfur and old people. The chair he gestures for me to sit in is vinyl and leaks stuffing. My breath catches in my throat a bit as he closes the door behind us.

Andreev leans back in his desk chair, which lets out a groan. "To what do I owe this pleasure, Ms. Dowling?"

"Well." I shift a bit in my seat. "I was thinking about my schedule for next year, and I think I'd like to take AP physics."

"Ah. Let me bring up your records." Andreev's hand trembles as it hovers over his mouse. I look away, glancing around the office. File cabinets are stacked upon file cabinets, overflowing with folders and papers. There's a counter behind his desk, covered with boxes of lab equipment. As far as looking for the flash drive goes, I've got my work cut out for me. The guy's a hoarder.

"I see here you are enrolled in calculus AB. Is good, but I recommend students complete calculus BC before taking physics." Andreev peers at me. "The math involved is very advanced."

"Oh," I say. "Well, I was really hoping to earn some extra science credits. Maybe through an independent study or research internship?"

Andreev pauses. He looks from me to the computer screen, which is probably still displaying my transcript. Suspicion works its way into his eyes: My lowest grades are in science. The whole extra-lab-period thing never worked for me.

"The research assistant positions in this department are

very competitive," he says. "But I think Professor Chavel is looking for a laboratory assistant for next year." He pronounces it "la-*bore*-atory," which actually sums up my feelings on the subject perfectly. "Unfortunately I only accept one student each year, and the position has been filled."

"That's too bad." I draw up my best puppy-dog eyes. "Isabella loved working with you."

Andreev pauses, and I can tell I've hit a nerve. My heartbeat stalls as I wait for him to speak. A small, crooked smile takes over his mouth. "It is interesting you tell me this. You see, despite my encouragement, Isabella did not apply for the position again this year."

His smile fades. I wait for him to call me on my lie and tell me to get the hell out of his office, but he folds his hands and presses his thumbs together. "It troubles me, this world we live in. Where such a brilliant and kind soul can be taken away in an instant."

A knock at the door startles Andreev, as if he were in a trance speaking to me. The door opens and Sebastian stumbles in, his eyes widening when he sees me. "Oh. Sorry, Professor." He holds up a manila folder. "Should I bring this back later?"

"Leave it on my desk," Andreev says, but I'm already standing up to excuse myself.

"Thank you, Professor," I say. I'm both nauseated and relieved to see Sebastian. He follows me out the office door, then Andreev calls his name.

"I have a meeting at the end of the day," he says. "Please continue what we were working on yesterday and lock up before you leave."

I can barely contain my excitement as Sebastian and I make our way to the stairs. "You're Andreev's research assistant?"

"*Oui*," Sebastian says with a grin. I fight off the urge to tell him to cut the crap, that I know he's as American as a Happy Meal. Instead, I smile back and say, "That must have been really hard to get," and watch him flush with pleasure.

"Oh, I didn't even apply." Sebastian runs a hand through his hair, making it stand up even straighter. "But I was one of two people to get a five on the AP physics *and* AP calc exams last year, so Andreev asked me."

I'm betting I know who the other person is. I wonder if Sebastian knows why Isabella didn't want the position again this year.

"So what are you researching with him?" I ask as Sebastian holds the stairway exit open for me. I sense him stiffen a bit.

"Boring stuff, really. We haven't found the Higgs boson or anything," he adds with a nervous laugh. I stare at him blankly. "Physics joke," he amends.

"Did you know Isabella Fernandez was his research assistant last year?" I ask him.

Sebastian cracks his knuckles. "Yes. I saw him the morning after she was killed. He had to cancel our meeting, he was so upset."

Or because he needed to get rid of damning evidence or a murder weapon.

The clock tower bongs twelve times overhead, letting us know there's still twenty minutes left to lunch hour. I don't know if Sebastian knows anything useful about Andreev and Isabella, but I'm 95 percent sure he has something I *definitely* need: a key to Andreev's office.

Sebastian has to go back to his dorm because he forgot his history homework. Seconds after we split up, someone calls my name. Brent jogs to catch up with me.

"Why aren't you at lunch?" he asks.

"Why aren't *you* at lunch?" I raise my eyebrows at him.

"Fair enough," he says, although he doesn't offer an explanation. But his voice has taken on a smug, singsong tone. "So . . . Sebastian, huh?"

My cheeks flare up. I keep my gaze fixed straight ahead. "Why not Sebastian?"

"Because. Sebastian is just . . . Sebastian." Brent's voice falters, and I can sense him staring at me as if he's trying to figure out if I'm serious or not.

"And what's that supposed to mean?" I ask innocently. "I think he's kinda cute."

"Sebastian is the destroyer of everything cool and enjoyable in this world," Brent says. "If you play a song for him and he likes it, he'll play it on repeat until you want to hang yourself. That's just what he does. He was my roommate freshman year. Ruined all my favorite movies for me, too."

"And yet you still hang out with him because . . ."

"He buys the beer." Brent shrugs. "And he's kind of grown on me. Like a little French hemorrhoid."

"Nice. Anyway, I just walked back with him from Professor Andreev's office," I say as we start walking to the dining hall. "It's not like that."

I wait for Brent to say he didn't think it was, because I'm so obviously out of Sebastian's league. But he just keeps walking, confusion building in his expression.

"You're taking biology," Brent says. "Why are you so interested in Andreev?"

"I'm not interested in him." I quicken my pace.

"Come on. I saw you cyber-stalking him in the library yesterday." His warm brown eyes soften. "I think I know what you're doing."

"I'm not doing anything." I pull my peacoat around my body tighter. "Can we please go inside? It's freezing."

"Look, I know you want to find out who killed Isabella. But Andreev?" Brent shakes his head. "He's just a half-senile old creep. You've got to leave this to the police."

"I'm only doing what the school won't let the police do." I lower my voice. "I'm not an idiot. I know the administration protects their own. If you want to tell on me, go ahead, but I'm not going to stop."

Brent looks over his shoulder and sighs. "Okay, in that case, what's our plan?"

I blink at him. "Huh?"

"Our plan." The corner of his mouth twitches. "Obviously you need help."

"Oh, really."

"Yup. You know nothing about the inner workings of this school, yet you want to infiltrate it. That's practically asking to get expelled. Plus, I'm afraid of what you'll burn down if left unsupervised."

I feel a rush of excitement. Brent knew my schedule before I did: That could mean he has access to administrative passwords and other things I can only dream of. Then a sobering thought hits me. "How do I know you're not going to tell Goddard or Harrow on me? The teachers here stare at you like they're wondering where you hide the halo."

"Ha," Brent says. "You must not know me very well."

"So you're a big badass now?" I laugh. "Sorry. Must have been the ironed tie that fooled me."

"Hey, say what you want, but you're not the only prep-school expellee around here." Brent grins at me. "And I don't iron my tie."

Dumbfounded, I trail after him. "You're shitting me."

"I shit you not. So does that mean I'm qualified to help you now?"

I chew the inside of my lip. I want Brent's help, and not just because I want to spend more time with him. Something is telling me to trust him—something about the way he doesn't fit in with his friends 100 percent and doesn't gush about how awesome boarding school is all the time.

"Depends," I tell him. "How comfortable are you with breaking and entering? Oh, and theft."

Brent looks me up and down as if he's deciphering if I'm serious or not. I guess he decides on serious, because he lowers his voice. "What do you need to break into?"

"I need to get into Sebastian's room," I say. "He has a key to Andreev's office."

Brent raises an eyebrow at me. "Ah, I can think of a really easy way to get you into Sebastian's room, but you probably don't want to hear it."

I roll my eyes, although I've already thought about that. Yes, the thought of seducing Sebastian to steal his key makes me want a skin-scalding shower, but if journalists can give up their lives in war zones to bring people the truth, I can give up some of my dignity.

The plan is flawed, though. It doesn't address the problem that Sebastian needs to be *out* of his room while I look for the key. Unless . . .

"How good are you at creating diversions?" I ask Brent.

"Just give me ten minutes and some matches—"

"*No,*" I squeak. "Are you insane?"

"Fine, fine. I was kidding. Sort of." Brent leans against the dining-hall entrance, even though by now lunch is almost over. "I have some ideas. Can you meet me outside the dorm Friday night? Say, like an hour after everyone gets back from dinner."

I nod, even though I don't want to wait that long. It's probably for the best though: I can't risk Sebastian getting suspicious.

"Hey," Brent says as I turn to go to class. "Boston Latin Academy. Eighth grade. That's all I'll tell you."

CHAPTER
FOURTEEN

Molly won't look at me when she walks into Latin class on Wednesday. She moves her braid so it's covering half her face, almost as if she's trying to shield herself from me. I want to grab her and shake her for being such a coward, but at the same time I feel terrible for her, and a little guilty. I never would have been as mean as the girls at her old school, but it's not like I would have helped, either. Mousy girls like Molly were kind of invisible to me at St. Bernadette's.

I pretend to be looking over my notes as Molly hovers at the back of the room, considering her seating options. She won't sit in the empty seat next to me, but her other choices are limited. My notebook pages flutter as she brushes past me, heading for the seat diagonally to my right.

I'm about to look away when she pauses, hovering over the empty chair next to Giant Clark Kent. Upton had said his name is Mr. Andersen. Molly looks nauseous as she backs away a step.

Then she turns and hurries to an empty seat on the other side of the room.

What the hell? I look over at Mr. Andersen to see if he noticed.

I can't see his face, but he's hunched over his computer, the back of his neck red. After a few moments, he turns and watches Molly scramble through her bag for a pen. The look of embarrassment in his eyes says he saw exactly what I saw.

Molly is afraid of him. And she might have just told me the reason Isabella dropped this class.

I watch Giant Clark Kent for the rest of the class. According to the cover of his notebook, his first name is Lee. I whisper his name, trying it out: Lee Andersen. He never makes eye contact with anyone, even when he's answering Upton's questions. He takes notes on his laptop all period, never switching to Solitaire or Tetris, like everyone else who uses their computers in class. The most movement he makes is picking methodically at the scabs on the knuckles of his left hand.

It's gross, but now I'm dying to know where he got those cuts. I wonder if Isabella fought her killer.

I'm so busy plotting out how I'm going to get more information on Lee that I don't realize Upton has called on me.

"Ms. Dowling. What is the nominative case of *dictator*?"

"Hold on a sec." I tuck my hair behind my ears and scan my notes, vaguely aware that the soles of Upton's ugly slingbacks are tapping against the floor. "Oh! *Dictatora*."

"Correct." She gives me a frosty smile, and the look on everyone's faces says I seriously violated some unwritten rule. Like I was supposed to admit I wasn't paying attention and let someone else give the right answer.

Upton watches me out of the corner of her beady rat eyes for the rest of the period. Every time she catches me looking at Lee, she bores her gaze into me.

It's a warning to leave Lee alone. I know that. But Upton doesn't know that, to me, a warning is a challenge.

After dinner, I head to the library to see what else I can find on Lexington Hall. Remy offers to come with me and study for

French, so I make some excuse about just needing to pick up a book really quickly. I don't want her asking questions, and besides, I've been doing practically *everything* with her and the girls lately. Blame it on the only-child thing, but I need some alone time.

I didn't realize how late we'd all stayed at the table talking after dinner, so it's pitch black out as I walk to the library. I also only have a little over an hour before the ten-o'clock curfew.

The library steps extend the entire length of the building. It reminds me of the steps of the American Museum of Natural History, and the homesick pit in my stomach grows a little.

I decide against asking the librarian for help and head straight to the second floor. Believe it or not, I'm actually pretty library-savvy. So I know if I go to the archives in the basement, I'll probably have to sign in and ask the person working down there to get the old campus maps for me. I might as well tap dance outside the headmaster's office and yell, "HEY! LOOK WHAT I'M DOING!"

My best bets are probably books on the Wheatley School's history—and I know they exist because Professor Matthews mentioned that one of the older teachers wrote them.

The second floor of the library is empty and quiet except for the hum of the lights overhead. I didn't expect anyone to be strolling the stacks instead of watching whatever crappy cable sitcom is on tonight, but I still get an uneasy feeling at being up here alone. I keep my eye on the stairway as I browse the stacks for the history section, the polished wood floor planks creaking under my feet.

I don't have to look far: There's a special section dedicated to the school's history. I run my fingers along the bindings, leaving a trail in the thin layer of dust covering them. I pause on a cranberry-colored binding with *A History of the Wheatley School* in peeling gold lettering.

I flip through the yellowing pages of the book until I find the index. The book was written in 1940. There's no chapter about

Lexington Hall or a fire, but there's a campus map in the glossary. The print and illustrations are minuscule. I can make out some familiar buildings, though: Amherst dorms, the clock tower, the William J. Brown Refectory, AKA the dining hall. There's a weird bunch of solid and dotted lines connecting all of the buildings. I scan the outer loop of campus until I see it—a square labeled "Lexington Hall."

I pull the map Barbara gave me out of my purse and compare it to this map. Right where Lexington Hall used to be, looming over the edge of the forest is . . . a parking garage.

I'm pretty sure that means nothing. I sigh and spend some time combing through the history books for mentions of Lexington Hall, but all I can find is that it was a regular old classroom building until it burned down in 1965 from an electrical fire.

As I flip through an edition that was written in 1960, a yellowed newspaper article falls to my feet. There's a black-and-white photo of a guy with a terrible mushroom cut. He's wearing the Wheatley School uniform blazer. The article is dated 1990. My heartbeat picks up as I read the headline.

What Happened to Matthew Weaver?

Donald and Joan Weaver have not taken down the photo of their son Matthew from the window of their diner in Wheatley. For nearly ten years, the smiling portrait of the sixteen-year-old has symbolized the hope of family and friends that one day Matthew might return.

The son of two small-business owners who never finished high school, Matthew Weaver was accepted to the Wheatley School in 1978 on a full academic scholarship. During his junior year, Weaver helped lead the nationally ranked Wheatley crew team to a victory at the Harvard Invitational.

Three weeks later, he left his dormitory in the middle of the night and never returned.

For years, police have been mystified by a case that has presented no suspects, no leads, and, above all, no body. Conflicting stories among Weaver's friends about what he was doing the night he disappeared prompted police to question members of the Wheatley crew team, which had previously been the subject of disciplinary action by the school for partaking in hazing rituals.

Police dropped the investigation after being accused of using the crew team members as scapegoats in the face of the family's pressure for answers. While Weaver's case remains open, investigators today maintain there is no evidence of foul play.

Weaver's parents feel differently. "We believe someone knows something about what happened to Matthew," Don Weaver tells us. "We only hope that enough time passes for them to gather the courage to come forward, so my family can have closure."

I fold the article and put it back. The similarities between Matthew Weaver's case and Isabella's are frightening. Not *axe murderer hiding in the shower* frightening, but *holy shit, this is messed up* frightening.

Over thirty years have passed, and no one knows what happened to Matt Weaver. How is that even possible? Even if someone was afraid of getting in trouble back when he disappeared, you'd think thirty years would be enough time to grow a pair and come forward.

A sickening thought hits me: Is the same thing going to happen with Isabella's case? Is the school just going to keep scaring people out of coming forward until the police have to declare her murder a cold case?

Now I'm really hungry for more details about Matt Weaver. Forgetting Lexington Hall and the reason I came up here, I flip to the front of the history book the article fell out of. This one was written in the early sixties—it's too early to have any mention of Matt Weaver. He must have disappeared around 1980 if this newspaper article was written in 1990.

I browse the shelf for the 1980s edition of *A History of the Wheatley School*. I can't find it; my eyes hurt from the lousy lighting up here; and I'm frustrated because I just wasted an hour searching for info on a building that doesn't exist anymore.

The library is pretty much cleared out by the time I get downstairs. The woman at the circulation desk spots me and smiles as I make my way to her. I tell her the book I'm looking for, and she types something into the computer.

"Looks like someone has it checked out." She frowns. "It was due almost a month ago."

"Could you tell me who has it?"

The librarian clicks around. Her expression darkens. "According to the system, Isabella Fernandez does."

"Oh." For some reason, I can't process the thought of Isabella doing something mundane like checking out a book. Dead people aren't supposed to have things like unreturned library books.

"She was my roommate," I tell the librarian, although I'm not sure why I do.

As I turn to leave, she gives me a sympathetic smile.

On the way back to my dorm, I tell myself Isabella probably checked out the book to do a report on Lexington Hall. It's the only thing that makes sense; at least it makes more sense than Isabella researching Matthew Weaver right before her own death.

There's no way Isabella could have known something similar would happen to her, right?

CHAPTER
FIFTEEN

I don't know what to do with the million questions haunting my mind, so the next morning, I sit down to e-mail Anthony. But I already have a message from him.

> I have something you should see. I can meet u at the school when u get out of class. Can't say anything more in e-mail.

His phone number is at the bottom of the e-mail. My fingers prickle with anticipation as I type out a response. Maybe Anthony found Isabella's flash drive, or some other clue. I'm so busy running through the thousand possibilities that I don't even feel my usual pang of disappointment when I get to breakfast and see that Brent isn't there. But Remy is missing today, too.

"Where's Remy?" I ask Kelsey and April.

"Doing Lex Luthor's bidding," Murali cuts in.

No one confirms he's talking about Alexis, but I know it's her.

"I don't see why Resident Council needs to have a fund-raiser at the same time as SGA," April says. "People aren't going to buy rose-grams *and* candy-grams."

"Isn't that the point?" Murali says. "Alexis is just trying to piss SGA off."

"Why? I thought she was on the student government," I say, waiting to be struck down for my ignorance. Instead, everyone kind of pokes at their food or looks into their coffee cups.

"Alexis is only a class representative for SGA," Cole finally says. "She's president of the Resident Council. She wanted to be SGA president."

The way he says it, I can tell that Resident Council is the equivalent of SGA's fat, ugly cousin.

"So who's president of SGA then?" I look around the table. It's got to be one of them, right?

"You asked for me?" Brent slips into the empty seat next to Kelsey, where Remy usually sits. He imitates the look of shock on my face. "What? I'm not leadership material?"

"So that's why Alexis doesn't like you," I say when Kelsey gets up for more coffee and Brent drags his chair next to mine. "And here I was thinking you just wouldn't sleep with her."

Brent snorts. "Trust me, if she ever got me naked, it'd be to hang me off a bridge by my—"

"EW!" April shouts. "God!"

"I prefer to be called 'Brent.'" He turns to me and lowers his voice. "We still on for tomorrow night?"

"As long as you're sure Sebastian will be in his room," I say.

"On a Friday night? I'm positive."

I take a long sip out of the Big Ben travel coffee mug Chelsea brought me from London. "Hey, do you know Lee Andersen?"

"Creepy Lee?" Kelsey is back. "Why are you talking about Creepy Lee?"

April shushes Kelsey. "That's so mean. What if he hears you? You know how he's always lurking."

Kelsey shudders and pushes her glasses up her nose. "I saw him hanging outside the girls' locker room with a *camera* once. I almost vomited."

"Did you tell anyone?" I ask, alarmed. "That sounds sick."

Kelsey shrugs. "Danielle Wilson was with me and asked him what he was doing, and he just mumbled that he was taking pictures of the new gym for the newspaper."

"That guy seriously just looks like he's going to snap and shoot up a Burger King someday," Cole says, shaking his head.

I notice that Murali is stabbing his potatoes a little harder than necessary.

"Murali and Lee are duking it out for valedictorian," Brent explains. "Lee knocked him into second place next year."

A piece of potato sails across the table and hits Brent in the forehead. "Screw you, number four."

"Number three." Cole's voice is quiet. "He's number three now."

Everyone is silent, but the uncomfortable looks on their faces are obvious.

Isabella was number three.

A thought crystallizes in my brain: A girl accusing a guy at a prestigious school run by an old boys' club of sexual harassment is a recipe for a scandal. But a girl in the top three of her class accusing the *valedictorian* of sexual harassment? That would be a scandal of epic proportions.

Sounds like a perfect reason to intimidate a student like Molly into shutting up about it.

The whole conversation leaves me without an appetite, so I leave my breakfast untouched. Two things are clear to me though: Alexis and Lee Andersen are two people I definitely don't want to be alone with. Whether or not they're scary enough to commit murder, though, is what I need to find out.

I'm anxious to get Brent alone and tell him my suspicions about Lee and Isabella, but it seems the school has other plans for me today. At the beginning of class, my biology teacher tells me Dean Tierney wants to see me in her office at the end of the period.

The administration secretary tells me to have a seat outside the dean's office. I steady my hands by applying rosebud salve. If this shit keeps up, I'm going to need to order it by the case.

"Anne?" Dean Tierney pushes the office door open. "Come in."

My heart catches in my throat when I see that Tierney and I aren't alone in her office: My father is sitting in one of the chairs opposite her desk.

He's here, in Massachusetts. I don't know what I was expecting after I hung up on him. My father has a reputation in the legal world of nearly knocking down the doors of people who don't return calls.

"Hello, Anne," he says over his shoulder. Dumbstruck, I walk over to him. He gets up and pulls me in a tight hug, but I can tell he's pissed off.

"You're supposed to be in Paris," I say when we break apart.

"I got here as soon as I could," my father says. He sits back down and I follow suit.

Dean Tierney gives a hawklike smile, showing off her gross snaggletooth. You'd think an institution that's practically crapping alumni donations could spring for an employee dental plan. "Anne, I asked you here because your father and I are concerned."

I swallow and glance at my father. "Concerned?"

"Yes. And I think you know why."

I stare at Dean Tierney, wondering what sort of brain seizure she had that made her go into education. Because with her personality, she'd make a pretty good butcher or undertaker.

"Jackie says you haven't seen any school counselors since Isabella died," my father cuts in.

Jackie? A horrible thought strikes me: My dad *knows* Dean Snaggletooth?

"My husband and your father went to law school together," Tierney explains, as if reading my thoughts.

"Oh," I say stupidly. *Tierney is the one who got me in to the school.* My palms begin to sweat; I'm sure she'd have no trouble getting rid of me if it came to it.

"We're concerned about how you're coping with the stress," Dad says. "Jackie tells me you don't feel safe in your room, yet you refuse to accept a new one."

"That's because someone stole my ID and used it to get into my room," I say angrily.

I expect my father to flip a shit over this, but he exchanges a look with Snaggletooth that lets me know this isn't the first he's hearing of the break-in. Tierney clears her throat.

"Ken, we checked with the Amherst RAs, and I can assure you that didn't happen."

My father nods and eyes me with concern. *He doesn't believe me.* Of course he doesn't believe me—he doesn't even trust me anymore. Not after the fire at St. Bernadette's. My fists curl with anger as Tierney prattles on about how fear and paranoia are a natural response to Isabella's murder. She assures my father that otherwise I'm adjusting fabulously to life at the Wheatley School, and the administration will do all they can to help me get over the whole dead-roommate thing.

Tierney gives my father and me a few minutes alone before he leaves. He tells me that I'm allowed to stay here, as long as I agree to see the school counselor and call home to check in every three days. I have to accept, because the only other option is going back to New York and getting homeschooled.

My father hugs me and speaks into my ear: "Don't be scared. You're safe here."

"I'm not scared." He squeezes me, and I don't tell him it's because I know I'm safe here. I'm too pissed off to be scared— pissed no one believes me about the break-in. Pissed no one seems to care if Isabella's killer is ever found.

Tierney makes it clear she's not done with me once my father leaves. "Have a seat, Anne. We need to schedule a time for you to talk to someone at Support Services."

"I don't think talking to someone about what happened will help," I say. "I prefer to deal with things on my own."

Dean Tierney gives me a pitiful look, as if that's what everyone says. "Sometimes dealing with things on your own is . . . unhealthy. It comes with the temptation to become involved in things it's not in your best interest to become involved in."

Her voice is cold and devoid of sympathy in a way that lets me know she's not talking about huffing spray paint. My tongue feels like it's stuck to the roof of my mouth, and my throat is tight. Her message couldn't be any clearer: *Stay out of Isabella's murder*.

But there's no way she knows I've been nosing around. I've been so careful. Someone had to have said something to her . . . someone with a reason to believe I was really meddling.

Someone like Professor Upton, I realize with a wave of nausea.

"Anne, you have a lot of resources here," Dean Tierney says. "Let us help you."

"Just like you helped me when someone broke in to my room? Or like you helped Isabella?"

Time seems to stand still after I say it, letting me absorb the full impact of how stupid it was. I've always had a problem keeping my mouth shut. My father says I got my big mouth from my Uncle Jason. He landed himself on a federal no-fly list after making casual jokes to a flight attendant about having an explosive in his pants.

Basically, Uncle Jason is a dumbass, and so am I.

"No one broke in to your room, Anne. And Isabella Fernandez's death was an unforeseeable tragedy." Dean Tierney's voice is clipped. "If I were you, I would avoid making false allegations to the contrary, especially when the school has been so accommodating of your . . . situation."

I swallow and nod. Message received: If I don't cut the crap, my ass is going back to New York, and homeschooling is my only chance at finishing my junior year on time.

Anger burns in my throat as Tierney hands me a card for the school counseling center and says I can go to lunch. How can she get away with threatening me like that? How can all of these jerks get away with screwing with a murder investigation just because they're rich and powerful?

It makes me so sick, and there's nothing I can do. At least not if I want to graduate from high school. I don't want to be one of the Martin Paynes of the world: a Trust-fund Fuck-up, destined to leech off his parents for the rest of his life.

I blink away the tightness at the back of my eyes as I leave the administration building. I should be worried about myself and my future, but I can't stop thinking about Isabella, and how if she were the daughter of a politician or the attorney general, the police would probably have found her killer by now.

It's not fair. And it's not fair for me to sit around and do nothing about it. Not when I got off with a slap on the wrist for almost burning my school down just because of my father. I'll be such a hypocrite if I don't at least try to get justice for Isabella.

I'm just going to have to be more careful with how I go about it.

Anthony is supposed to meet me in the student center, but he's a few minutes late. I pass the time Googling Dean Tierney on my phone. Obviously she wants me to be afraid of her, and I want to make sure I have a reason to be.

According to the school's Web site, Dean Tierney was on the Wheatley School Board of Trustees before taking over for Dean Watts two months ago. There's a picture of the board; Tierney is the only woman on it, and according to the caption, she's the only member who didn't go to Harvard. She graduated from Smith College in 1983. All of the board members except her are Wheatley School alumni.

I scroll down the page, where there are more pictures of the board members doing board-memberly-like things, which, as far as I can tell, are limited to playing golf and accepting lots of money from people.

There's a sickening taste in my mouth as I hover over a photo of a board member and Dr. Harrow shaking hands with a man in a suit who looks like he gets regular spray tans. I don't need the caption to confirm that it's Senator Steven Westbrook: The familiar horsey nose and too-straight, too-white smile are enough.

Senator Steven Westbrook makes historic $1 million gift to the Wheatley School.

I could seriously barf. Alexis's father practically owns the school. Harrow might as well have his tongue hanging out and a collar around his neck, because the look he's giving the senator clearly says *I am your bitch.*

I pause on the last picture. The board is presenting some sort of award to a younger-looking woman with a short, cropped blond haircut.

Dean Margaret Watts receives prestigious Wheatley School Service Award.

The picture is dated from October of this year. Something is seriously bugging me about it, though. Something in my brain is sending off signals that it can't be right.

Dean Watts is facing the camera, her entire body in the frame. She's wearing a simple gray pencil skirt and suit jacket, but her stomach is undeniably flat and smooth.

Barbara told me Dean Watts was out on maternity leave—no, she specifically said that Dean Watts was *having her baby.* I add up the months in my head. There's no way Dean Watts is pregnant in this photo, and even if she were, it would have to mean she left school to have a zygote, not a baby.

Why would Barbara lie about why Dean Watts left?

"Sorry I'm late. Ready to go?"

I look up and see Anthony. He's holding a motorcycle helmet.

"What . . . is that for?" I ask.

"It's for you." His eyes gleam wickedly. His hair is pulled into a stubby ponytail at the nape of his neck, so I can see all of his face: his full upper lip, strong jaw dotted with stubble. I have to admit, it's a good look for him. I catch the girls selling rose-grams in the lobby staring at him on the way out, and I'm shocked at my primal urge to snarl at them.

Anthony stops at a beat-up but clean red motorcycle parked at the curb in front of the student center. He crumples up the yellow ticket on his windshield and throws it to the ground without looking at it.

"You shouldn't litter," I say, ignoring the wild thumping in my chest. I'm wavering between *There's no way in hell I'm getting on that thing* and *Hell, yes, let me on that thing.* I've always wanted to ride on the back of a motorcycle, but I imagined it would be through the streets of Greece with a hot guy named Theo who just rescued me from a boring-ass tour group.

"Do you even have a driver's license?" I ask Anthony.

He stares at me like I couldn't have asked a dumber question if I'd tried. "Of course I do. You don't?"

"Why would I?" I say. "I live in Manhattan." I'm not about to admit to him that I don't even know how to drive.

Anthony just shakes his head and hands me the helmet. "Hop on."

I wince as I put the helmet on, trying not to think about the last time Anthony washed his hair. "Where are we going, anyway?"

"Police station." Anthony squeezes the handle of his bike, and the engine revs. "My buddy at school has an older brother on the squad. He's got something to show me."

It's clear Anthony isn't going to shout over the sound of the engine to tell me more, so I swing one leg over the back of the motorcycle.

"You're gonna want to hold on," he says over his shoulder.

I look down at my arms and wrap them around Anthony's

waist. His stomach feels solid through his T-shirt. I feel Anthony tense up at my touch. I say a silent prayer that this ride will be over fast.

My legs wobble as I slide off Anthony's bike. He gives me his hand to steady me. He's avoiding my eyes, like he's embarrassed I spent the last fifteen minutes groping him, even though if he didn't drive so damn fast, I wouldn't have had to hold on so tightly.

"Are you going to tell me what this is about?" I ask as Anthony leads me to the side of the police precinct. It's a four-story building made of beige stone. There are bars covering the windows over the front entrance.

"There's something wrong with the security feed from the night Isabella was killed." Anthony takes out his phone and dials a number. He lets it ring a few times before hanging up. Moments later, the side door opens. A young officer in uniform gestures for Anthony to come inside, his eyes filling with concern when they rest on me.

"I thought it was going to be just you," he says to Anthony.

"No, she's cool. Don't worry."

The officer does look worried, though, as he offers me his hand. He's probably in his twenties. Military-looking. "Dennis."

"Anne," I say, following him and Anthony down the corridor. Another officer walks by, picking his head up from his folder when he sees us.

"Taking my lunch now," Dennis says, nodding to him.

The officer looks from Dennis to Anthony and me and nods back as if to say *Hell if I care*. Dennis leads us into a room at the end of the hall and shuts the door.

"I could get in trouble for this," Dennis says. "But if it were my sister, I'd want to know everything that was going on."

Anthony's face is stony. "Thanks, man."

We're silent as Dennis slips something into the DVD player

in the corner of the room. A wave of paranoia hits me as I realize the black-and-white images on the screen are still shots taken outside of Amherst.

"I had no idea there were security cameras," I murmur as Dennis plays the tape and I see me, Remy, April, and Kelsey sneak out the back door. "Crap."

"They're unmanned at night," Dennis says. "Used just as a precaution. Probably why people were able to get away with sneaking out for so long. Watch, though."

Anthony and I keep our eyes on the screen. I recognize a few of the other people sneaking out, but there's no Isabella. We watch me herd April and Kelsey back into the dorm, and, an hour later, we see Cole walk Remy back.

And then, at 3:15 A.M., the security feed goes dark. NO SIGNAL, it reads.

"There was a power surge in the dorm," Dennis explains. "Probably from the wind. But it doesn't matter, because the medical examiner says Isabella died between eleven and two."

"That doesn't make sense," Anthony says. "She didn't leave the dorm during that time frame, according to the tape."

I suddenly feel dizzy. "Could she have been killed inside the dorm?"

"Highly unlikely," Dennis says. "Aside from the fact we didn't find blood in the dorm, the killer would have had to carry her body all the way to the woods—and somehow evade the security tape."

"But it went dark at three fifteen," Anthony shoots back. "Maybe whoever killed her turned the camera off before moving her body."

"We confirmed there was a power surge," Dennis says. "It's nearly impossible her killer got that lucky. Evidence says she was killed in the forest between eleven and two, despite what the tape says."

"Then Isabella took another way out of the dorm," Anthony finally says. "One the security camera can't see."

Dennis nods, almost mechanically. "That would be the most logical explanation."

"So what's the problem then?" Anthony demands.

"We can't figure out how she did it," Dennis admits. "All of the doors are within range of the camera, and the first-floor windows have heavy-duty locks on them."

"But that doesn't make sense." There's an edge to Anthony's voice now. "She had to have left."

"There's another explanation. It's not a popular one." Dennis's voice is low. "But there's a small chance someone could have tampered with the tape."

Goose bumps ripple across my arms. If someone tampered with the tape, it means Isabella's killer was probably on it.

"Someone at the school had to have messed with it." Anthony's hands clench into fists at his sides. "Why aren't you arresting them for interfering with the investigation?"

"It's not that simple," Dennis says. "The records don't show anyone entering the security office from the time the guard left at ten P.M. and the next showed up at eight A.M."

"Fuck their records." Anthony shoves the chair he was leaning against. The screeching of metal on linoleum makes me jump. "They're hiding something, Den. They know who did this, and they're protecting them."

Dennis doesn't respond to this. His eyes are on the TV, where we just watched the tape. I don't believe that someone tampered with it. Isabella was smarter than all of us. If she wanted to sneak out of the dorm without being seen, even by the security cameras, she would have found a way.

But becoming invisible?

CHAPTER
SIXTEEN

Anthony is silent as we leave the police department. He's super pissed off still, so it takes me the entire ride back to school to gather the nerve to ask him what I've been meaning to all afternoon.

"Hey," I say after he parks, "I found out some stuff."

He raises an eyebrow at me, but I can see his curiosity is outweighing whatever's left of his anger. "Is it about the flash drive?"

"I'm still working on that. Did Isabella ever talk about a guy named Lee Andersen?" I ask.

"She didn't talk about her love life with me, if that's what you're asking." The area between Anthony's eyebrows creases. "But as far as I know, Iz never even had a boyfriend."

"I'm not talking about a boyfriend. I think this guy might have been bothering her . . . maybe even stalking her."

Anthony's expression is pained. "Isabella never would have said anything to us about something like that. She would have been too afraid of worrying my parents and making my dad sicker."

"That's pretty selfless," I say.

"No." Anthony looks angry again. "It's stupid. Especially if this guy killed her. What do you know about him?"

"Not much," I say. "But once I have proof she complained about him, it should be enough for the police to—"

"You can't go to the police. Not unless you have something solid."

"Um, why? You're the one who told me I should leave all this to the police anyway."

"That was before." Anthony pauses and looks around, but we're alone outside the student center. "That was before I looked into things a little more."

I feel a coil of unease unfold in my stomach at the thought of Anthony knowing something I don't. "And?"

"I knew there had to be a reason the cops are so afraid of stepping on the school's toes," Anthony says. "So I asked around, and I found out a Mass senator's daughter goes here. The same senator who donated a shitload of money to the Police Benevolent Association and voted to increase police pension and retirement benefits."

I feel like the air has been squeezed out of my chest.

"Alexis Westbrook," I say. "Steven Westbrook's daughter."

"Yeah, that's him. You saying you know her?"

"Unfortunately." I chew the inside of my lip, debating whether or not to tell Anthony my suspicions about Alexis. I go with not. I don't need to risk setting him off again, and I figure if I'm going to accuse a senator's daughter of murder—even if it's only saying it to Anthony—I'd better have more to back it up than the fact that Alexis is a bitch.

"Look, Steven Westbrook can't buy off the entire police force," I say. "Even *he*'s not that powerful."

"You sound pretty sure of yourself. Who do you think tampered with the security tape, if it wasn't someone at the school? Gremlins?" Anthony's eyes flash. He's mocking me. Anger swells in my chest.

"They don't even know for sure if the tape was tampered with. All I'm saying is that I don't think it's the police we should be worried about," I say.

"Why? Because all police officers are good?" Anthony snorts and shakes his head. "Maybe where you're from."

"I'm from New York, jackass. Not some magical place where bad things never happen."

Anthony laughs. He actually *laughs* at me. "Got it. I'm sure your life was so tough there that Mommy and Daddy had to send you to school here."

"Shut up," I snap. "Just shut up. You don't know anything about me, and you know what? I don't think we can help each other."

"Fine." The anger dissolves from Anthony's face and for a moment I can see the hurt he's been hiding beneath the tough-guy act. Now he just looks like someone who's sad and angry because his sister died and no one will give him answers.

But the violence in his expression comes back as quickly as it left. "Go ahead and think I'm being paranoid. The only reason you don't believe it is because you're too scared to admit that if you can't trust the police, everything you were taught to believe is a lie."

"You don't know what I believe," I say to his back as he climbs onto his motorcycle.

Anthony speeds away from the curb without looking back at me, and I can't shake the thought that maybe I *don't* know what I believe anymore.

CHAPTER
SEVENTEEN

I can't sleep that night. I'm anxious that Brent and I won't be able to pull off Operation Sebastian, and I'm angry at Anthony—angry because he didn't seem to care that we may never see each other again, and angry because he exposed the gaping hole in my plan.

What am I supposed to do if I figure out who killed Isabella? Will the police even believe me? Will they charge me with interfering with an investigation? Or worse, if Anthony is right and the police are corrupt, how do I know I won't wind up like Isabella?

Anthony can't be right, I decide. The police are doing all they can to find Isabella's killer. They just really suck at it.

It's Friday evening. Dinner is in an hour, which means it's about three hours 'til showtime. I narrow the pile of clothes on my bed down to a cashmere black V-neck and a gray sweaterdress. I go with the V-neck and put my hair in a ponytail to draw more attention to the subtle bit of skin I'm showing. I really don't need to go overboard for a guy like Sebastian: I could probably show up to his room wearing garbage bags and still achieve my goal.

But since I'm seeing Brent too, I spray some perfume on my wrists and put on a pair of dangling silver earrings.

I have time to kill, so I wander the dorms looking for Remy. I find her in the basement, doing laundry.

"Why are you so dressed up?" she asks when she sees me. She hasn't changed out of her uniform yet.

"Oh, I don't know. Got bored, I guess," I lie.

The stair door creaks, and a tall blond girl walks into the room.

"Hey, Jill," Remy says.

"Hi." Jill smiles at Remy, and I don't miss the obvious nasty look she throws me before turning to one of the washing machines and beginning to unload her clothes. What the hell did I do to her? I look at Remy to see if she noticed, but she's leaning against her dryer, head tilted back in a dramatic sigh.

"I'm so bored. What should we do tonight?" She looks at me expectantly, and it hits me: I'm pack leader now. I get to decide these things.

"Um, there's actually this thing that I have to do." I examine my cuticles casually. "With Brent."

Remy squeals, and Jill looks over at us, her hand frozen on the dryer door.

"It's for class," I tell Remy quickly, aware of Jill's laser gaze. I don't need her starting rumors about me doing *things* with Brent Conroy on a Friday night.

"Jill, are you coming?" an impatient voice yells from the stairwell. Alexis's.

"Yeah," Jill calls back, her face red as she slams the dryer door and leaves without looking back at us.

"Um, did I miss something?" I ask Remy. " 'Cause I barely know that girl, and she looked like she wanted to choke me."

Remy's mouth forms a small *o*. "Omigod. I'm such an idiot."

"Why? You didn't do anything," I say.

"No. I did. Crap." Remy puts her hands on her cheeks. "Jill is totally in love with Brent."

"Oh." I don't know why this tidbit of information makes me nauseous. I mean, I pretty much assumed half the school is in love with Brent.

"But it's okay," Remy blurts. "They're just friends. I know you like him, and I think he really likes you, so . . ."

"Brent and I are just friends, too," I say coolly, even though I'm imagining Jill getting hit in her perfect little nose with a softball.

"Didn't look that way at the party," Remy says.

I hate thinking about that night, and I guess it shows on my face, because Remy's smile fades. I remember the security tape and bite the inside of my lip.

"Hey, Remy. Is there another way to sneak out of the dorm?" I ask. "Besides the back door?"

"Not that I know of." She eyes me. "You know what would happen if you got caught now, right?"

"Don't worry, I don't want to sneak out. I'm just curious."

"Oh. Well, they put alarms on all the doors so unless we dig ourselves out of here, looks like we can't sneak out anymore anyway." The dryer buzzes, and Remy begins to unload her clothes.

But there *is* a way out. I know because Isabella used it the night she was killed.

I look around the laundry room, thinking maybe there's a door down here that we don't know about. There's only the stairs leading up to the first floor.

But I notice something else. The basement is small. Too small. Basements are supposed to be the same size as the first floor of the building they're under, right?

I look around and notice there are only windows on one side of the room. They're high up on the wall, level with the ground outside. I stare at the opposite wall. It's like the basement is divided up into two rooms, but there's no way to get to the other side. The first floor lounge is the only place with stairs to the basement.

"Ready?" Remy asks me, cocking her head to the side.

"Yeah." I shoot a glance back down the stairs as I follow Remy, wondering where I can get a floor plan of Amherst Dormitory.

"So tell me what you think you'll find in Andreev's office again?" Brent asks, after he signs me into the boys' dorm after dinner.

"Hopefully something that tells me why she didn't want the research position again this year," I say. "It sounds like it was super competitive."

Brent nods as I follow him into the elevator. He pushes the button for the fourth floor. "A recommendation from Andreev could get a monkey into MIT. It was a pretty big deal for him to want the same student two years in a row. He kept Isabella after class almost every day when school started . . . probably to see if she changed her mind."

"It sounds like he was obsessed with her," I say. "Maybe she quit because he made a move."

"I don't know if that fossil has it in him," Brent says. "She could have seen something in his research she wasn't supposed to see."

I don't tell Brent I'm already considering that possibility, because I don't want to explain how I found out about Isabella's missing flash drive. Just the thought of explaining my relationship with Anthony to Brent gives me a headache.

It also makes me feel guilty, because I'm really into Brent, but I can't deny that lately, Anthony is the last thing on my mind before I fall asleep. Even though Anthony thinks I'm nothing but a spoiled brat and I basically told him to screw off yesterday.

"Getting cold feet?" Brent asks.

I shake my head and put on some more lip salve. "Let's do this."

Sebastian's face floods with surprise and delight when he opens his door and sees me leaning against the frame. He's so surprised, he forgets his accent when he greets me.

"Do you have a few minutes?" I twirl a lock of hair around my finger. "I'm trying to do the French homework, and I just don't understand the short story we were supposed to read."

"Of course. Come in," he says. He doesn't question why I'm doing Monday morning's homework on a Friday night, but that's the whole point. Say what you want about guys like Sebastian, but at least they're dependably predictable.

Sebastian frantically pushes a pile of books and laundry off his bed while I scope out his room. My gaze rests on the black leather messenger bag on his desk chair. I cross my fingers that he keeps the key in there. Or in the worst-case scenario, that Brent's plan gives me enough time to figure out where else Sebastian could keep the key.

"You don't have a roommate?" I sit down next to Sebastian on the bed, hoping I can keep my gag reflex in check for long enough to pull this off.

"No. I 'ave, ah, a medical condition, so they gave me a single. Lucky, no?" He inches closer to me and grins.

Ugh, gross. Sebastian actually thinks I want to hook up with him. He's either delusional, or I deserve an Oscar for my performance so far. "Very lucky," I purr. "So . . . the short story?"

"Oh." Sebastian scrambles through the pile on the floor until he finds the packet Monsieur Gillette gave us. "I think it's about a man who wants to win a race."

Wrong. The main character of the story is a mouse, and I'm pretty sure the entire thing is a metaphor for communism. I try to count the minutes that have gone by. Where the hell is Brent? He should have put phase two of the plan into motion by now.

"It's really a boring story," Sebastian murmurs, closing the centimeter gap between my leg and his.

That jerk, I realize. Brent is totally messing with me right now by stalling. I'm going to kill him. Actually staying in Sebastian's room long enough for him to make a move was *not* in our plan.

"Maybe you could help me with the questions we're supposed to answer about it," I say, trying to disguise that I'm inching away from him by making a big show of sliding the elastic off my ponytail.

"You have beautiful hair," Sebastian trills. "May I touch it?"

Now I'm *really* going to kill Brent.

The frantic knocking at the door nearly makes me sigh with relief. Sebastian apologizes to me and answers it, his face twisted with annoyance.

"What do you want, Conroy?"

"Dude, I heard Kyle is doing a surprise room check tonight," Brent says. The door is obscuring his face. "Just a heads-up."

Sebastian looks disturbed by this. "But we just had one last week. What am I supposed to do with all that leftover beer?"

"Hell if I know," Brent says. "But you better get rid of it. Now."

"Now isn't a good time," Sebastian whines, with a look over his shoulder at me. I shrug at him sympathetically.

"How many bottles of beer are there?" I ask. "You could hide them in one of the washing machines downstairs until the room checks are over."

Sebastian contemplates this as Brent sticks his head in the room. "Anne! Fancy seeing you here." His grin takes up half his face. When Sebastian turns his back to me again, I mouth the words *You're an asshole.*

"You have to guard the elevator for me," Sebastian says to Brent, panic creeping into his voice.

"Just put the bottles in your laundry basket and cover them with clothes," Brent says. "No one'll know. I've got to go ditch my own stash."

The door closes, and Sebastian looks from me to his closet, clearly torn. I can practically see his thought process: There's alcohol in his room, which is bad, but there's also a girl in his room, which probably doesn't happen often. Luckily, the fear of getting expelled wins out, because Sebastian lets out a grunt and starts loading the beer in his closet into his laundry basket.

"I'll be right back," he tells me.

"Don't walk too fast," I say innocently. "The bottles will clink together."

He nods and then he's gone.

Phase two: complete.

I don't waste any time digging into the pockets of his messenger bag. I push past an expensive-looking wallet, a pair of Armani sunglasses (gross), and empty gum wrappers. I nearly stab myself on an uncapped pen when I get to the bottom of the pocket, but there's no key.

Trying not to panic, I search the main pocket. There's nothing but notebooks and stray papers.

Okay, so the key isn't in his bag. I look around the room, my palms beginning to sweat. Where would I keep a key, if not in my purse? My gaze lands on Sebastian's desk. I yank open the main drawer.

It doesn't take long to find a key on a frayed MIT lanyard that looks as old as Andreev. Jackpot. I pause with my hand on the key, suddenly aware that Sebastian left his Wheatley ID on his desk, next to his laptop.

The fact that he left his room key here only buys me another minute, tops. But Sebastian left his laptop on, the "level failed" screen of some military shooter game still blinking.

I can't help it. I minimize the game and open Sebastian's documents. I type "Andreev" into the search bar, my breathing growing shallower with every second it takes the results to load.

"Come on," I whisper. The search brings up two documents, as a knock sounds at the door. Brent.

I ignore the second knock and log into the Wheatley e-mail portal. I don't have time to read the documents, and even if I did, I couldn't risk Sebastian seeing that someone opened them in Word. I compose an e-mail to myself and attach the documents to it, my legs threatening to give out beneath me as I wait for them to upload.

Brent's knock at the door grows frantic as I send the e-mail and click out of everything. I slip the key into my back pocket and stumble out into the hallway, my heart racing.

"What the hell took you so long?"

"What the hell took *you* so long?" The amount of adrenaline surging through my body is making my voice hysterical. "He actually asked to touch my hair!"

As we approach the elevator, the panel overhead lights up to let us know the door is about to open.

"Shit. That might be Sebastian." Brent takes my hand and pulls me into the supply closet across from the bathroom. He closes the door just as the elevator pings outside.

Brent and I are sandwiched between two shelves filled with rolls of toilet paper and paper towels. Our chests are pressed together, his rapid heartbeat matching mine. He hasn't let go of my hand yet. His warm breath on my neck sends sparks all the way to my toes.

"That was close," he whispers. I can barely make out the shape of his face in the dark.

"Yeah," I say, waiting for my normal breathing rate to return.

"So," he says.

"So."

"How are you going to get him his key back before he realizes it's missing?" Brent lets go of my hand. My cheeks burn with disappointment, but luckily it's too dark for him to see that.

"I was hoping I could just slip it back into his bag before he meets with Andreev again," I say. "But I don't know if that leaves me enough time to break into Andreev's office."

"I have a better idea," Brent says. "As long as you're comfortable with breaking a couple of Massachusetts laws."

CHAPTER
EIGHTEEN

An hour later, Brent and I are waiting for the T. In my possession is a fresh copy of the key to Andreev's office, courtesy of Hank's Hardware. Brent agrees to play *Call of Duty* with Sebastian tomorrow so he can slip the original back into his desk before he even realizes it's gone.

"You're pretty useful," I tell him, over the sound of the train grinding to a halt in front of us. "I think I'll keep you around."

"You owe me," he grunts, but I can tell he doesn't mind that much. I have to pause for a minute and wonder why he's helping me, especially when one wrong move could get us both expelled. Could all of this just be an excuse for him to spend time with me?

I study his profile as the train doors open and we find seats. His knit cap is pulled over his ears, and his cheeks are pink from the cold. I can make out faint freckles on his nose that probably get darker in the summer.

"You're staring at me," he says.

The train lurches forward and my body slides into his. "I was just thinking of something. How did you know I was in Brit lit before I even got my schedule?"

"I have resources."

"Yeah, well, your resources might help me get information I need about Isabella." I glance around, just to make sure no one from school is on the train. "Do you have access to class rosters?"

"Let's say I do." Brent cracks his knuckles. "How would that help you?"

"I don't know exactly. But I'm pretty sure Isabella dropped Upton's Latin class to avoid Lee Andersen. I want to know if they had any other classes together."

"They were both in my calculus class last year." Brent's brow creases. "I know we call him Creepy Lee and everything, but as far as I know, he's never even talked to a girl."

"He wouldn't have to talk to Isabella to stalk her." Acid swirls in my stomach at the thought. "I confronted Isabella's friend Molly about it, and she got all freaked out. Said Isabella never should have gotten her involved." I stop myself from picturing the scars on Molly's arms. "Whatever happened between Isabella and Lee, someone definitely told Molly to shut up about it."

Brent bobs his head and taps his foot in rhythm, considering this. "If you had access to the teachers' portal, you could pull up anyone's schedule and transcript. And any history of disciplinary action."

The thought sends a thrill coursing through me. St. Bernadette's had a teachers' portal, but I never could crack that bad boy. My skill sets are more old-school: lock picking and smooth talking.

If I had my very own hacker, there's no limit to what I could do.

"If I had access," I repeat, waiting for the punch line.

"Yes. If you had access, it would mean you probably talked to Dan Crowley," Brent says. "This is all hypothetical, by the way. I'm not saying Dan got me onto the portal so I could play a prank on Murali involving fake reports from all his teachers about his excessive gas passing in class." He pauses. "That would be really immature."

I roll my eyes. "You're unbelievable. My surprise at you getting kicked out of your old school is wearing off."

"That's not good. I'm all about the surprise."

Remy, April, and Kelsey are watching *Sex and the City* in the third-floor lounge when I get back to Amherst, but I sneak past them and go straight to my room. If I wanted to watch a bunch of rich women drink wine and complain about their problems I'd hang out with my mother's friends. Plus, I have to check out those documents I e-mailed myself from Sebastian's computer.

I send my mother a text to reassure her I haven't been murdered this week and wind up scrolling through my old messages. A lump rises in my throat when I find the message my father sent me the night before Isabella was killed.

It's a picture message of Abby curled on the sitting-room couch, with the caption *We miss you, princess.* I burst into tears when I first read it, not just because I was crazy homesick, but because the note from Daddy meant he finally forgave me for getting kicked out of St. Bernadette's.

I should have been happy he wasn't pissed at me anymore, but the message had really made me lose it. Isabella came into the room and saw me crying. To get me to stop bawling and smile, she played me this totally ridiculous video of a honey badger killing and eating snakes.

I really, really wish I were home, or that Isabella were here. For a moment, I consider calling Anthony. Even though he couldn't be more different than his sister, they have the same crystal-gray eyes. And since I can't go home, I just want something to feel familiar right now.

I check the news alerts I set for any mention of Isabella's case. There aren't any new stories since I last checked this morning.

The files I found on Sebastian's computer take forever to load. They're probably nothing of value to me; I didn't exactly have time for a well-thought-out search of Sebastian's documents.

The first file looks like a half-finished report of some sort. It's titled "Antihypertritons and Colliding Nuclei Experiment." I try to read it, but before long, my brain is spinning and I've accepted that trying to understand science this advanced is a waste of time.

The next file asks me for a password before I can open it.

This document has been locked by user E. ANDREEV.

I've officially hit a wall.

Before I shut my laptop off, I realize there was something else I wanted to look into. I Google "Margaret Watts" and browse the results. The first hit is her faculty page on the school's Web site.

The page you requested cannot be found.

Huh. I check the links to Dr. Harrow and Dean Tierney's pages, but they're not broken. I return to the search results and click on the next hit on the school's Web site, a news story about the award Dean Watts received in the fall.

The page you requested cannot be found.

Okay, seriously, what the hell? The school really needs to fix their Web site—unless someone took down the pages mentioning Dean Watts on purpose.

The limited bits of information I have on Watts swirl around in my head. I know that she wasn't pregnant in the fall, which was only a few months ago. That definitely means she couldn't have been having her baby when I got here two weeks ago. So why does the school want everybody to think she's on maternity leave?

I look up Margaret Watts in the White Pages, but there are no hits for the Boston area. Every other Margaret Watts is either too old or too young to be Dean Watts, according to the search results.

I lean back in my chair and press my fingers to my temples, feeling a killer tension headache coming on. My leads aren't giving me much to follow through on. First I had a roommate who's invisible to security cameras, and now I have a disappearing Dean of Student Activities and Affairs.

I knew the administration at the Wheatley School was powerful . . . but powerful enough to make people disappear?

CHAPTER
NINETEEN

The girls want to go to a place called the Good Beane for brunch the next day, so tracking down Dan Crowley will have to wait until dinner. I'm trying to decide what annoys me more, the crappy coffee or the waiter wearing an I HATE NEW YORK T-shirt, when April suggests we go shopping somewhere called Newbury Street.

Naturally, that gets my attention. "Where's Newbury Street?"

So far, all that anyone's mentioned of shopping since I got here is the Wheatley Mall. And the only time I've even been to a mall is when we visited my dad's family on Long Island. Why anyone would want to shop in a place that smells like stale pretzels is beyond me.

"Oh my God, you've never been to Newbury Street?" April pauses, her hand poised to adjust her hair. She's wearing it down, with a lock of hair on one side pinned back. The same way I wear my hair most days.

"Anne, have you been into the city at all yet?" Remy asks me this with the same voice my mother uses to ask me if I've been taking my vitamins. I shake my head.

The three of them babble on about how we *have* to go now, and all I can think of is how I don't want to lose any more time I could be using to follow up on my leads.

But I guess I have been kind of obsessed with this whole murder-investigation thing, and it wouldn't kill me to take today off to act like a normal person. Especially if there's shopping involved.

Newbury Street, as it turns out, is the only thing I've seen in Boston so far with the potential to rival the awesomeness of New York. The buildings are a lot like the ones on the Upper East Side—charming, made of brick and brownstone—and they house everything from a Betsey Johnson to a Pinkberry.

It's enough to think that maybe if I get stuck in Boston forever, I won't have to shoot myself after all.

Everyone humors me as I bounce from one side of the street to another, trying to take everything in, even though it's clear it'd be impossible to do that in a day. I feel some of the weight on my chest lift: I'm in the city again, even if it's not *my* city.

We stop in the Sephora on Boylston because I'm almost out of rosebud salve. Watching my new friends play with all of the makeup testers confirms that we're finally in a territory where I know more than they do. In fact, once you take away the prep school uniforms and dump them into the wild, they seem pretty self-conscious and vulnerable.

Here in the city, no one knows Remy's father is the mayor of Concord or that April's father is the president of Boston University. Away from campus, I'm not such an outsider.

Kelsey is sniffing her new shampoo as we leave the store, and with a pang in my chest, I'm thinking how it's exactly something Chelsea would do, when Remy stops us. It takes me a moment to realize that they know the blond woman carrying a Whole Foods reusable bag walking toward us.

"Hi, Mrs. Redmond," Remy says, her voice getting pitchy like it does when she's nervous.

The woman gives us a thin smile and I realize, duh, Redmond.

This is Cole's mother. They have the same tall, lean build and angular face.

"Hi, girls." Mrs. Redmond pauses awkwardly. Her hands go into the pockets of her coat. It's one of those ugly quilted ones that look like a giant oven mitt.

"Mrs. Redmond, this is Anne," Remy says, saving me from standing there like a mute idiot. "She's new at school. She's from New York."

"It's nice to meet you, Anne," Mrs. Redmond says. I search her face for any indication that she's already heard about me. If she has, she's hiding it well.

"You have a lovely son," I tell her, and this almost gets her to smile. Remy tenses next to me, and I think I see April stifle a laugh.

"Be careful getting back to school, girls," Mrs. Redmond tells us. "I hope you weren't planning on staying out too late. What happened to that girl is just terrible."

The way she says *that girl* makes me sick. Everyone in the state knows Isabella's name by now.

"Ugh," Remy says, after we've put a block between Mrs. Redmond and us. "She was *so* awkward. She still hates me."

"You dumped her son," Kelsey says. "And you're the only one good enough for him, remember?"

This is all news to me. "You dated Cole, Remy?"

"For, like, three months." Remy's face is red. "He's over it. She should be, too."

I don't know why I'm so surprised that Remy and Cole were together. It unsettles me a little bit, though, because what if one of the girls dated Brent? Would that make it weird for everyone if he and I ever become more than friends? Do I even want Brent to be my boyfriend? I mean, I hate being tied down. The last thing I need is to get attached to something in Massachusetts when I already have one foot out the door.

I'm mulling over all this as April stops us at a shop that sells loose tea leaves. I can't help but stop in the doorway, where there's a rack stacked with newspapers. My stomach lurches at the headline on a flimsy, tabloid-ish paper that can only be Boston's equivalent of the *New York Post*.

Murdered Wheatley Student Came from a "Violent" Family, Acquaintances Say

I move out of the doorway and flip to the story without thinking.

> Sources close to the family of Isabella Fernandez, the seventeen-year-old Wheatley School student found murdered last week, say the quiet Somerville residents have a violent past. An official at the public high school attended by Fernandez's twin brother, Anthony, calls the teenager "troubled." Last year, Fernandez had an altercation with another student that left the latter hospitalized.
>
> Fernandez's family could not be reached for comment. Police officials say they have not yet named the victim's brother as a person of interest in the murder, but they are "looking into" these new developments.

"Anne, are you okay?" Remy puts her hand on my shoulder, and I realize I'm shaking. Hard.

Anthony. A killer. His *sister's* killer. It can't be right. Not when he convinced me that maybe we could find Isabella's killer together.

Not when I fell asleep the other night remembering the way I felt on the back of his motorcycle as my hands slid over his midsection. . . .

But if Anthony wanted to distract me from figuring out he killed his sister, it would make sense he'd encouraged me to believe someone at the school did it. And if he knew the police were investigating him, he could have been trying to keep me away from them by making me believe they couldn't be trusted.

Nausea rolls through me. Anthony could have been leading me on a wild-goose chase this whole time.

CHAPTER
TWENTY

I track down Dan Crowley at dinner. He's sitting at a noisy table of guys I've never really noticed before, although some of them look vaguely familiar from class. They all freeze and get silent when they see me. Some stare at each other like they're wondering if they're hallucinating or not.

"Hey, Dan," I say as if we're old buddies. "Can I talk to you for a sec?"

A look of suspicion crosses Dan's face. His red hair is gelled into a mohawk, and he's wearing a tiny silver earring. The sad thing is, it's the boldest display of individual style I've seen at this school. "About what?"

"Something for Matthews's class," I say, a little exasperated that I have to lie. I give Dan my best *Please don't make this difficult* smile. He glances back at his friends and follows me to an empty two-person table by the window.

"You need a grade change, don't you?" he says when we sit down.

I'm so taken aback at his forwardness that all I can do is nod.

"Who told you to come to me?" Dan leans back in his chair,

chest puffed out slightly. He's posturing: He knows he has something I want. The power dynamic between us has changed.

"He asked me not to tell you," I say.

Dan leans forward and drums his fingers on the table. "I don't do this for just anyone. I could get in deep shit, obviously."

I fold my arms across my chest and level with him. "Name your price."

Dan actually looks surprised at this. "I don't want money from you."

"But you want something." I raise an eyebrow. Dan's pasty skin turns pink.

"Kelsey Emmet," he says. "You're friends with her." I nod. "Put in a good word for me."

"You're serious?" I say. "That's all you want?"

It's Dan's turn to nod now. But now I'm suspicious.

"How do you know I won't get you in trouble?" I say.

"I don't." Dan shrugs. "But I figured out you were okay when I saw you shut up Alexis Westbrook in class last week."

"Thanks," I say, even though I'm not sure he meant to compliment me.

"So what class do you need a grade change in?" Dan lowers his voice. "I could probably do it Monday morning."

"You mean I can't do it myself?"

"I'm not going to mess it up, if that's what you're worried about. I've done this tons of times."

"It's not that," I say. "It's just . . . there was something else I wanted to check on the teachers' portal."

Dan's forehead creases. "What is it?"

God, he's nosy. "Someone's discipline record, okay?"

"Is this about Isabella Fernandez?" Dan whispers, making his slight lisp more pronounced.

My insides go cold. "So what if it is?"

Dan's face looks conflicted for a minute, as if he's debating whether or not this is something he should get involved in. But at least I don't have to worry about him telling anyone what I'm trying to do, because he'd have to implicate himself as well. Plus, he doesn't seem like the type to squeal.

"Okay, but you can't just go screwing with the portal when you've never used it before," Dan says. "I'll have to be there to help you. Meet me in the science computer lab Monday after class."

That's perfect: I need to be in the science building to break in to Andreev's office anyway.

I should be finishing my art-history paper, but instead, I'm combing through my e-mails for the one from Anthony. The one with his phone number.

Obviously this can't end well, but I can't help myself.

I can't gather the nerve to call him, so I send him a text message:

Hey . . . it's Anne. You there?

I'm positive I'm going to faint from nerves the second I send it. When a minute goes by, then five, I'm convinced he's not going to respond. I turn back to my paper just as my phone lights up.

yeah. didn't think you wanted to talk to me anymore

I saw the front page of the news today, I type back. *Is it true?*

What ensues, I'm convinced, is the longest five minutes of my life. He's definitely not going to respond to that.

But by the time I finish peeling all of the nail polish off one hand and am arranging the flakes in a pile on my desk, I have a new text from him:

it's not as bad as they made it sound. And then a few seconds later, this: *i didn't kill my sister*

He must interpret my silence as not believing him, because he sends another message after a few minutes:

i have an alibi. i was with my ex-girlfriend the night isabella was killed

This is supposed to reassure me, probably, but my chest feels tight. So Anthony was with a girl. What do I care? Sure, I'm attracted to him, but it's not like I actually thought anything would happen between us.

My stomach drops as I think back to the article about Anthony. If it's true, and he put some kid in the hospital, would I be stupid to believe him that he didn't kill Isabella?

Am I stupid for not being afraid of him?

Alexis is out to lunch with her parents Sunday afternoon, so Remy and I are doing our French homework in her room. Or, I'm doing *my* French homework, and Remy is freaking out that the warm-chestnut dye she put in her hair is going to turn it orange.

I tried explaining that for her base color, that would be pretty much impossible unless we were in a lame sitcom, but she ignored me.

"I should wash it out early." Remy sits on the opposite edge of her bed from me and gnaws at her thumbnail.

"You still have five minutes," I say. "Try to chill."

"This was a terrible idea. And I dripped a little dye on Alexis's rug." Remy points to a minuscule brown spot with her toe. "She's gonna kill me."

I move my French textbook from my lap to the bed. "What's the deal with her, anyway?"

"What do you mean?" Remy's not looking at me.

"You know what I mean. Everyone seems afraid of pissing her off, but no one actually wants to be friends with her."

"That's not . . . completely true. I know she seems like a total bitch, but Lex has been through a lot." Remy shoots a glance at the door. "Her Dad only cares about his campaign, and her stepmom is a total psycho. Lex's real mom and little brother died in an awful car crash when she was five."

Something catches in my throat. That does sound terrible, but I can't bring myself to feel sorry for Alexis. "She did something to make you guys stop hanging out with her, didn't she?"

Remy avoids my eyes and tucks her feet beneath her, and it becomes clear to me that she'll be a tough nut to crack. She's still got some sense of loyalty to Alexis, for whatever reason. Maybe it's because they were friends when they were kids. Maybe Alexis has something on her. Who knows?

"Remy, you can trust me," I say. "I won't tell anyone."

"It's not like that," Remy sighs. "I mean, everyone knows. It's no secret. She just did something really messed up, and it was embarrassing. Anyway, I really don't want to talk about it. And I have to wash my hair out now."

"Okay." I can't tell if she's mad that I pried. She gets up and leaves me in her room.

Leaves me. In her room.

Alexis's room.

I stay seated on Remy's bed, frozen. It's not that I'm too scared to go through Alexis's stuff. But probably, if I had the choice, I'd rather snoop around the cave of a particularly violent bear.

When am I going to get another opportunity like this, though? Remy will be in the bathroom for at least ten minutes washing the dye out of her hair. This could be my only chance to see if Alexis is hiding anything that could connect her to Isabella's murder.

Think, Anne. Think like a cop. What would you look for if you had a search warrant?

I have no idea what Alexis could have stolen from my dorm room, so the most obvious thing to look for is a murder weapon. A knife, I remember with a wave of nausea. But Alexis is too smart to hide something that damning in her dorm room.

The blood . . . Isabella's neck wound was so grizzly that her casket had to be closed at her wake. There must have been a lot of blood. Whoever killed her had to have gotten some of it on their clothes or shoes.

Think, think. What was Alexis wearing the night Isabella was killed? I saw her earlier that night at dinner. And I *know* some part of my brain processed what she was wearing.

I make sure not to disturb anything in Alexis's closet as I try to jog my memory. Alexis has everything arranged by color. I didn't think mentally stable people actually did that, but I remind myself I'm not positive I'm dealing with a mentally stable person. There's a rainbow of cardigans and V-necks along with an array of neatly pressed uniform sweaters. I push aside a bunch of stiff-looking pastel sundresses and grunt with frustration. Why can't I remember what she was wearing?

Maybe none of these clothes are jogging my memory because Alexis got rid of the clothes. It would make sense, if she didn't have time to wash the blood out or if they were so stained it'd be no use anyway. I move my attention to the far end of the closet, and that's when I see it: a crisp white button-down shirt.

It's not what Alexis was wearing the night Isabella was killed, but now I can see her in my head. Wearing an identical button-down shirt in powder blue.

I triple-check the closet, but the blue shirt isn't there. It's not in her dresser, either, or the small pile of laundry at the bottom of the woven bamboo hamper at the foot of her bed.

Her bed. I plop down on the ground and roll onto my side so I can get a look underneath. No clothes. No bag they could be stuffed into. Underneath Alexis's bed it's dust- and junk-free.

So what happened to the clothes she was wearing the night Isabella died?

I'm barely to my knees before I hear the door open. The rage in Alexis's eyes is indescribable.

"This is a joke, right?" she hisses as I scramble to my feet.

"I um, dropped my earring." I wince. I'm not even wearing earrings.

"Do you think I'm retarded or something? What the hell are you doing in my room?"

"I could probably ask you the same thing about what you were doing in my room," I say innocently.

"What are you talking about?" The panic that flits in Alexis's eyes for half a second is the only indication she's lying.

"You know exactly what I'm talking about."

Alexis takes a step toward me. "You might have charmed your way into a spot at this school, and you might have charmed your way to the top of the social ladder, but I swear, if you keep sticking your nose where it doesn't belong, you're going to seriously regret ever leaving New York." Alexis's eyes flash in a way that makes me think that maybe I should believe her.

"Sounds like you're afraid of what I might find, Alexis. Like something you stole from Isabella?"

Alexis's hand flies up, and for a split second I'm sure she's going to slap me. I think maybe *she* does, too. Instead, she smoothes her headband down and hisses, "I didn't kill that meddling little bitch. But it doesn't surprise me that someone did."

That's when Remy opens the door. Her face says she can tell she's walked into a war zone. "Um. Hey, Lex."

"I'm going to go," I say to Remy, and she doesn't question why. With one foot out the door, I see Alexis give me a look that makes me remember something Anthony said the day he came to collect some of Isabella's things.

You might as well attach a target to your back.

I think I just did.

CHAPTER
TWENTY-ONE

To: dowlinga@Wheatleyschool.edu
From: conroyb@Wheatleyschool.edu
Subject: Change of plans

Anne,
I hate to do this, but I forgot there was an SGA meeting after classes today. Normally I'd roll in late (surprise), but I'm already on thin ice with our advisor. Let me know if I can make it up to you.
Brent

P.S. Be careful.

Annoyance surges through me. He's backing out of breaking into Andreev's office with me. At least he had enough sense not to use those exact words in the e-mail. Who knows who's reading them?

Whatever. I don't need him there. I mean, I wanted him there, but I don't need him.

I follow Dan's instructions and meet him in the basement computer lab. Luckily, it's empty, but I get the feeling Dan knew it would be.

"No one comes down here," he explains. "The computers are ancient."

I look up at the water-stained ceiling. Somewhere in the walls, pipes clang together. "Let's get this over with," I say.

The computer we sit at loads painfully slowly. I notice Dan eyeing me before he finally says, "Is it true that fire you started shut your school down for a week?"

An annoyed sigh escapes me. "The school only closed for a day. And I didn't start the fire on purpose."

"Oh. Still, it'd be cool if someone burned a building here down and we didn't have to go to class."

"Careful what you wish for." My thoughts drift to Lexington Hall, room 180. A room that doesn't exist anymore. I wish I knew what used to be there. Or what Isabella thought was there.

The computer rasps and honks its way to life, and Dan enters an address into the Internet browser. Slowly, a page titled ICampus loads.

"There's no way they can trace this back to us, right?" I ask.

"Technically, they could trace the IP address to this computer, but they'd have to notice suspicious activity first," Dan replies. "Just poking around on here isn't suspicious. Especially since I make sure to log in as a different teacher every time."

"How did you figure out how to do that?"

"It was easy, once I figured out their pattern for generating passwords. Teachers can't create their own." Dan pauses. "We're not the only ones at this school who aren't allowed to think for ourselves."

The layer of bitterness to Dan's voice surprises me a little. But it also makes me feel like I can trust him, so once he's logged on, I ask him to search the student directory for Lee Andersen.

"Andersen?" Dan's eyes widen. "What do you think he did?"

I ignore Dan and peer at the search results. There's a tiny red flag dated last April next to his name. "Does that mean he got in trouble?"

"It means a teacher wrote an incident report. We should be able to access it." Dan clicks on the red flag, but an error page loads.

"Something wrong with the Internet?" I ask.

"Computer says the connection is fine." Dan's upper lip creases and he goes back a page. He clicks the red flag again but gets the same error message.

"That's so weird," he says. "It's like someone deleted the report."

"Yeah. Real weird," I mutter. "There's nothing else?"

"Not on here," Dan says. "But teachers and RAs can always go straight to Dr. Harrow. Reporting stuff on the portal is a formality." Dan looks like he's deep in thought. "I wonder if that report on Lee had anything to do with his broken nose."

"Lee had a broken nose?" I ask. "When?"

Dan rubs the faint outline of a goatee on his chin. "End of last year. I don't know, the busted nose was weird. The kid doesn't talk to anyone. Hard to imagine him getting into a fight."

Did Isabella break Lee's nose? It's hard to imagine her hurting even a lab rat, but I get the feeling she could be fierce if she needed to protect herself.

"Do you think Lee Andersen killed Isabella?" Dan looks absolutely enthralled. I want to slap him.

"I don't know. Can you get me Lee's and Isabella's schedules from last year?" It's a place to start: If Lee was harassing Isabella and a teacher reported it, I can narrow the teachers down to the ones they shared.

"Sure." Dan pulls up Lee's in one window and Isabella's in another. I scan the screen, but Dan is faster. "Looks like they had calculus, American history, and Latin together."

This turns my stomach. Isabella had to see this creep three times a day. "What about this year?"

Dan clicks around. "Doesn't look like they had any classes together."

"They did, until Isabella dropped Latin," I say.

Dan is studying the screen. "Take a look at this. Isabella took the first half of AP calc last year, then switched to statistics this year. That's weird."

Not if she custom-made her schedule to avoid Lee. I check his schedule, and sure enough, he's taking the second half of AP calculus this year.

"So what are you going to do with all of this?" Dan asks me.

"I don't know," I say honestly. "This isn't enough to prove Lee was stalking Isabella. Don't say anything to anyone about this, okay?"

"I won't." Dan looks unsettled though. "Dude, Lee lives on my floor. I could be sharing a bathroom with a psychopath. I'm dead-bolting my door tonight."

I think of how I couldn't find the clothes Alexis was wearing the night of the murder. I don't tell Dan that it's possible there are two psychopaths in the junior class.

CHAPTER
TWENTY-TWO

After I part ways with Dan, I take the stairs up to the third floor, where the science teachers' offices are. Andreev is the last teacher to leave. He locks the door behind him and stuffs his key into his briefcase, oblivious to the fact that I'm watching him from behind a statue of Ben Franklin inscribed with the words GENIUS WITHOUT EDUCATION IS LIKE SILVER IN THE MINE. After the stairwell door closes behind Andreev, I wait five minutes before I emerge and cross the hall to his office.

I have to battle with the key once it's in the lock. Panic fills me as I think maybe I have the wrong key after all, but when I lean against the door, the doorknob clicks. I'm in.

I close the door behind me and take in the room. Really, where am I supposed to start? I'd call this place a pigsty, but that wouldn't even be fair to pigs.

Andreev's desk seems like the most logical place to store a flash drive. I comb through his drawers, my eyes peeled for something purple. The bottom drawer doesn't open when I yank it.

It's locked. I jiggle the handle just to be sure. But any thirteen-year-old with a bobby pin can pick a file cabinet. I would know, because that's what I did when I was thirteen and my dad took my cell phone away and hid it in a file cabinet in his office. He upgraded to a more heavy-duty lock after that.

I slide the bobby pin out of my hair and wiggle it around in the drawer's lock. I've done this lots of times before, but it's still frustrating and takes lots of patience. A thin line of sweat is forming at my brow by the time I hear the satisfying *click*.

I open the drawer, and I'm shocked to find it's empty except for a plastic bag. Andreev's passport is inside. There's also a red book with a gold crest on the front. This looks like a passport as well, but I don't recognize the language on the cover. I rifle through it: There's a picture of Andreev inside, but this passport is issued to "Konstantin Milenko."

I compare the photo with the one in Andreev's U.S. passport. They're definitely of the same person. So who the hell is Konstantin Milenko? The foreign passport has got to be fake. With my phone, I take a picture of the cover of the red one so I can figure out later what language it's in.

As I make my way through the rest of the bag's contents, I'm certain of one thing: It looks like Andreev was, or is, planning to leave the country. There's a red ATM card printed with the same Slavic-looking letters as on the passport, and more than a thousand U.S. dollars.

My palms are sweating as I place everything back in the bag, trying to arrange the items like I found them. Being a suspect in a murder investigation seems like a compelling reason to leave the country to me.

There's only one other thing in the drawer besides Andreev's *how to disappear from the United States* kit: a Post-it note with a list of four words. They're not in English, and on a closer glance, I realize they're not even words. There are numbers sandwiched between the unfamiliar letters.

Passwords. They've got to be passwords.

I'm saving a picture of the Post-it note to my phone when I hear the stairwell door slam. My heart leaps into my throat, and

I close Andreev's desk drawer. I grab my bag and peer out the pane of glass on Andreev's door.

It takes all I have not to vomit everywhere when I see Sebastian and Andreev at the end of the hallway. *Shit.* I was positive Andreev had left for the day. He took his coat and briefcase with him!

There's absolutely zero chance of me getting past them. My only option is to cry hysterically and hope Andreev feels badly enough for me to leave my body in one piece so my parents can bury it.

I'm almost paralyzed with fear until one word pops into my head. *Hide.*

I spin around and examine my options. Under the desk is not one of them. They'd see me in a second. But then there are the cabinets beneath Andreev's counter where he keeps his lab equipment.

There's about five square feet of free space under the sink. I crawl into it, curving my body around the pipes. My head is practically touching my toes as I close the cabinet door, and my heart is slamming against my chest so hard I'm seeing black spots.

Andreev's door clicks open and I suck in a breath. "This had better be important, Sebastian. I'm late for a meeting."

Breathe. Breathe. Just don't let them hear you.

"I'm sorry, sir," Sebastian says. "I didn't know who else to go to."

"Well, what's this about, then?" I hear the sound of groaning leather. Andreev must have sat down. The thought of him getting comfortable makes me even more aware of the way my joints are complaining.

"There's a detective watching me," Sebastian blurts. "He stopped me and asked me about Isabella yesterday morning."

The silence that follows is so painful, I'm sure they're going to hear my heart beating. Finally, Andreev speaks. "Well . . . what did you tell him?"

"I said I only knew her through class, but I could tell he didn't believe me." Sebastian drops his voice to just above a whisper. "Sir, I e-mailed her asking for help a few weeks ago. She never responded, so I kept trying—"

"You imbecile," Andreev growls. "How many times did you e-mail her?"

"Three or four." I can practically hear Sebastian wincing.

"Didn't I forbid you to contact her about our work together?" Andreev's voice shakes, as if he's trying not to yell. "Surely you know how this looks to the police. Harassing a girl through e-mail weeks before she's killed."

"I wasn't harassing her!" Sebastian sounds panicked. "You threatened to fail me, and I knew she'd made more progress than I did—"

"I did no such thing. I simply alerted you to your incompetence, which you have proved yet again." Andreev pauses. "Sebastian, you are aware of my life's work, correct?"

There's a short silence, so I assume Sebastian's nodded, because Andreev continues, "Then I do not need to remind you what could happen to both of us should we be dragged into a murder investigation."

"But I had nothing to do with that," Sebastian says.

"I know you didn't, dense boy. But think of how this will look to the police." Andreev's chair groans again. "Tell them you needed Isabella's help with homework if they bring up the e-mails. Say nothing about your position and the work we do together."

"I don't want the position anymore," Sebastian says. "Not if it's going to get me into trouble."

Andreev lets out a sharp laugh. "You say that as if you are not replaceable. Go ahead. Quit. Maybe I will then find someone of value to me."

Sebastian is silent. I wonder if, like me, he's considering the fact that the last person to quit Andreev's internship wound up dead.

The muscles in my legs are cramping to the point that I'll be shocked if I ever regain use of them, so I just want this conversation to be over so I can get the hell out of here. But then Andreev says something that sends me reeling:

"I suggest you go to the dean or vice-principal if this detective becomes bothersome to you. You'd be surprised how . . . well equipped they are to handle these situations."

There's acid at the back of my throat, and I'm sure I'm going to throw up, stop breathing, or both. *Please let me get out of here.*

"You have complicated things, Sebastian," Andreev says before the door closes behind both of them.

CHAPTER
TWENTY-THREE

This time, I'm not as stupid. I wait ten minutes until I'm sure Andreev has left for good. Ten minutes to regain feeling in my legs and let my raging heartbeat calm down.

Then I get my ass out of there. I don't even slow down as I'm going down the stairs. My legs are still weak from being cramped in that horrible position, so my ankle gives out beneath me and I slip down the last three steps.

I cry out and put my hand over my mouth instinctively, even though I doubt there's anyone left in the building. Ignoring the pain in my left foot, I run all the way around the back of the building and don't stop until I've put a considerable distance between me and the edge of the forest.

Because for the first time since Isabella's murder, I'm scared. Not the shocked, *How could this happen to someone I know?* type of scared or the way I feel every night when I double-check that my door is locked.

I don't have a word for this type of scared. But I feel it in every corner of my body, and it's enough to make me want to run back to New York and pretend I never got involved in any of this. Because this is not a game. There's no telling what Andreev would have done to me if he'd found me in his office, and there's no telling what the school will do to me if they find out how much I know. I have a feeling I'll be lucky just to get expelled.

Andreev said Sebastian should ask the administration for help if the police become *bothersome.* Is that what happened to Isabella? Did she become *bothersome* to someone?

I can tell Remy is dying to ask what happened between me and Alexis in her room on Sunday, but the first time we're even close to being alone is dance class Tuesday morning. Even then, she can't get rid of April long enough to talk to me.

I'm glad, because I definitely can't tell Remy the truth about Alexis's missing clothes. If she knew I suspected her roommate of murdering Isabella, she'd either (a) think I was nuts and stop talking to me and complicate everything, or (b) believe me, freak out, and complicate everything.

Either way, I figure all of this is complicated enough already, so as we're stretching at the dance-studio barre, I take the bait as April leads the conversation to Valentine's Day, which is this Friday. I haven't given much thought to it this year, because it seems silly to me to be worrying about who might send me a rose-gram when there's a murderer running loose in Wheatley.

All right, maybe I've thought about it once or twice. It's not like I expect anything to happen, though. If Brent hasn't made a move by now, I doubt he'd make one on Valentine's Day. It's too predictable. Too vulnerable. And I doubt a guy who's kept me at an arm's length since I met him would ever let me catch him being either.

Ms. Dawson, our teacher, instructs us to come to the center of the floor for warm-ups. She's rail-thin and probably in her late twenties, and she takes herself very seriously. I don't like her. But I do like dance class, for the most part. It's something I'm good at, even though that wasn't enough to save me from getting kicked out of Donna Claire Ballet Academy in the eighth grade for excessive talking.

Normally we're allowed to talk during warm-ups as long as we keep the volume down, so the hush that's spread over the group tells me something's wrong. When I turn and see Detective Phelan in the door of the studio, I feel a sense of dread and know he's here for me before he gestures for me to come to him.

"Officer, you can't just pull students from my class without warning," Dawson says, her face pink. No doubt worrying she'll be fired if she lets him take me.

Detective Phelan gives her a look that says *Shove your MFA up your ass; this is a murder investigation.* He beckons to me, and I follow him outside the studio.

"Where are we going?" I ask, suddenly aware that I'm wearing only yoga pants and a tank top.

"For a walk. You can get your coat and meet me outside."

I do, my hands shaking as I enter the locker room. Why is Detective Phelan here? If it's something that couldn't wait until after classes are over, I'm sure it can't be good.

"Did you find out who killed Isabella?" I ask him when I meet him on the steps outside the athletics building.

Detective Phelan shakes his head. "I know you think that if we haven't found whoever did this by now, we never will, but that's not the case. These things take time." His voice is far off in a way that lets me know there's something he's not telling me.

A bird whistles in the tree above us. We're on the path that leads to the forest. My chest constricts for a minute, worried that he might be taking me to the place they found Isabella's body, but we make a left to stay on the path that forms the outer loop of the campus.

"Anne, I'm here because I want to help you," Detective Phelan says. "And I can only do that if you're honest with me."

Wait. Help *me*? For a split second, I think he's figured out what I've been doing, maybe he's been watching me. But then I really get what he means when he says: "Did you and Isabella get along, Anne?"

I stop, and every instinct telling me to trust Detective Phelan drains from my body. "Yes. We spent a lot of time together. I mean, because we wanted to. Not just because we lived together."

Detective Phelan nods. "You never fought?"

My skin crawls with the feeling he's setting me up. "Of course not."

He clears his throat. "Anne, someone's come forward. They said they knocked on your door after they heard yelling, and Isabella was crying. The day you moved in."

"What? When? That never happened—" I freeze. "Wait. That's all wrong. You don't understand."

I can't get the words out. I'm so paralyzed with rage. Alexis.

"Isabella was singing that night, not yelling," I manage to say. "We weren't fighting. She was only crying because we were watching *Les Mis*. You can't believe Alexis Westbrook. You can't . . . you can't think I killed Isabella."

"We're just trying to fill in the pieces," Detective Phelan says.

"Well, I'm not one of them." There's anger bubbling in my voice. "I barely knew Isabella. Why would I want to kill her?"

Apparently, Detective Phelan can't answer this, because he changes the subject. "Can we go back over what you were doing the night she died? I just want to make sure I know everything."

"I already told you everything," I said. "I left Isabella around ten. I came back with my friends April and Kelsey after one and stayed in their room when Isabella didn't open the door or answer her phone. You can ask them about it."

"April Durand and Kelsey Emmet confirmed you were with them," Detective Phelan says. "We also talked to some of your classmates who were also at the party." He clears his throat. "One says the three of you were drinking heavily."

My stomach dips. Not because two cups of wine hardly counts as drinking *heavily*, but because I get why Detective Phelan is acting like he can't trust what I say.

When I first spoke to him, I didn't tell him the three of us were drinking at the party, let alone that April and Kelsey were wasted by the time we got back from the dorm. I just didn't want to get us all in trouble, because what did it matter if we were drinking? I didn't think it would change my story, at the time.

But now I see it changes everything. If April and Kelsey were drunk that night, they can't claim with 100 percent certainty that I stayed in their room until morning.

And I can just see how a prosecutor would spin it: me, the out-of-control arsonist, killing Isabella in an accidental, but drunken, rage. The security feed that could prove I was in the dorm until morning crapped out at three. Plenty of time for me to figure out how to get rid of the body before the hiker found her in the morning.

I'm so angry my brain can only form one word: *Alexis.*

"Alexis," I say. "You can't listen to her, Detective. She hated Isabella, and she hates me. She may have even broken in to my room. She's the one you should be questioning."

"Anne, I'm not questioning you," he says. He pauses, and I can tell the tidbit about Alexis hating Isabella is news to him. "How come you didn't tell me earlier that Alexis Westbrook and Isabella were enemies?"

"I didn't find out until a couple of days ago." I stop myself there. This already looks bad enough for me without me admitting to all the snooping around I'm doing. "You have to believe me."

"I want to, Anne. I said I'm trying to help you here, right?" He rubs his chin. "I believe you didn't kill Isabella."

He says it the way my mother said she believed me that the fire in the auditorium was mostly Martin's fault: like he wants to believe me but can't completely. Because as charming or pretty as I am, it's like Bailey said. Trouble always seems to find me.

I'm exactly the type of girl the media would have a field day over if I were accused of killing Isabella.

"Then you won't mind if I go back to class," I say to Detective Phelan. I turn on my heels, in the direction of Amherst, as he calls out to me. Of course I'm not going back to class now.

But I'm definitely not sticking around for him to see me cry.

CHAPTER
TWENTY-FOUR

Remy is at my door. "Anne. Please let me in."

I don't say anything. I'm lying on my back, my cheeks warm and stiff with dried tears. I can't even think of all the work I missed today, or how bad it looks that I didn't show up for classes after a detective came looking for me. And I definitely can't talk to Remy.

I knew Alexis was going to make me pay for snooping in her room, but I never saw this coming. It's so manipulative, so horrible, so . . . *Alexis*. If only I hadn't underestimated her.

"Anne." Remy knocks again. "Please. I don't believe what they're saying."

I wonder if that's supposed to comfort me. Of course there are rumors already. Alexis has had at least four hours to spread them, with me locked away in my room, unable to do damage control. I wonder if she threw in one about me sleeping with every guy at the party, just for shits and giggles.

Wait. The party. Alexis wasn't there. Didn't Detective Phelan say someone saw me, Kelsey, and April drinking? It couldn't have been Alexis, so who the hell was it?

Eventually, Remy gives up. By the time dinner rolls around, I'm tired of sitting on my ass feeling sorry for myself. I press a cucumber-infused wipe to my face, hoping it'll soothe some of the redness, and change out of my dance-class clothes.

Then I head to the dining hall to face the music and find out who other than Alexis feels so threatened by me that they'd go this far to screw me over.

A hush spreads over the dining hall as I make my way to our table. Even Murali, Cole, Phil, and Brent are silent as I sit down. *I don't trust any of you anymore,* is the first thought that crosses my mind. *I don't trust anyone.*

When Kelsey sees me, she bursts into tears, and for a second I forget how shitty I feel for myself and wrap my arms around her.

"I'm so sorry," she sniffles. "This is all my and April's fault."

"It's not. It's okay. I can deal with this," I tell her.

"The evidence is all circumstantial anyway," Cole says. "They can't prove anything."

"I don't need a lawyer, Cole," I snap. "I'm not a suspect. This is all just someone's lame attempt to set me up. Someone who's trying to hide something."

I know how loud I'm being, and I don't care. Alexis is at the table next to us, with Lizzie and Jill and whatever other spineless souls Alexis has managed to recruit. Good. I want her to hear me. I don't care anymore.

"My parents are going to kill me if they find out about this," April mutters. I want to slap her, not only because of how selfish she sounds, but because the remark sends Kelsey, who obviously hadn't considered this possibility, into another fit of sobs.

"All right. Enough." It's obvious that I'm going to have to handle Thing One and Thing Two before I attempt to take care of myself. "Both of you come with me. Now."

April and Kelsey stand up obediently, and Remy, who's been sitting in silence up until now, motions to follow.

"No," I say. "You stay here."

She looks hurt, but I don't care how unfair I'm being, punishing her for her loyalty to Alexis. For leaving me with April and Kelsey the night of the party.

I usher Kelsey and April into the bathroom, ignoring the countless pairs of eyes that follow us. I check to make sure that all the stalls are empty before rounding on them.

"Someone who was at the party screwed us," I say, all business. I'm back to my old self: in control. Calm under pressure. Not letting anyone see me cry. It's how I came to rule St. Bernadette's, but more is at stake now. "I need to know who."

April and Kelsey look at each other. "It had to be Jill Wexler," April says.

Slowly, it's like a fog has been lifted from my thoughts. "She's the one who likes Brent."

"She's in *love* with Brent," Kelsey says. "Oh God. She probably saw you two flirting at the party and flipped out."

"Well, do you blame her?" April shoots back. "He's been leading her on *forever*—"

April clamps a hand over her mouth, but there's nothing more to say. "I'm sorry. I didn't mean—"

"Don't," I say. "Just don't. I really don't care. I have bigger problems."

It's true. But mixed in with the million types of anger and betrayal I'm feeling right now is the kind that makes me want to make a tiny Brent voodoo doll and run it over with a truck. I want to revert back to my fifth-grade self and write *I hate brent conroy* all over anything I can get my hands on.

"So Jill's the one who told the police we were drinking," I say, pushing Brent out of my head. "But I know Alexis put her up to it. She lied to the cops about me and Isabella fighting, and it's got to be to cover her own ass. So you two better tell me everything you know, because like it or not, you're involved now."

April is silent, her mouth hanging open, but I can see Kelsey battling with something inside her. I can see her remembering how I gave her advice about Justin, and how she really wants to help me, too. But there's fear in her eyes.

She's stronger than I give her credit for, though, because she finally says, "The SGA election speeches last year. Alexis wanted to be president, but someone replaced her campaign video with a tape of her saying some really messed-up things." Kelsey swallows. "Someone spied on her to get the video, and Alexis told us it was Isabella."

My head is swimming. "Why would Isabella do something like that?"

"Alexis was making her life hell last year," Kelsey says. "Leaving her these sticky notes all the time. It got so bad Isabella had to use the bathroom on a different floor because Alexis was always picking on her."

"But no one could prove Isabella made the video," April says, her voice hushed. "Zach Walton was in charge of video for the speeches, and he swears he didn't see anyone mess with his laptop."

"But he's friends with Peter Wu, who was running against Alexis. He's probably the one who switched the tapes," Kelsey says. "Anyway, all I'm saying is I believe she did it. I would have done the same thing if I'd heard Alexis saying that horrible stuff."

"What kind of horrible stuff?" I ask.

"It was really bad," Kelsey whispers. "Stuff that could destroy her father's campaign."

"Goddard said he'd expel anyone who even thought about putting the video on the Internet," April adds. "I guess it scared Isabella enough, because almost everyone's forgotten about it by now."

Everyone except Alexis, I think. If she publicly humiliated Alexis once, what was to stop Isabella from doing it again once she graduated and didn't need the scholarship to the Wheatley School anymore? Alexis could have set Isabella up—lured her into the woods, maybe promising her a lot of money in exchange for the tape, only to decide killing her was the only way to shut her up for good.

"Anne, what are you going to do?" Kelsey asks, her face and voice anxious.

"Nothing," I lie. "Just tell the truth if the police come to you, okay?"

None of us feels like watching the entire student body gossip about us as we eat our salads, so we agree to head back to Amherst together. Brent jumps up from his seat as he sees us heading for the door.

"Anne," he says, his expression strained. Does he know his little girlfriend is setting me up to spend the rest of my life in jail?

"No," is the best retort I can come up with, because I'm shaking. Because I know he's probably been leading me on just like he's been leading Jill on. I push past him, but Kelsey and April hang back to answer his demands as to what my problem is.

Good. I'd rather walk back to the dorm alone anyway. But as I take one final glance over my shoulder at Brent arguing with April, I collide with Alexis. She balances her bowl of fruit in time to keep it from spilling everywhere, but a strawberry topples out and lands on my shoe.

"Sorry," she says. When she realizes we have an audience, she smirks and adds, "Don't kill me."

I want to lunge at her, to shove those strawberries down her throat until she chokes. But that's what she wants, right? She wants everyone to think I murdered Isabella.

Well, she better try harder, because now that's she's made this personal, there's no way I'm giving up on finding the real killer.

CHAPTER
TWENTY-FIVE

All of my resolve crumbles when I get back to Amherst. I curl up on the couch in the first-floor lounge, seconds away from dialing home and asking my parents to come pick me up. When I get tired of feeling sorry for myself, I consider all the missing pieces to Isabella's murder that I don't have.

The tape Isabella used to humiliate Alexis. Isabella's flash drive and Andreev's research. The missing discipline report on Lee Andersen.

All I know for sure is that any of them could have killed Isabella.

I'm sitting upright again when I spot Remy, Kelsey, and April outside the lounge window. I really don't want to talk to them anymore tonight, but it's going to be hard to avoid them. Even if I try to make it upstairs quickly, they'll probably be inside in time to ride the elevator with me.

I glance at the basement door. Hiding in the laundry room alone isn't ideal, but I just can't face the girls right now. I hurry down the steps.

As I expected, the laundry room is empty. Sure, it's a little creepy down here, but it might not be a terrible place for me to hide until the rumors about me go away. Or until the end of the year. I walk the length of the laundry room, because I'm going to go crazy if I don't keep moving.

That's what I wanted to do tonight, I remember. I wanted to see if there is a floor plan of Amherst, if there are any other ways out of here that the police may have missed.

I run my hand over the walls beneath the stairs. It looks like it could be a closet of some sort. Like the type Harry Potter lived in. But there's no door. I knock on one wall. I can't tell if it's hollow inside or not.

My gaze locks on the bookshelf against the stair wall. Now why would a laundry room need a bookshelf?

I approach it, my heart racing, and examine it from every angle. It could definitely be blocking a door. I grab hold of one side and pull it toward me, wincing at the awful sound the wood dragging across the concrete floor makes.

The bookshelf only budges a few inches, but I have a clear view of what's behind it.

A door.

I tug at the bookshelf until there's enough space for me to fit behind it. The door is made of a heavy wood; I have to lean my shoulder against it, but it opens.

I step into the tiny space beneath the stairs and use the screen of my phone as a light. The space beneath the stairs extends into some sort of hallway.

Except it's not a hallway exactly. It's sloping downward, and there's a stone arch over it. I get closer and hold up my phone for more light as I read the inscription on the arch.

ABANDON ALL HOPE, YE WHO ENTER HERE.

I can't help it: I shiver. Suddenly everything makes sense: the system of dotted lines linking the buildings on that old campus map. Isabella never leaving the dorm, according to the security tape. Even Remy's comment: *Unless we dig ourselves out of here, looks like we can't sneak out anymore.*

This hallway is a tunnel.

My first instinct is to follow it all the way to the end, but I know that would be stupid, with only an almost-dead iPhone for light. The tunnel is pitch-black. I hold my phone up to the side and see there are empty sconces on the walls. It smells like mildew and dirt down here. These tunnels probably haven't been used in years.

I have so many questions: How did Isabella find out about the tunnels? Who else knows about them? I definitely need to be careful who I let know about this. If Isabella used the tunnels to sneak out the night she died, her killer could have met her down here.

Which means he or she knows about it, too.

Using my feeble light, I make it about twenty feet down the tunnel until it splits off in two directions. On the wall in front of me is a plaque engraved with four words.

LIBRARY →
REFECTORY ←
AMHERST DORMITORY →

This is crazy, I think. There are entrances to the tunnel in at least three places on campus. Who knows where else it leads?

Panicked, I think of how I left the Amherst entrance to the tunnel uncovered. I need to leave now and come back when I can think of a better way to cover my tracks. Also, I'm going to need a real flashlight if I'm going to go farther into the tunnel.

I replace the bookcase and hurry back upstairs. I can barely contain myself once I lock my door behind me. I figured out how Isabella evaded the security camera! Suck on that, Wheatley Police.

I'm dying to tell someone about the tunnel—and about Sebastian's conversation with Andreev—but I don't trust anyone here anymore. Trusting Brent didn't exactly turn out too well, and if I thought people were watching me before, it's only going to be about a thousand times worse now.

There's really only one person I can talk to about any of this. I don't even wait until I get back to my room to text Anthony: *I found something. What are you doing tomorrow afternoon?*

CHAPTER
TWENTY-SIX

Just as I'm thinking I'm not being totally fair to be so pissed at Brent, he strolls into Brit lit and sits two tables away from me. No wave hello. No smile. He won't even look at me.

White-hot anger surges through me again. No wonder I got the sense Isabella was holding something back about Brent. His *I don't hook up with boarding school girls* act is just a way for him to lure us in and string us along, and now that he got caught, he wants nothing to do with me.

The way Brent seemed to ignore Remy and the other girls when I was around makes sense now. Why pay attention to the girls who already have you figured out when you can go after the clueless new girl?

But at least focusing on picturing heavy objects flying into the back of Brent's head distracts me from the people who are staring at me. Because there are a lot of them. And the few who have seemed to learn that staring is rude are whispering to their friends, carefully shooting me glances when they think I'm not looking.

I wince as a crumpled piece of paper lands on my desk. I squeeze my eyes shut and open it.

KILLER, someone has written in purple ink.

I whip my head around. Alexis is two tables behind me, her hair falling in a curtain to the side of her face as she talks to Brooke, Jill's snobby, pig-nosed other half. I glare at Alexis until she looks up at me and mouths *What?*

I roll my eyes at her. She didn't even bother to hide the purple pen resting on her notebook.

I turn around and rip the paper in two, completely aware that everyone is watching me. I'm glad they're watching, because it's all the more reason I'm not going to show that Alexis is getting to me.

There is one person who doesn't seem to care that people are calling me a killer, though. Dan Crowley plops down next to me before class starts, like we're BFFs now or something. For the most part, I don't mind. Until he opens his mouth.

"Hey, Anne. Um . . ." He uses his pinky to twirl the silver ring in his ear. "Did you talk to Kelsey yet?"

"Not to be rude, but I've had more important stuff on my mind."

"Oh. Yeah, I heard about that." Dan drops his voice. "Look, it's just a stupid rumor. Try to ignore them. That's what I did in ninth grade. My roommate was a dick and lied about me looking at naked pictures of Zac Efron before bed. The whole thing blew over in a week."

"Really, Dan, I appreciate your concern, but two *totally* different things."

Professor Fowler slaps his literature anthology down on his podium. "Mr. Crowley and Ms. Dowling. I've started class. If you'd like to continue your conversation outside, by all means . . ."

At least this has the effect of shutting everyone up. I watch the back of Brent's head for a reaction, but the most movement he makes is borrowing a pen from the kid sitting next to him.

I turn to the next blank page in my notebook and notice that Dan's become twitchier than usual. He's drumming one set of fingers against the table, and the other against the keyboard of his laptop. He keeps stealing glances at me, until I finally mouth, *What is it?*

He tilts his laptop screen to me so I can get a better view, and loads a blank page. Then he types, *I found out something.* He erases it right away.

I swallow and write a single question mark on the corner of my notebook so he can see.

I got curious about why someone would delete a discipline report. The words are gone almost as quickly as he types them out. *So I looked into who has the power to do that.*

When he pauses, I raise an eyebrow at him as if to say *Go on.*

Only an administrator can delete reports. So that means Goddard, Harrow, Watts, or even Tierney, depending on when it was deleted.

My stomach sinks, even though I had a suspicion someone high up was covering for Lee. But there's more, because Dan is still typing.

Teachers can also delete reports they wrote.

I check to make sure Fowler isn't watching us, before I scribble across the top of my page, *Is there any way to find out who wrote the report?*

Dan hesitates, then types, *There's no way to prove it, but I logged in as the 3 teachers Lee shared with Isabella. Only one has filed a discipline report in the last nine months.*

"Who?" I whisper, completely forgetting where we are.

Dan puts a finger to his lips. The name is gone from his screen before I can even process it.

Professor Upton.

Why?

That's what I want to know. Why did Upton file a report on Lee? I've only been in her class for three weeks, and it's obvious to me that he's her shining star. She's always calling on him and making that approving clicking noise and staring at the rest of us as if to say *Why can't you all be as smart as Lee?*

Something changed since last year. Upton went from being willing to turn Lee in, to a spy for Dean Snaggletooth. She let Isabella drop her class, and if the administration told her to stay out of the whole thing, she may have even let Lee kill her.

Why?

Or rather, how? How could she let something like this happen? Just so she could keep her job?

The thought makes me so sick I almost forget Anthony is waiting for me in the visitors' parking garage. I insisted that he meet me there this time. Security is bound to recognize his motorcycle by now, and getting caught for an unpaid ticket won't help his not-so-squeaky-clean public image.

Not that mine would be any better, should the media get wind of Alexis's story. The thought is so paralyzing I have to think of other things so I don't turn around and find the quickest way out of Massachusetts.

But when I see Anthony, leaning against the wall of the parking garage, one foot propped up behind him, I almost lose it. Everything floods my brain at once: almost getting caught in Andreev's office, Isabella humiliating Alexis, Detective Phelan showing up yesterday, Jill and Brent.

Brent—the perfect example of how cute guys always get me into trouble.

"What's wrong?" Anthony's face softens, just a little bit, and I'm overwhelmed with the urge to run into his arms. But that's definitely something I can never do. Anthony's already made it clear that I come from a world he hates, and how can I blame him, when that world might be responsible for his twin sister's death? The only reason he wants anything to do with me now is to get closer to the truth. He could never see me the way I'm beginning to see him.

How did I end up wanting the only two guys in Wheatley I can't have?

I motion for Anthony to follow me around the back of the garage, to the edge of the forest, even though Goddard has declared it off-limits. I can't risk anyone hearing us, though, and ironically, the place where Isabella was killed is the safest.

Anthony doesn't ask questions as he follows me down a path blanketed with brown pine needles. When we're deep enough into the forest that the parking garage is out of view, I spill everything.

Well, almost everything. I'm not about to tell him what happened with Brent, but I tell him about Andreev, Lee, and Alexis. I recount my conversation with Detective Phelan, my throat tight like I'm about to cry the whole time. I don't, though, because Anthony is the one person I definitely won't let myself cry in front of.

When I end with Alexis and the tape Isabella supposedly made, Anthony is quiet.

"Sounds like you've had a shitty week," he says, and I have to laugh a little in spite of myself.

"So you actually broke in to that teacher's office?" Anthony's eyes are wide. I nod. "Wow. You really . . ."

"What?" I ask.

"I don't know," Anthony says. "I was wrong about you, that's all."

"Glad to hear I have your approval." I roll my eyes at him, even though it really is nice to hear him admit he's wrong for once.

I'm leading him out of the forest and back toward Amherst when he says, "They're just trying to scare you. The cops. There's no way they think you did it."

"Why would they want to scare me?" I ask.

"To get you to talk, or to rat out someone you might be covering for." Anthony shrugs. "They'll keep bullying you as long as they think you know something."

"Is that what they're doing to you?" I ask, nervous to push further than that. But he knows what I mean.

"No. I knew my reputation at school would get out," he says. "But that news story about me was wrong."

"I thought you said it was true."

"I did fight a kid last year," he says. "And he did need stitches. But that was all. If I'd really put him in the hospital, I would have been expelled. Even public schools have standards, you know," he adds, his voice bitter.

"Look, we need to get something straight," I say. "I don't give a crap that you go to public school, Anthony. So you can stop acting like *I'm* the one who's making you feel inferior."

I can tell I've surprised him, because he shuts up. After a few minutes of walking in silence, he cracks a smile and says, "I can see why she was friends with you. My sister.

"She really drove me nuts," he adds after a pause, because I guess it's impossible for him to say something remotely nice without ruining it.

Darlene is on duty, so I don't have to sign Anthony in to the dorm. I just quickly wave to her and tell her he's here to get the rest of Isabella's stuff.

"Are you trying to tell me I need to wash my clothes more often?" Anthony asks once we get to the laundry room. Thankfully, it's empty, but I figured it would be. Almost everywhere on campus is dead during 3:00 and 4:00 P.M., or what I call "get in to Harvard time." This is when all of the clubs and organizations and sports for people who really don't know how to play sports meet. Like Ultimate Frisbee.

"Help me move this bookcase," I tell him. He stares at me, so I repeat myself.

"What are we doing . . . ?" He asks, his voice trailing off as he sees the door the bookshelf was concealing. "Whoa. How'd you know this was here?"

"Look around the basement. Doesn't it seem a little small for a building this size?"

I gesture for Anthony to follow me through the door while I find the flashlight in my bag. Mom insisted I pack one with the rest of my stuff because "you never know when you might need one." But I don't think she had something like this in mind when she said that.

"Holy shit," Anthony says as I shine the light down the tunnel. "This school has tunnels?"

I tell Anthony how I read up on the school's history and found that the tunnels were used during really severe weather. The state ruled them unsafe after Lexington Hall burned down. They said students could get trapped down there, and the school supposedly sealed off all the entrances, and no one has been allowed to use them since.

"Except they didn't seal off every entrance, obviously, because we just used one." Anthony pauses and runs his hand over the inscription pointing us toward the library. Even though there's barely any light, I can see his face is calculating.

"Anthony, this has to be how Isabella snuck out of the dorm without being caught on camera," I say.

Anthony nods, his face far off. "Let's see where this thing leads."

I suggest we make a right where the tunnel splits into two, since it will bring us east. The forest is on the eastern edge of campus.

The deeper we descend into the tunnel, the more uneasy I feel. There's the sound of water dripping off in the distance, and it seems like the vaulted ceiling is getting lower. Since I have no idea what I'm going to find down here, I'm glad Anthony is with me.

"Check this out." He points to another inscription on the wall.

INFIRMARY ←
MONROE HALL →
LEXINGTON HALL →

"Let's go this way," I say to Anthony. "Lexington Hall is the building that burned down. There's a parking garage there now, right by the forest. That's got to be how Isabella got out of here."

We make a right. The toe of my shoe snags on a crack in the ground and I lurch forward, the flashlight flying out of my hands. Anthony's hand is at my waist, sending a flush up to my cheeks. I scramble to pick up the flashlight. As I stand up, I follow its beam up the wall. There's a door in front of me, with the number 103 inscribed on it.

I take off past the door, Anthony trailing behind me. As I expected, the tunnel opens up into a room: a dank and dark basement like the tunnel entrance in Amherst's basement. And there are more doors. I frantically shine the light on each one.

I know it's here somewhere. I know we're in the basement of what used to be Lexington Hall. My heart almost stops as my beam lands on a door.

Room 108. *Lexington Hall 108.*

I don't waste time giving Anthony an explanation. I jiggle the doorknob. It's locked, but not for long, because luckily, I brought my wallet. Thank you, Visa.

Anthony gapes at me as the door squeaks open. "Jesus. How did you do that?"

The truth is: practice, luck, and an older lock. But my adrenaline is flowing now that I've found room 108, and I'm feeling reckless. Flirtatious, even. So I say, "I have a lot of skills you don't know about, Anthony."

Through the dark, I see his lips settle into a smirk.

We step into the room and I suppress a gag. It smells about a thousand years old in here.

A 180-degree motion with my flashlight reveals what the room holds: wall-to-wall filing cabinets. I feel a surge of disappointment. I don't know what I was expecting to find here, but if there's anything useful, finding it is going to be like searching for a needle in a haystack.

"Look." Anthony stoops to pick up a folder lying face open on the ground. I help him pick up the contents. "It looks like someone tried to put this back in a hurry."

I hold my flashlight to the name on the file. ELAINE MICHAELS. I browse the inside of the folder, which is yellowing at the edges. From her transcripts, I learn that Elaine Michaels graduated in 1984. There's also a grayscale photo of her that makes me pause.

I've seen her before. But that's impossible, since I've never met anyone named Elaine Michaels.

"What else was in that file?" I ask Anthony. He hands me a bunch of papers, pointing to the one at top.

"This looks pretty recent," he says. ALUMNI CONTRIBUTIONS, the top of the paper reads. I grab it from him and examine it. Elaine Michaels made two contributions of fifteen thousand dollars: one in 1990 and then another in 1996. But by then, she was Elaine Redmond.

Cole's mother. That's why I recognized her.

"What does this have to do with my sister?" Anthony asks, an impatient edge to his voice.

"Probably nothing," I admit. I can't help being frustrated. Isabella obviously knew about this room and the tunnels, but that doesn't mean she was the one who pulled Mrs. Redmond's file. Even if she was, how could Cole's mother have anything to do with her death?

I run my phone light over the filing cabinets again, pausing on the W's. I open the drawer, coughing as dust drifts up to my nostrils.

"What are you looking for?" Anthony asks.

"I'm just curious about someone. Matthew Weaver."

"The missing kid?" Anthony is behind me, his breath warm on my neck. "I remember the *Dateline* special on him a few years ago. Why are you interested in him?"

"Don't you think it's worth acknowledging the fact that no one from the school came forward when *he* disappeared, either?" I run my fingers over the labels on the folder. WATSON, WEXLER, WILSON . . . but no Weaver.

"There's no file on him," I whisper.

Anthony's whole body suddenly freezes.

"What?" I ask.

"Do you hear that?" He looks toward the door. That's when I hear what he hears.

Voices. Two of them.

We're not the only ones down here.

CHAPTER
TWENTY-SEVEN

Anthony and I move in perfect synchronization. I lock us inside the room, and we press ourselves against the wall beside the door. Moments later, a beam of light passes across the glass pane in the door.

"Is there anyone down here?" A gruff voice calls out. It's older. Not one I recognize. Probably belongs to a security guard.

"I could have sworn I saw a light in one of these rooms," the other voice responds.

"Wouldn't be the first time you saw things, Ray." The doorknob jiggles, and I tense against the wall, drawing in a sharp breath. Next to me, Anthony grabs my hand. It's not protective or sweet like the way Brent grabbed my hand. No, Anthony's message is clear: *Calm the hell down or we're screwed.*

"It's probably some kids messing around," Ray says. "Let's go."

"We're the ones who're supposed to keep the kids out of here," his companion snaps. "Are you sure you saw a light?"

Ray hesitates. "I guess not. These rooms are locked, anyway. Kids can't get in."

The light passes across the glass again, and then there's blackness. When the voices disappear, we sneak back out of the room and run.

It's dark, but we can't risk using the flashlight again. We can't go back the way we came, either, unless we want to run into the guards.

I tug on Anthony's sleeve and pull him with me in the opposite direction, feeling the wall to guide us. The tunnel floor is slanting upward. We're getting closer to ground level. An entrance has to be nearby.

"Here," Anthony whispers, at the same time as I stub my toes on a slab of concrete.

Stairs. We fly up them, emerging in a narrow concrete stairwell.

Anthony pushes the door at the top of the stairway open to reveal a parking garage. That's when we see the sign on the other side that says SECURITY ONLY.

And then the security SUV coming around the corner of the garage.

We run down a level, but we'll never outrun the SUV back to campus. If we're seen in the administration parking garage, security will put two and two together that we were the ones in the tunnel.

There are a couple of cars left parked in the garage. I slam into Anthony, taking us both down so we're concealed by a huge, Secret-Service-looking vehicle.

The security SUV idles past as if the driver never saw us.

I allow myself to breathe, and realize I'm sitting on top of Anthony in a position that's a little, uh, friendly. I motion to get up, but he puts his hand on my waist. I barely have time to process what the look on his face means before he's grabbing me. Kissing me.

And I don't just let it happen. I push it further, opening my mouth and letting his tongue find mine. I don't care that my knees are digging into the concrete and the stubble on his chin is scratching my face. In this moment, every ounce of care I have in the world is replaced by desire.

His lips move to the area just below my ear and I lace my fingers through his hair, which is surprisingly soft. Just when I think I'm gonna go crazy, his voice is in my ear.

"Anne. We have to get out of here."

And just like that, it's over. We don't look at each other as we get up, and I'm glad, because I can feel what a mess I must look like right now.

We don't talk about what just happened as I walk him back to the visitor garage. I ask him if he can have Dennis look up where Margaret Watts—the missing dean—lives now, and he says he'll call me when he hears something.

But I catch him looking back at me before he hops on his motorcycle, his expression matching what's going through my head.

Holy shit. That was the most amazing kiss I've ever had.

Every nerve ending in my body is still going crazy by the time I walk back to Amherst. What is wrong with me? I've kissed lots of guys, but none have ever had this effect on me. It's like someone doped me up, and now I can't focus or stop touching my lips, replaying every second they were touching Anthony's.

Guilt pokes through all of the giddiness I'm feeling, though. I just kissed my dead roommate's twin. Isabella is dead—her killer still on the loose—and the best I can do is make out with her brother.

How could I let this happen? My only defense is that we were overcome with adrenaline and didn't realize what we were doing. Not acknowledging the kiss was probably our way of confirming it was a mistake.

Because considering the position we're both in with the police, getting involved with each other is *definitely* a mistake.

I force myself to stop thinking about Anthony. I need to focus on my schoolwork, on piecing together the information I have about Isabella's murder, on keeping my latest encounter with the police from my parents. Kissing Anthony is a distraction I can't afford.

When I get back to my room, I make myself a cup of chai tea and attempt to get my homework done. Except after fifteen minutes, I realize I've answered the question "What modernist painting movement depicts emotion instead of physical reality?" with "37." I close my textbook.

I find myself Google-searching for *Abandon all hope, ye who enter here*. It takes me about three seconds to learn where the quote is from.

The Divine Comedy. Dante. The inscription at the entrance to the tunnel is supposedly the same one as at the gate of hell.

I hope all it means is that whoever built the tunnels had a good sense of humor.

My mind is running in circles. I desperately want to know how Isabella found the tunnels, and if her killer knows about them, too. If Lee found an entrance to the tunnels from the boy's dorm, he could have followed her to the forest. And as a teacher, Andreev might have been the one to tell Isabella about the tunnel entrances in the first place.

I suddenly remember the photos I took in Andreev's office. I'd been so wrapped up in the fiasco with Alexis and Detective Phelan that I'd forgotten all about them. I look at the one of the foreign passport first, zooming in to get a better look at the insignia. It doesn't match the one on the images of Russian and Ukrainian passports I Google. I have no idea what country it could be from, but since the name *Konstantin Milenko* doesn't generate any search results, I'm guessing it's a fake.

A false identity seems like a good way for Andreev to leave the country and evade American authorities.

I scroll to the next picture: the list of what I hope is passwords. There's a good chance one of them opens the document I stole from Sebastian's computer, since Andreev was the one who locked the file. Too bad there's no Russian alphabet on my keyboard so I can type the passwords in.

But what if Andreev wanted to double-cover his ass in case someone found—or in my case, stole—his passwords? The passwords are probably in English, I realize, and he only wrote them down in another language as a type of code.

It's a smart move, because how am I supposed to translate words when the alphabet is totally foreign to me? It could take me hours to look up each letter and try to make sense of the words.

Unless . . .

I scroll through the list of contacts in my phone to see if I have her number—Irina Peterson, who sometimes sat with my friends at lunch back at St. Bernadette's. I was always kind of jealous of her killer hair. Anyway, she's half Russian, and I've heard her speak to her mother in Russian on the phone before.

I find Irina's number and send her the picture, along with a message asking if she can help me figure out what the words mean. Five, then ten minutes go by with no response. I imagine what Irina is thinking: First I disappear from St. Bernadette's after burning a part of it down, now I contact her after weeks of silence with a request to translate a bunch of vague words that might not even be written in Russian, for all I really know.

So, yeah. I'd probably ignore me, too.

My heart starts hammering when a knock sounds at my door. I'm nervous it could be a detective wanting to grill me more, or the million other people who essentially have the power to ruin my life right now. I glance through the peephole, and let out a little sigh of relief when I see it's only Remy.

"Hey," she says as I open the door, "I wanted to— Oh! Your face." She leans in a little. "Have you been kissing someone?"

I glance at the mirror on my closet door in a panic. My chin is red and raw from Anthony's stubble. How am I supposed to fix this by dinnertime? I mean, I've got some calming toner with chamomile, but I'm not a miracle worker or anything.

Remy's reflection blinks at me.

"It's just a rash," I blurt.

She nods like she's still trying to figure out who I could have been kissing. But she doesn't push it. "Anne . . ." she says, "I had no idea what Alexis was doing."

I pause, because I hadn't even considered that Remy might have known. "Okay."

"I should have stood up for you from the beginning," she says, "but I was afraid of hurting Alexis's feelings, because she already thought I was replacing her with you. Even though she and I don't even talk that much anymore. . . ."

I don't know what's funnier—the thought of me needing Remy to stand up for me, or the idea that Alexis has feelings. "She's not just pissed because she thinks I'm going to become your new best friend, Rem. She feels threatened by me, so she's trying to destroy me."

"Why would she feel threatened—"

"Remy, I know Alexis hated Isabella. I know about what happened with her SGA speech. And unlike everyone else, I'm not just going to look the other way."

Remy looks like she's been slapped. "What are you say— Oh my God, Anne." Horror registers on her face. "There's a difference between hating someone and actually *killing* them!"

"Not if the person you hate has the potential to ruin you," I shoot back.

"You don't know Alexis like I do," Remy says. "She'd never *kill* anyone. And I don't think you really knew Isabella, either." There's an angry urgency to Remy's voice that shocks me. I've never seen her worked up like this. "Making that video was manipulative. *She* was manipulative."

"I thought no one could even prove she made it."

"Prove it, no, but I know she did," Remy says. She bites her lip, and her face scrunches like she's holding back tears. "I know because I saw her watching us in the lounge. I'm in the stupid video, too."

CHAPTER
TWENTY-EIGHT

Now I understand why Remy sounded so annoyed when she said Alexis did something embarrassing: She meant that it was embarrassing for her too. I have to sit down, because the thought of Remy being involved in all of this makes my head spin about a hundred times faster.

Remy sits next to me. "We thought Isabella couldn't hear us. She was on her computer in the lounge with us, but she had her headphones on. I never would have thought she was listening to me and Alexis the whole time, let alone *taping* us with her Webcam."

She squeezes her eyes shut, as if she's fighting off a headache. "It was a week before the SGA elections, and Alexis was mad because people were accusing her of taking down Peter Wu's campaign posters. She said some pretty awful things about him. All I did was sit there and let her rant like always, but it was still mortifying when the whole school saw the video, you know?"

I nod. I think I know who Peter Wu is, since I've only seen

one Asian guy in the junior class. He sits with Dan Crowley and two other guys in the dining hall.

"Anne, you have to believe me that Alexis didn't have anything to do with Isabella being killed," Remy says. "Sure, she was really pissed about not getting to be president, and she was worried about the video getting out and embarrassing her dad, but that was almost a year ago. Why would Alexis wait until now to do anything about it?"

I don't tell Remy that there are a million reasons why, because I'm not ready to consider the fact that Isabella may have decided to blackmail Alexis with the video. I don't want to believe that Isabella was *that* manipulative. I want to keep remembering Isabella as I saw her before she was killed—as the quiet, helpful girl who kept to herself.

Even though I'm realizing that was probably never the real Isabella.

I'm dying to get my hands on that video, but Remy's made it clear that if she knows who might have a copy, she's taking that information to the grave—which obviously only makes me more curious. What could Alexis have said that was so bad?

After the scene I made yesterday, I'm dreading going to dinner. Remy doesn't need to twist my arm too much to get me to go with her, April, and Kelsey, though, because if I start holing myself up in my room during meals, it'll look like I'm hiding.

Brent is already at the table when we get to the dining hall. He nods to all of us, avoiding my eyes. It almost depresses me, how cute he is. He threw a gray-and-black-striped sweater over his button-up uniform shirt and even styled his hair tonight. For a minute, I'm paranoid he'll see the redness lingering on my chin and figure out what I was doing earlier. Then I remind myself that even if I hadn't been making out with Anthony earlier, Brent and I would be just as awkward with each other right now.

I don't have time to worry about all that, though, and I'm barely in my chair when Cole says, "Guys. My dad called me today. The DA is trying to get a warrant from the judge for the police to search all the dorms."

Everyone is quiet, processing what this means. It's April who finally speaks up. "But that would mean they think a *student* killed her."

"You're a genius, April." Brent spears a tomato in his salad. "They'll never get a warrant."

His dig at April is so quick, so subtle, that I wonder if I'm the only one who notices it. April's face is frozen, her lips parted as if she doesn't quite get what just happened.

"You never know," Murali says. "They could have probable cause."

"To search every dorm room on campus?" Brent shakes his head. "Not a chance. Probable cause means they would have evidence against a specific person."

My stomach plummets as I wonder if it could be me, although the only "evidence" against me is a steaming pile of Alexis Westbrook's bullshit. Plus, the police have already searched my dorm room.

Could it be that they have something on someone else—someone like Lee or Alexis?

I push myself away from the table and wander to the line for wraps. Three freshmen girls in front of me whisper to one another and look away from me. They look like a pack of scared baby deer, so I can't even gather the energy to be annoyed.

The skin on the back of my neck prickles as I inch forward on the line. I hear his breathing behind me. There's a foot of space between us, but his presence is suffocating me.

I glance over my shoulder to confirm it's him. Lee stares back at me in a way that tells me he's been watching me the whole time.

I quickly look forward again, unease spreading through me. I sense him shifting behind me. My insides go cold, and I can't explain it, but I just know he's the one who hurt her.

I keep my eyes trained straight ahead. I smile at the wrap lady and nod, yes, I would like grilled chicken with sun-dried tomato, my usual. I grip the corners of my tray and don't look back at Lee until I've put a safe distance between me and him.

And I watch him get off the wrap line empty-handed.

Bile rises in my throat. Was he just trying to freak me out? Why else would he wait on line and not get anything?

Head bowed, he skulks over to a two-person table by the window, where a scrawny kid with a really round head and even rounder glasses is sitting. Even sitting down, Lee towers over the other kid by a foot or two.

The boy acknowledges Lee, then shoots uncomfortable glances around the dining hall as if he doesn't want to be caught dead with him. I see Cole refilling his soda from the corner of my eye and approach him.

"Who's that kid with Creepy Lee?" I ask him.

Cole glances over. "That's Peepers. Lee's roommate."

For some reason, Lee having a roommate feels bizarre to me. I guess in my head I pictured Lee living alone in some dank cave like an ogre, instead of in a dorm room with an actual person.

It dawns on me how valuable Peepers could be. With glasses that big, he's bound to notice something like his roommate leaving in the middle of the night just before Isabella's body was found.

"Hey. He's really bummed," Cole says.

"Who? Peepers?"

"No." Cole nods his head toward Brent. When I look over at him, he pretends to be completely absorbed in tearing a dinner roll in half. His cheeks are pink, though, and he looks miserable. Was he watching me and Cole because he's jealous?

"Is that supposed to be my fault or something?" I grumble.

"He thinks you've been avoiding him."

"I have been. Whatever I have to do to stay out of jail," I say.

Cole rests a hand on my arm. He smells like an Abercrombie & Fitch store. "Look, Brent's really messed up over this. He doesn't like Jill . . . he's just afraid of hurting her feelings."

"Cole, I appreciate what you're trying to do, but nothing is stopping him from talking to me himself."

Cole looks over at our table and back to me. "Before this all went down, he was talking about asking you to stay with him over spring break. Meet his mom and stuff. I'm the only one who has even met Brent's family."

"So I'm supposed to feel special or something? He had a million opportunities to make a move and he didn't."

"You're special," Cole says. "He actually likes you, and he's afraid of screwing things up."

For some reason, this hits me really hard. Back at home, I could have dated any guy I wanted, but I chose losers like Martin and seniors that were about to leave for college anyway. The ones I avoided were the ones I actually liked—I mean, I'd have rather had them around as friends instead of hooking up with them and making things weird.

I allow myself to look at Brent again, briefly, as Cole and I walk back to the table together. I miss him, a lot, but the last thing I need right now is him projecting all of his trust issues onto me.

I've got enough issues of my own right now.

Cole tells me I can probably find Peepers in the library after dinner. Also, I probably shouldn't call him Peepers, because he doesn't know that's his nickname.

I find Peepers, whose real name is Arthur R. Colgate III, according to the leather notebook in front of him, sitting at a study carrel on the first floor. He's reading a Stephen King book the size of two Bibles mashed together.

"Is that for a class?" I ask, sitting on the opposite side of the carrel.

Peepers peers at me over the top of the book. His glasses swallow half his face and magnify his eyes. It's mean, but I get how he earned his nickname. "No. I just like to read in here."

"Noisy roommate?" I ask casually.

"The opposite," Peepers says. "He barely talks. He's just *always* there."

"That's got to get annoying." I trace the grooves in the carrel's wooden surface with my finger. "You live with that guy Lee, right? The valedictorian?"

Peepers nods. "I didn't want to, but I filled out my housing form late, so . . ."

I nod, even though I'm pretty sure Peepers got stuck with Lee because neither of them could get a single room. "That's a bummer. He doesn't do any clubs or anything after school to give you time alone?"

"Not really," Peepers says. "But he does go home every Saturday night."

"Every Saturday?" Isabella was killed on a Saturday night. I was hoping he could tell me if Lee disappeared for a few hours the night of her murder, but if Lee went home that Saturday night, there's no way I'll be able to find out if he came back to campus or not.

Peepers nods and my heart sinks.

"Hey," he says. "You were Isabella Fernandez's roommate, right?"

I nod. "Did you know her?"

"Just through class and stuff. She was nice." Peepers shrugs.

"Lee liked her, didn't he?" I ask.

"Lots of people liked her. Like I said, she was nice."

I can tell I'm going to need to use fifth-grade language on this kid, so I say, "No, I mean, he *like*-liked her."

"Oh. Yeah. I mean, she was the only girl who talked to him." Peepers's eyes probe mine. He lowers his voice. "Until the thing with the picture, at least."

"Picture?"

"Isabella didn't tell you about that?" Peepers's eyebrows knit together. I shake my head.

"You didn't hear it from me," he says. "But Lee painted a picture of Isabella for the spring art show last year. She saw it and freaked out and stopped talking to him. And then Dean Watts wouldn't let Lee enter the picture in the show."

My stomach swirls at the thought of Lee holed up in his room, painting a portrait of Isabella without her knowledge. "I can't believe he did that."

"I don't think he meant to freak her out. And he tried to apologize. A bunch of times. She just told him to leave her alone."

Trying to apologize for something is one thing, but keeping at it after being told to back off qualifies as stalking, in my book. No wonder Isabella switched her schedule around to get away from Lee. Maybe she thought having one class with him wouldn't be so bad this year—except she shouldn't have had to think that way. She should have been able to take whatever damn classes she wanted, and the teachers should have done their job to keep that creep away from her.

But what if not everyone let Isabella down? It sounds like Dean Watts tried to help her . . . at least before she was replaced by that T. rex Tierney.

Everything I know is pointing to this: Lee stalking Isabella was a problem for the administration. And if I can track down Dean Watts, maybe I can prove just how far they were willing to go to make the problem go away.

I say good-bye to Peepers and tell him to enjoy his book. As I turn to leave the study area, he mumbles something.

Something that sounds an awful lot like "Good luck."

CHAPTER
TWENTY-NINE

I wake up on Valentine's Day feeling as if there's a weight on my chest. Maybe it has to do with the package I got yesterday afternoon. The card said *Love, Mom and Dad* but I know my mother made it on her own. My father doesn't know that those chocolate hearts with marshmallow in the middle are my favorite candy. The package was full of them, along with a note saying my parents are looking forward to seeing me at the end of March for spring break.

Spring break means I get to go home for a week. I get to sleep in my own bed and see my friends and walk Abby to Central Park if the weather is nice enough. All of this should make me happy, but counting the days until the end of March is super depressing. Home is still so far away.

But I'm not one to wallow, so I put on my uniform and curl the ends of my hair and go to breakfast.

When I get to art history, Professor Robinson is distributing rose-grams with a scowl on his face that says he truly believes this whole production is a personal insult to his livelihood.

Everyone is too giddy, waiting to see who sent them one, to care about how Robinson will take this out on us once he's done.

There are already five roses waiting for me when I take my seat. I open the heart-shaped pieces of paper folded around the stems. They're all from Sebastian. Beside me, Murali is laughing so hard, tears are threatening to spill over his dark lashes.

"You're just jealous because you didn't get any," I tell him. As if to help prove my point, Robinson sets two more roses down in front of me with a grunt.

"Who are *those* from?" Murali cranes his neck as I open one of the cards. The handwriting inside is unfamiliar. It's not neat and slanted, like Brent's, but squashed and scratchy.

> Anne,
> I'm not good at figuring out what's supposed to go here.
> Happy Valentine's Day.

It's not signed.

"Looks like you have a secret admirer," Murali croons. On the other side of him, Cole chuckles, and for a minute I wonder if maybe he sent it. Murali snatches the card from me and they examine the handwriting while I open the card on the other rose. This one is written in block lettering, and I have to roll my eyes when I see the message is a poem.

> ROSES ARE RED,
> VIOLETS ARE BLUE,
> YOUR ROOMMATE IS DEAD,
> MIND YOUR OWN BUSINESS, OR YOU WILL BE, TOO.

The blood rushes from my head. I reread the poem until the words blur together.

"C'mon, let's see what poor lovesick bastard sent this one." Murali grabs the card out of my hands, which have gone numb.

His forehead creases as he reads the inside. "What the hell is this?"

"A sick joke." I will myself to grab the card back from Murali. I'm trembling a little, even though I should probably be laughing at the stupid poem. I mean, it's not even creative.

"Yeah, well, it's not funny." Murali's expression darkens. "You've got to show that to Dr. Harrow."

"He'll say the same thing: It's just a sick joke." I crumple up the card and shove it in my bag. I think of Snaggletooth's reaction when I told her someone broke in to my room. If she even told Harrow what happened, he probably had the same one.

Those types of things don't happen at the Wonderful Wheatley School.

Murali looks unconvinced as Robinson shuts the lights off and projects an O'Keeffe painting onto the blackboard.

"Don't tell anyone about this, okay?" I whisper to Murali. "It's just some idiot's way of messing with me."

Murali nods as if he wants to believe me. I want to believe me, too, because a sick joke is easier to swallow than the alternative.

Isabella's killer is watching me.

Molly isn't in Latin class. For some reason, I'm more distracted by this than by the threatening rose-gram sitting at the bottom of my purse. I try to focus on Upton's lecture, but my eyes keep wandering to Molly's empty seat.

I wanted to confront her about what Peepers told me. Maybe if she knows I already know about Lee and the picture, she'll tell me what went down to make Isabella drop out of Upton's class.

I look over at Lee, not surprised to find him staring at me already. Instead of looking away, I lock eyes with him, as if to say, *Did you write that stupid rose-gram? Because I'll find out, you creep.* He averts his eyes back to the screen of his laptop. I crane my neck to see if there's anything on the table in front of him with his handwriting on it.

Sending me a threatening poem seems a little too confrontational for Lee, but there's always the chance he saw me talking to Peepers and got spooked. Maybe he thought the rose-gram would be enough to get me to back off for a while.

I have two text messages when I get out of class. The first is from Irina, apologizing for taking so long to get back to me. She's dancing with the Alvin Ailey Company now, and rehearsals for their spring show have been running late. But she translated the words I sent her . . . and by the way, did I know the girl at my new school who was murdered?

I remind myself to thank Irina later as I check the next message. My heart flip-flops when I see it's from Anthony.

Got an address for Watts. Call me.

I race back to the dorm and wait until my door clicks behind me before I call him. He picks up right before the call goes to his voice mail.

"Hey," he says over the sound of a drill.

"Hi. Stuck at work on Valentine's Day?"

"Yeah." He laughs. It's a nice sound. He should do it more often. "Not like I had anything better to do tonight, though." I flush, not sure how to fill the awkward pause that follows. Luckily, Anthony does. "You have a pen? I've got that address for you."

Anthony tells me Margaret Watts lives in Wayland, which is about thirty minutes from Wheatley. She recently changed her phone number to an unlisted one.

"So who is this woman?" Anthony asks, after I repeat the address back to him.

"She was a dean at the school," I say. "I think she got fired for . . . trying to help your sister."

"With what?"

I don't want to tell him Lee was stalking his sister, because I don't know how he'll react. But at least if he flips out, I'm safe on the other side of the phone. I draw in a breath and tell him about Lee, leaving out as many details as possible.

Surprisingly, Anthony sounds calm when he says, "She never said anything about this guy. Are you going to talk to Watts?"

"I want to, yeah. I was hoping to do it in person so she can't hang up on me." I twirl a lock of hair around my finger. "If only I knew someone who could give me a ride."

"I have work at four tomorrow. We could go around ten in the morning if you want."

I tell him I'll be ready, and just as I think he's not going to acknowledge that anything has happened between us, he says, "I hope you liked that rose thing."

Then he hangs up.

So Anthony sent me the other rose-gram. He must have stopped and bought one from the girls in the student center before we went to the police precinct. Which means he sent me the rose before we even kissed.

Maybe I'm wrong about why he kissed me, and it wasn't just adrenaline after all.

My cheeks burn as I remember how Anthony's rough lips felt on mine. Suddenly, it's not just my face that's on fire, but I command myself to stop thinking about him as I reopen Irina's text message.

There is only one English word in the translated passwords—BIRCHWOOD—but the others look like names of Russian towns or streets. I pull up the locked document from Sebastian's computer and type in the first password. Just as I'm afraid one more wrong attempt will send my computer into lockdown mode, the password PRAVDY1245 causes the entry box to disappear.

The document loads, and all I can think is *Holy crap. I did it.* Well, technically, Irina did it. But still.

As I expected, I don't understand anything that's in the document. In fact, I don't see how anyone can make sense of the jumbled letters and numbers on the screen. It's like a secret code or something.

I scroll through the entire eighteen pages of the document

until I see that someone has inserted comments next to some of the sequences of numbers.

Letters. Each sequence of numbers corresponds to a letter.

Oh my God. This really could be a code.

I instinctively close the document, my head spinning. So this is what Andreev's "research position" involves: code breaking.

I replay Andreev's conversation with Sebastian in my head. Sebastian had said Isabella made more progress than he did. Does that mean Isabella was close to cracking the code before she quit the internship? It would make sense, why Andreev wanted her back so desperately. But that doesn't answer why Isabella quit in the first place.

Sebastian, you are aware of my life's work, correct?

My fingers race across my keyboard, typing in Andreev's name. There's nothing on the school's Web site about what he did before he was a teacher, but I'm surprised to see he's only been teaching here for the past three years.

I revisit the abstracts for the journal articles the search engine turned up. Although I can't access the full text, I can read a preview of Andreev's bio. And what I find makes me nauseous.

He worked at Sandia National Laboratories. A nuclear-technology research facility.

CHAPTER
THIRTY

There are men in black masks in my room. One tells me he wants the flash drive and jams a gun in my face. It's so dark I can't see how many of them there are, but they're pulling me out of bed, and Isabella is telling me to run, and I'm screaming . . .

I wake up, paralyzed by terror. I'm sitting up, my legs swung over the bed, ready to run as if the whole nightmare were real.

The part of my brain that's making my heart slam against my chest isn't convinced the dream *wasn't* real. Maybe there are no masked men in my room, but Isabella's scream is still splitting through my head. And it sounds so real it hurts.

Still shaking, I get out of bed and throw on every light in the room. Then I turn on my computer and delete the files I stole from Sebastian. It was stupid of me to hack them in the first place. Obviously, whatever Andreev has Sebastian doing is illegal and dangerous—maybe even dangerous enough to have gotten Isabella killed. Either way, I don't want anything to connect me to them on my computer.

I turn off the lights and climb back into bed, feeling through my sheets for my phone. When I don't find it, I look in the crack between my bed and the wall. I don't see it, but it had to have fallen there, because it's not on my bed or the floor.

I turn the lights on again and crouch so I can get a look under my bed. I see my phone in the far corner, but there's not enough space for me to squeeze through and grab it. I climb back on my bed and shove my hand between the mattress and the wall— and jump a little when I come in contact with cold metal.

What the hell? I feel around a little more. The metal thing has a handle. A security box? What's it doing under my bed?

I tug on the handle, but the box won't fit through the space between the wall and my mattress. I get a clothes hanger from my closet, flatten myself on the floor, and poke under the bed with the hanger until I feel it latch onto the handle. I drag the box from under the bed and sit cross-legged with it on my lap.

The box is plain and black with a keypad on top. But whose is it? My first thought was Isabella's old roommate, but no one would buy a heavy-duty security box like this and just forget she hid it under her bed.

This has got to be Isabella's. Hiding it under *my* bed was too clever for it not to be hers. I shake the box gently, but it makes little noise.

I run a finger over the keypad. Breaking into Andreev's office and the room in the basement of Lexington Hall was one thing, but cracking open something Isabella obviously didn't want anyone to find just feels wrong.

I bite my lip and enter 4-3-2-1 onto the keypad. A red light flashes, telling me I have the wrong code. I return it to its spot under the bed, a little relieved. Isabella wanted to keep whatever is in it locked away, and I should respect her wishes.

At least for now.

I don't fall asleep again after that, but before I know it, sunlight is streaming through my window and I have to get ready to meet Anthony.

I can't stop playing with my hair while I wait for him to meet me outside the student center. How do you greet a person when, the last time you saw him, you were on top of him on the floor of a parking garage with your tongue in his mouth?

Somehow, a hug just seems inappropriate.

I settle for an awkward "Hey," when he slides off his motorcycle, removes his helmet, and shakes his hair from his eyes. A few wet pieces cling to his forehead.

"Hey." His eyes travel the length of my body. There's a hungry look in them that makes me flush to my toes. "Ready?"

Anthony pulls over after about five minutes. Confused, I take off the helmet. He points at the convenience store across the street. "I need to grab a coffee," he says. "Not used to being up this early."

"It's ten o'clock."

He holds the store door open for me. "Yeah, well, when you don't have to work until four, it might as well be the ass crack of dawn."

I linger by the magazine rack while I wait for Anthony to make his coffee. I would grab one too, but a quick look around the store says this place is violating about twenty different Board of Health laws.

That's when I see her. Isabella, staring at me from the cover of *People* magazine. It's the same school portrait from her funeral, but there's also an older photo of Isabella and Anthony on a dock. Anthony is holding a fishing pole.

WHO KILLED ISABELLA? The headline asks.

I sense Anthony behind me, and my stomach drops. I turn in time to see the anger explode across his face. He yanks the magazine off the shelf and rips the cover off. I grab his arm as he reaches to do the same to the other copies. "Anthony, stop!"

This gets the cashier's attention. "Hey, man, what do you think you're doing?"

Anthony tears another cover off and slams the magazine to the floor. "What do *you* think you're doing, selling this garbage?"

I'm stepping in front of Anthony in a pathetic attempt to stop him from flipping the whole magazine rack over, when the cashier yells for us to get out or he's calling the cops. Anthony storms out. Before I follow him, I stop and pay for the magazines he destroyed. And his coffee.

"What the hell was that about?" I'm ready to tell Anthony off when I find him sitting on the curb, his face in his hands. "Hey. You okay?"

He looks up at me, the corners of his eyes red. "It didn't feel real. Isabella being gone. I'd walk by her room sometimes, just to try and make myself feel something, but it still felt like she was away at school." Anthony doesn't say what I know he's thinking: Seeing Isabella's face on the cover of that magazine finally makes her death feel real to him.

He rubs his eyes. "Those fucking reporters don't get it. My sister is dead, and they're making *money* off it. They don't care how much it hurts us. How much that goddamn picture can hurt."

I don't know what to say, so I reach out and cup the side of his face. He holds my hand there and closes his eyes, and warmth swells deep in me somewhere. Everything that's happening is so wrong, but for some reason, I wish I could put this moment on pause forever.

"My mom took that picture three years ago. We used to go to Hyannis every year," Anthony says. "Isabella and I were fighting in the car. Probably about something stupid . . . I can't even remember now. Mom had a meltdown and told us we were ruining the last vacation we'd probably be able to take as a family." Anthony pauses. "When we got home, they told us my dad was diagnosed with MS."

"I'm so sorry, Anthony," is all I can manage to say.

He opens his eyes, and I realize I'm still touching his face. I let my hand slide down his neck. His skin is hot. I push aside the neck of his T-shirt, revealing an intricate black design. A tattoo.

I let myself trace the outline of the design. Anthony shudders and closes his eyes again. We sit like that for I don't know how long, until Anthony stands without looking at me.

"Let's go."

Margaret Watts lives in a development filled with uniform white condos. When Anthony pulls up to the curb, a cocker spaniel appears in the glass door next to Watts's condo. It barks at us once before running away.

"So I was thinking you might want to wait here," I tell Anthony. "Chances are she's going to be weirded out enough as it is once I tell her I'm from the school, and if she finds out who you are—"

"No, I get it," he says. "Better to keep her away from the riffraff."

"Why do you always do that?" I demand.

"Do what?"

"Assume that people are judging you. That I'm judging you." I put my hands on my hips. "Stop it. Because I actually like being around you. And I'm guessing that's not something you hear a lot."

Anthony blinks at me, and I'm struck by how much he looks like Isabella right now. Young. Vulnerable. I wonder if the tattoos and leather jacket and crappy attitude are his way of hiding how insecure he really is.

"Okay. I'll wait here."

I breathe a sigh of relief and walk up to Watts's door. I ring the bell and listen to footsteps padding down stairs. My heartbeat quickens as the door opens.

"Yes?" The woman's eyes go up and down, trying to place me.

"Hi. Are you Dean Watts?"

Her face instantly clouds over. "Is this a joke?"

"No! I mean, I don't know what to call you," I say. "Is Ms. Watts okay?"

"Do I know you?" She narrows her eyes at me.

"We never met. My name is Anne. I'm a student at the Wheatley School," I say. "I was Isabella Fernandez's roommate."

Dean Watts motions to slam the door. I grab hold of it. "Wait! I want to talk to you."

"I don't know what you're trying to pull, but it's not funny. Let go of my door."

"Not until you talk to me. Please. I think you can help me."

Her eyes probe mine, filled with the same confusion Anthony had in his when I told him I wanted to find out who killed Isabella. "I can't."

"I know about Lee Andersen," I blurt, before the door slams in my face. It swings open again and Watts stares at me, her face drained of all color.

"Then you know why I can't talk to you," she says.

"I know you tried to help her," I say. "Is that why you left?"

Dean Watts lets out a sharp laugh. "Left? They fired me and refused to give me a recommendation so I could find a new job. All of the schools I applied to wouldn't even give me an interview. They ruined my life."

"How could they do that to you?" I ask.

"They just can, Anne. And if they find out why you came here, they'll do the same to you." A tear rolls down her cheek. "Just stay away from him, okay? I couldn't protect Isabella. As soon as I heard she was killed, I knew I'd never be able to forgive myself for not fighting hard enough for her."

"What do you mean? No one believed that Lee was stalking her?"

"Even if they did, do you think it would have made a difference?" she asks. "Michael Andersen is the chair of the Wheatley School Board of Trustees. The headmaster told me to deal with Lee quietly."

"So why did they fire you?" I ask.

"I told Lee to leave Isabella alone," Watts says. "He did, for a while. Until Isabella came to me and said he was leaving notes and letters at her desk. I couldn't ignore that."

Upton's class, I realize. "What about the proof? The letters, the painting he did of her? Couldn't you go to the police?"

Watts shakes her head. "I made the mistake of showing the evidence to Goddard. I never saw it again."

A chill runs through me. This is so much worse than I ever could have imagined.

"You should go, Anne," Watts says. "Leave this to the police. If he killed Isabella, they'll find out."

"If I believed that, I wouldn't be here," I say, before her door closes in my face.

CHAPTER
THIRTY-ONE

I tap Anthony's shoulder and lean into him. "Pull over!"

"We're on the turnpike," he calls to me over his shoulder.

"I don't care! Pull over!"

Anthony slows, looking for a space on the side of the high-way while the drivers behind us zip past, leaning on their horns. I stumble off the motorcycle and lean over, giving in to dry heaves. I let them shake my entire body, as if there's something poisonous inside of me that I'll never be rid of.

Anthony stands to the side. I can't look at him. I'm afraid all I'll see on his face is disgust. How could he not be disgusted with me, when my parents are writing checks to the headmaster who killed his sister?

Because that's what Goddard did, if he purposely ignored the fact that Lee was stalking Isabella. Even if he's not the one who cut her throat, he's just as responsible.

I finally bring myself to look at Anthony. His face is strained, as if it's taking all he has not to fly into a rage over what Watts told me. Maybe he knows he can't freak out, now that the police are waiting for him to prove he's the Violent Brother with Anger Issues. Or maybe he's just waiting until he gets home to do it.

"I burned part of my old school down," I blurt. "That's why my parents sent me here. It was an accident. Sort of. I should probably be in jail, but I'm not, because my dad is a lawyer." I pause, and add, "He's kind of a dick."

Anthony's face is expressionless. "Why are you telling me this?"

"Because I'm afraid of you being right about me," I admit.

Slowly, Anthony's face changes. His eyes fill with a hungry intensity, like he wants me or hates me. Maybe both. "Now who's afraid of being judged?"

I open my mouth to protest but he's pulling my face to his. A sigh escapes me as his lips find mine, drowning out the sound of cars speeding by. There's urgency to it this time, and I know this kiss isn't meant to reassure me or comfort me. There's a message in the way he's holding the sides of my face: *Don't fall apart now. This is about her.*

"This Goddard person," Anthony says when we break apart. "You really think he's covering for the guy who stalked my sister?"

I picture the headmaster. Empty eyes under thick gray eyebrows. His twisted, patronizing smile. The portrait of money and privilege. "Absolutely," I say.

"Then what are you going to do?"

"Isn't it obvious?" I hold Anthony's gaze. "I'm going to take the son of a bitch down."

Deep down, I knew it would come to this. But the thought of what I have to do still scares me. The last time I did something like this, I wasn't scared. Not because I was braver. I was just stupider.

Because I should be scared of breaking in to Goddard's office.

Scared of getting caught, scared of what I might find. But mostly scared of getting caught and being dead to my parents forever if I get expelled.

Being brave isn't the same as not being scared, though. It means going through with something even if it totally terrifies you.

At least, that's what I'm telling myself so I don't chicken out.

A stunt this risky requires careful planning, though. I can't afford another close call like the one in Andreev's office. If I'm going to pull this off flawlessly, I need to sneak in and out of the administration building completely undetected after it closes.

The tunnels are my best chance at that. So Sunday night, after studying for a French exam with Remy, I go to the library and find the Wheatley School history book—the one with a campus map before Lexington Hall burned down and the tunnels were closed.

I study the lines indicating the tunnels more closely this time. On Lexington Hall and Amherst, there are black dots. I trace the tunnel to the boy's dorm and to the library. There are black dots over those buildings as well. As far as I can tell, the only buildings without dots are the student center and a handful of classroom buildings.

Entrances to the tunnel. That's what the dots indicate, probably. I breathe a sigh of relief when I see one on the square symbolizing the administration building.

Okay, so, I can get into the administration building through the tunnel. That just leaves me to figure out how I'm going to get into Goddard's office. I return the book to the shelf and put my coat on. That will have to wait until tomorrow morning, when I can get into the administration building and scope things out.

I have to fight with the wind to push the library door open. Campus is eerily empty, I realize with a wave of unease. I reach around in my bag and let my fingers curl around the sharpest item I have—a pair of tweezers.

I'm being ridiculous. I've walked through some of the scariest parts of New York City before. And how am I supposed to defend myself with tweezers? Pluck someone to death?

I'm halfway down the path leading to the center of campus when I hear leaves crunching behind me. My grip on the tweezers tightens, and I pick up my pace, ignoring the singsong voice in my head.

ROSES ARE RED,

VIOLETS ARE BLUE,

YOUR ROOMMATE IS DEAD,

MIND YOUR OWN BUSINESS, OR YOU WILL BE TOO.

I spin around, figuring I have a better chance at scaring off the person behind me if I look him or her in the eye. Make him think I'm not afraid, even though I'm one muscle clench away from peeing myself. But a shadowy figure is already darting back around the side of the library.

The person followed me out here, I realize. *Someone is following me, and he was probably in the library with me the whole time.*

I take off in the opposite direction. As much as I want to know who's following me, that doesn't matter as much as staying alive. My gut is telling me it's Lee, and he's got about a hundred pounds and a foot and a half on me. I don't have a chance of defending myself.

Footsteps on leaves sound again behind me, but this time they're quicker. I break into a run. The footsteps behind me keep getting louder, faster, and I'm about to scream when he reaches out and grabs my arm.

I jerk around and freeze, seconds away from jamming my tweezers into Brent's neck.

CHAPTER
THIRTY-TWO

"What the *hell*, Brent?" I demand, shaking myself free of him.

He holds up his hands. "I'm sorry. I should have let you know it was only me. Please don't stab me."

"You're lucky I don't do more than that!" I practically shriek, barely hearing myself over the sound of my heart palpitations.

"I said I was sorry! I didn't want you to walk back alone." Brent's eyes find mine in the dark. "I heard about the message you got. It freaked me out."

"Yeah, well, I can take care of myself," I tell him. "I'm not dumb."

"Really? Because taking off with Isabella's brother seems pretty dumb to me, Anne."

I'm caught between being pissed off that he's apparently been watching me since yesterday, and smug that he seems to care I'm spending time with Anthony. "You don't even know Anthony."

"I don't have to," he says. "The police think he killed Isabella. That should say it all."

"The police also think *I* killed Isabella. Next, they'll be saying one of the Muppets did it." I square off with Brent. "What's really your problem with Anthony, Brent?"

He gapes at me. "I'm just looking out for you."

I laugh and set off in the direction of the dorms. "Okay."

"You think I don't know why you're mad at me?" Brent says, trailing behind me. "Anne, I grew up with women. Three sisters and a mother—and a dad who was always traveling. I'm not stupid. This is about Jill."

"What about Jill, exactly?" I ask. "You leading her on, or her trying to get me arrested?"

"Alexis is the one who gave Jill the idea to go to the police." Brent taps his chin in pretend thought. "I wonder if Alexis is the one telling everyone I've been leading Jill on all these years? Nah, that doesn't sound like her."

I glare at him.

"Jill and I are friends. I've told her repeatedly that I don't want to be anything more," Brent says. His eyes twinkle. "She *was* fine with it, except now she's mad because she can tell I'm really into this other girl."

I raise an eyebrow at him, although I can't help feeling fluttering in my stomach. "What's this other girl like?"

Brent smirks. "Petite. Brunette. Wicked smart and doesn't take my shit." His face widens with mock horror. "Oh my God! She's my mother!"

I pick up my pace so he can't see me grin as he tries to catch up with me. "Hey. I've been dying to talk to you. Let me help you again." His voice becomes serious. "Someone threatening you isn't a joke. If you're not going to go to Harrow about it, I can help you find out who it was."

We're in the quad now, which isn't as empty as the outer loop of campus. People are streaming in from the dining hall and athletic complex. Any one of them could be the person who threatened me.

"Fine," I tell Brent. We part ways to go back to our dorms, but moments later he's calling over his shoulder to me.

"I hope this means you'll sit next to me in Brit lit again!"

"You're the one who wouldn't sit next to me!" I yell back.

He smiles at me before disappearing into his dorm. The same way he smiled at me when he first laid eyes on me in Harrow's office. And just like that, I'm under the Brent Conroy spell again.

Guiltily, I think of Anthony. I remember how it felt to kiss him. I realize I want it to happen again.

Looks like I'm the one complicating things now.

CHAPTER
THIRTY-THREE

There's finally an update in Isabella's case.

The police found her cell phone.

All the news story says is that the phone was recovered at the city dump, and it's been too long since the murder to determine how it got there. The killer erased Isabella's call history before ditching the phone, but the phone company records show a number of calls between her and a disposable cell phone the night she was murdered.

By lunch on Monday, everyone has heard, and judging from the hush that's fallen over the dining hall, you'd think it was the morning after Isabella was killed, all over again.

Everyone is quiet, their eyes fixed on food they're not eating. Their faces are scared, as if the fact that the police found Isabella's phone is a sobering reminder that her killer is still out there. But I know better now.

They're scared for themselves. In theory, anyone here could have called her. Anyone could be the next target of the police's questioning.

As soon as I get to Latin, I know something is wrong. I kind of have a knack for sensing these things. The day our cleaning lady found a bottle of vodka under my bed and told my parents, I just *knew* they were at home waiting to eat me alive. True story.

I can't explain what feels wrong when I take my seat. We don't have an exam today, and we're not getting one back. Upton has her back to me. Lee is in his seat, biting his nails and looking as nonthreatening as he could possibly be.

Molly.

Why can't I remember the last time I saw her? I definitely know she wasn't in class on Friday, but it's Monday now.

I think back to the weekend. I don't remember seeing her in the dining hall. Or in the dorm. My legs jiggle beneath me. *Relax, Anne. She could just be sick. Or late.*

Sick enough to be bedridden for over three days, though?

Upton's voice is far away. Someone taps my shoulder, and I realize I'm supposed to pass my homework to the front. When Upton begins to hand out tonight's homework, I raise my hand.

Upton nods to me, the area between her eyes pinching.

"Um. May I have an extra homework packet for Molly?" I ask.

I sense all eleven bodies in the room stiffen. Upton is short enough to click her nails against her desk while standing. I wait until I can't take the sound anymore before saying, "Molly's been out since Friday. I could bring her the homework."

"That won't be necessary." Upton doesn't look at me as she instructs everyone to turn to page 297. I stare around the room, searching for some sort of indication that Upton is acting bizarre. No one will look at me.

My gaze rests on Molly's empty seat again. What if someone's threatened her too? Or even worse? Upton is about ten minutes into her lecture when I can't ignore the fear building in me any longer.

I stand up.

The silence in the room turns into confused murmuring as I pack up my things. This gets Upton's attention. She turns away from the blackboard, the chalk nearly falling from her fingers as she sees me.

"I don't believe I've excused anyone yet, Ms. Dowling." Her voice is saccharine, but her eyes say *Leave this room and it'll be the last thing you do.*

"I need to be excused," I say, just as sweetly, even though I'm trying not to shake.

I need to find out where Molly is. Even if she's really just sick and in the dorm, I need to know. Now. Because I may have put her in danger by trying to get her to talk.

"Anne. Sit down." Upton's face says she's not playing anymore.

But I never was. I hold her gaze, aware of the way the room has tensed, as if Upton and I are pit bulls waiting to rip each other's throats out.

She doesn't call after me as I leave the room.

The halls of Amherst are so quiet, I feel a totally inappropriate urge to scream. On the door at the end of the hall, pink wooden blocks spell out MOLLY.

It's the same type of corner room Sebastian has. A single room.

"Molly," I call into the crack. "Are you in there?"

No response. I peek under the threshold, but the lights are off. "Molly!" I pound on the door this time. "MOLLY."

A door opens across the hall, nearly causing me to jump out of my skin. It's only Emma, the second-floor RA. "Anne? Shouldn't you be in class?"

"Where's Molly?" I demand. "Is she okay?"

Emma shrugs. "Probably."

"What do you mean, 'probably'? Aren't you her RA?"

"Not anymore," Emma says. "I got a call this morning that she wouldn't be back."

I freeze. "A call from who?"

"From the dean, obviously." Emma sounds mega-annoyed now. "If you need to talk to Molly, why don't you call her or something?"

Black spots swim before my eyes. Suddenly I'm back on my floor, talking to Darlene, and it's Isabella who's missing. My chest cavity is shrinking. This can't be happening again.

Anyone could have called Emma, pretending to be Tierney. Molly could be dead, and who would notice?

I push past Emma. I don't know where I'm going until I get there.

The administration building.

My heart hammers as I ascend the spiral staircase. Portraits of presidents and senators stare back at me from the walls, almost accusingly.

I practically freeze when I get to the second floor. Dr. Harrow's office looks empty. So does Tierney's; her receptionist is even missing. I tiptoe down the hall and around the corner. At the end of the hall, there's a conference room. I crane my neck to see through the pane on the door.

I can only see the tops of heads, but I'd recognize that ugly L'Oréal shade of copper hair anywhere. Tierney. I stretch to see who else is sitting at the table with her, but the door creaks open. I freeze and press myself against the wall. It's not like I'm doing anything wrong—minus the cutting-class part—but I still don't want to be seen lurking around the administrator's offices. Luckily, the footsteps stop in the middle of the hall. There are two sets of them.

"We had an agreement," a low voice snaps. It takes me a second to place it.

It's Dr. Harrow's.

"You broke our agreement the second you dragged Lanie into this," a second male voice responds. "You greedy bastard."

I swallow, feeling the back of my neck begin to perspire.

"I'd watch who you're calling a bastard," Harrow growls.

"Unless you want a murder investigation tied to your presidential campaign."

And without looking around the corner, that's how I know who the man is.

Senator Westbrook.

CHAPTER
THIRTY-FOUR

Blackmail.

It's the only explanation for Dr. Harrow's threat: *Unless you want a murder investigation tied to your presidential campaign.*

I run out of the administration building so fast, I forget why I went there in the first place—to ask Dr. Harrow what happened to Molly.

I thought I could trust him over Dean Snaggletooth. Now it sounds as if he knows something about Isabella's death—something that could be tied back to Senator Westbrook.

The tape. I want to kick myself for not realizing it sooner. If Dr. Harrow has a copy of the tape Isabella made, he could be blackmailing Alexis's father with it. That sure would explain the "historic" gift the senator made to the school.

There's nothing more historic than your daughter completely fucking up your career.

But why would Alexis kill Isabella if her father was taking care of the situation? And who's Lanie?

I really need to get my hands on that video and see for myself if it's worth killing over. But first, I have to make sure Molly is okay.

I get back to Amherst as people are trickling in from class. I head straight to my room and compose an e-mail.

To: frankm@Wheatleyschool.edu
From: dowlinga@Wheatleyschool.edu
Subject: Where are you?

Molly,
Are you okay? Emma said you're not coming back. What happened? Did they threaten you? Please e-mail me back.
Anne

Dinnertime rolls around without a response from Molly. The only thing that gets my mind off of her is the way everyone in the dining hall is staring at me with a mix of fear and awe. Apparently walking out of Upton's class has elevated me from someone to be feared to a somewhat legendary status, according to my friends.

"I heard you almost slapped the Botox right off Upton's face," Brent says with glee as I choose a seat.

Everyone glances from me to Brent, as if it's news to them that we're on speaking terms again.

"It wasn't like that," I say to no one in particular.

"You're my hero." Murali sidles up next to me. "I dropped Latin freshman year because Upton is such a C U Next—"

"We get it, Murali." Remy rolls her eyes. "Jeez, give Anne some space before she starts to think *you're* the one that sent her that rose-gram."

"What rose-gram?" Brent's eyes are suspicious. Only me, him, and Murali know about the threatening message.

"From her secret admirer," Remy says with a grin. Brent quirks an eyebrow at me to let me know this is news to him.

"You mean the one Zach Walton sent to her?" April pipes up. We all turn to her. "What? I saw him write Anne's name on one of the ones he bought from a freshman."

"I don't even know him," I say, feeling my jaw go numb. "Why would he—"

"Because you're a hottie," Remy giggles. "Poor Zach's got a crush."

But I know Zach didn't send me *that* rose-gram. Anthony did.

"Where is Zach?" I demand.

A few fingers point to Dan Crowley's table. Next to Peter Wu is a kid with a mushroom cut that almost covers his eyes. He's in one of my classes—I can't remember which right now—but he's also the boy that stood up on the train going to Isabella's wake so I could sit next to Molly.

Why would he threaten me? I've never even talked to him before. I'm still staring when he looks up and sees me. Something barely detectable flashes in his eyes.

He gets up, his back to me, and acts like he's heading for the soda fountain.

And then he slips out the door.

CHAPTER
THIRTY-FIVE

I don't stick around to hand out explanations. I abandon my chicken salad and take off after Zach. He's fast, but my ever-unflinching willingness to cause a huge scene gives me the upper hand here.

"HEY! Don't run from me!" I scream once we're in the lobby. Zach is almost at the door. The woman who checks our cards to let us into the dining hall looks up, and Zach is forced to stop. He hesitates for a minute and I catch up to him.

"Hi," I say. "I'm Anne. But you already knew that, since you threatened me and everything."

"I don't know what you're talking about," he mutters.

"Bullshit, you don't. April Durand saw you write that rose-gram to me. That should be enough to convince Dr. Harrow."

Zach's ferret-like face pales.

"Not a smart move, Zach. I'm probably not the only one who thinks your message makes it look like you killed Isa—"

"I didn't kill her! Isabella was my friend," he says. "And I didn't want to send you that rose-gram. I had no choice."

"What are you talking about?"

Zach pushes open the dining-hall door, and for a second I think he's going to run again. But he steps outside and waits for me to follow. He wants to be out of earshot.

"Someone made me send that rose-gram. I'm sorry. Please don't tell Dr. Harrow."

"What do you mean, someone made you?" I demand.

"Isabella and I were friends," he says. "We did something together last year . . . something that could have gotten us in serious trouble."

"You mean the video of Alexis Westbrook," I say.

"Could you keep your voice down?" Zach says, even though I'm barely speaking above a whisper. He shoves his hands in his pockets. "Yeah. Our friend Peter was running for SGA president against Alexis and Brent Conroy. Someone was taking Peter's posters down. Isabella thought she could catch Alexis admitting to it on tape, but she said something else."

"Where do you come in?" I ask.

"It was my idea to show the tape at the SGA debates, anyway. Isabella gave me the footage, and I edited it on my computer to make the sound louder and everything." Zach's expression darkens. "When Alexis told Dr. Harrow what we did, we deleted everything so we wouldn't get in trouble. And I thought no one else had a copy of the video . . . until I got an e-mail last week saying Isabella saved the original."

"Who sent the e-mail?" My head is spinning.

"It was a fake address." Zach swallows. "Whoever it was uploaded the file to the e-mail to prove they have the video now. They said they could prove the video was edited on my computer and they would tell Dr. Harrow if I didn't do exactly what they said."

"And they told you to threaten me?" I ask, a little incredulous.

Zach nods. "They told me exactly what to say. I didn't want

to, but this person could get me expelled. Or the Westbrooks could sue my family. Please don't tell on me."

I search Zach's face for a sign he's lying. But all I see is the same scared, sad face I saw on the way to Isabella's wake.

"It was really stupid of you to threaten me," I tell him. "I won't tell Harrow about it if you promise to tell me if you get another e-mail like that."

Zach nods. "I just . . . Isabella promised me she destroyed all copies of the video. The old Isabella would never lie about something like that."

I feel a prickle on the back of my neck. "What do you mean, 'the old Isabella'?"

"She changed after the whole video thing," Zach says. "She stopped hanging out with me. When I confronted her about it, she admitted she was seeing someone. A guy."

"I thought the police said she never had a boyfriend?"

Zach shrugs. "I don't know. She was probably lying to me about that too. She wouldn't even tell me his name."

My mind is running in circles. Isabella may have had a boyfriend, after all—or she could have lied to Zach to distract him from something else she was doing. Like trying to break the code for Andreev.

There's only one person who would have gotten Zach to threaten me: Alexis. I'm almost positive she stole my ID to get into my room and steal Isabella's copy of the video.

With a surge of anger, I remember the sleepless night after she broke into my room. I think it's time for me to teach Alexis that it's not nice to go through someone else's stuff.

CHAPTER
THIRTY-SIX

"You know, a person's coffee says a lot about them," Brent tells me over the rim of his hot chocolate. I glance down at my own nonfat soy cinnamon dolce latte.

"That's so not a thing," I say. It's Tuesday after classes, and we're in a coffee shop off-campus so we can talk in private.

"Sure it is," Brent said. "You ordered the most complicated thing they offer."

I glance at his hot chocolate, not sure if he meant that as a compliment. "You didn't even get coffee. What does that say about you? Mysterious? Not to be trusted?"

I realize what I've said, as Brent's smile melts a little. Oops. There's that Awkward Thing between us again.

Brent clears his throat. "Ask me anything about myself, and I swear to tell you the truth."

"Are you trying to prove I can trust you or something?" I roll my eyes, despite how tantalizing the offer is.

"Go ahead. Anything."

"Fine. Why'd you get kicked out of your last school?"

Brent leans back in his chair and folds his hands behind his head. He lets out a half whistle/half sigh. "Anything but that."

"Nope. Not interested in anything else. Sorry."

Brent scratches his neck as I stare him down. For the first time, I notice the fleck of copper in his right eye. "I got caught cutting class . . . with a girl."

"They expelled you for that?"

"It wasn't so much the cutting class part. . . . Anyway, you don't want the details." Brent actually looks embarrassed.

"Oh," I say. "*Oh.*"

"Hey. No judging." Brent's cheeks are pink. "Now it's your turn. What do you have to tell me that you couldn't say on campus?"

I put Brent's story out of my head, because I don't like thinking about him doing expulsion-worthy things with another girl. In the *eighth grade* no less. So I tell Brent everything Zach told me, watching a small crease form between his eyes.

"Honestly, Zach sounds like he's full of shit," he says when I'm done. "Why would Alexis go through the trouble of blackmailing him? If she wanted to threaten you, why not do it herself?"

"Why would she do it herself if she could have Zach do it?" I shoot back. "Let's say I did report the threat to Harrow. April saw Zach write the message to me. There wouldn't be any way to trace it back to her."

"Okay, say that's true. How did Alexis get her hands on that video?" Brent asks. "And why would she risk sending it to Zach and having him upload it for the world to see?"

"I'm pretty sure she stole it from our dorm room right after Isabella died." I tell Brent about the break-in. "And Zach has nothing to gain from uploading the video of Alexis except getting kicked out of school and being slapped with a lawsuit."

Brent contemplates this. "True."

I let the silence sit for a moment as we sip our drinks. "I just don't know how I'll be able to pull off getting the video from Alexis's room. She's going to be guarding it like a cobra now that she caught me snooping once."

"This is President's Day weekend," Brent says.

"What does that have to do with anything?"

"Well . . . everyone goes home President's Day weekend." He lifts an eyebrow at me.

"Huh." I sit back in my chair. "Go on."

"We could stay and do some poking around. Of course, you don't want anyone getting suspicious, so you'll have to tell anyone who'll listen that you're going back to New York for the weekend," Brent says. "But think of the damage we could do."

My stomach flutters, and I don't know if it's at the thought of having Brent to myself for the weekend, or the realization that I really could go back to New York this weekend if I wanted to. I could hop on a train Friday night, and I wouldn't even have to come back until Monday afternoon.

The thought is tempting, but I can't waste the opportunity to look for answers. Not when I feel as if I'm finally close to the ones I want.

"Don't look now, but lover boy is outside," Brent deadpans.

I nearly knock my coffee over. Does he mean Anthony? Because the thought of Brent and Anthony in the same room tops the list of things that make me seriously uncomfortable. Right above people using the word *delicious* to describe things that aren't food, and men's UGG boots.

Stomach in my throat, I look outside. "Oh. It's just Sebastian."

Brent's eyebrows form a V. "Who'd you think I was talking about?"

I ignore him and watch Sebastian press a button at the crosswalk. He looks up at the red light barring him from crossing the street and rocks back and forth on his heels.

"Brent, does something seem off about Sebastian to you?"

Brent shrugs. "His new mustache makes him look like a sex offender, I guess."

Somehow, I've managed to avoid Sebastian since that night in his room. I only have a view of his profile from here, but his face looks thinner. Paler. I wonder where he's going.

Find out, a voice in my head says.

The crosswalk light turns green.

"Be right back," I tell Brent.

I stay twenty feet behind Sebastian. He's moving quickly, so if I put any more distance between us, I might lose him.

Sebastian turns onto Massachusetts Avenue and pauses outside a coffee shop. I can't help feeling a little disappointed, until I realize we passed about a bajillion other coffee shops on the way here.

There's got to be something special about this one.

Sebastian goes inside, and I wait a few minutes on the sidewalk, blowing warm air into my hands. My alpaca wool gloves aren't cutting it today.

I peer into the window of the café. It's crowded, but Sebastian towers over everyone. He's sitting by the far wall, staring at . . . a computer screen.

This is an Internet café.

My breath catches in my throat. We have perfectly good Wi-Fi back at school. Why else would Sebastian walk twenty minutes away from campus to use the Internet unless it's to do something he doesn't want anyone to see?

I pull my crocheted cap over my ears and step inside the café. I perch myself at a table in the corner with a diagonal view of Sebastian. He reaches into his messenger bag, looks over his shoulder, and plugs a flash drive into the computer.

A purple flash drive.

CHAPTER
THIRTY-SEVEN

I'm up and leaning over his shoulder in an instant.

"Nice flash drive, Sebastian."

His whole body tenses, but he doesn't turn around. Slowly, he reaches to pull the flash drive out of the computer.

I lay a hand on his shoulder. "Going somewhere? You just got here."

Sebastian turns his head up at me, fear skirting across his face. "Anne," he squeaks, "funny seeing you here."

"Yeah. Real funny. Where'd you get that flash drive, Sebastian? Did you steal it from Isabella before or after you killed her?"

"Whoa, hold on." Sebastian lifts his hands up, as if he's surrendering. "It's mine."

"*J'accuse*, Sebastian." I sit in the empty seat next to him and drag myself uncomfortably close. He flinches. "I wonder if the police will buy that, once Isabella's brother says that's the same flash drive missing from her stuff. Doesn't help your case once you add that to the e-mails you sent her before she was killed."

Sebastian pales, and squirms in his chair. "You know about those?"

"I know a lot more than you think, Sebastian." I put my face inches from his and lay a hand on his knee. To the casual observer, we probably look like a couple. "Now tell me why you have Isabella's flash drive."

"I didn't know it was Isabella's," Sebastian blurts. "He gave it to me. Andreev."

My stomach twists around itself. "Your internship isn't really an internship, is it?"

Sebastian hesitates.

"C'mon. He's using you, isn't he? To figure out some sort of code?"

"It's more complicated than that," Sebastian says.

"I've got time," I tell him.

Sebastian swallows. "Andreev came to me at the end of last year. After the AP exams. He said he was impressed with my scores and wanted to offer me a job." He lowers his voice. "Technically, students aren't allowed to be paid for on-campus internships, but he said as long as I didn't tell anyone what we were working on, he would pay me when the time came."

Sebastian looks at the door and wipes his hands on his pants. "He had lots of odd rules. I had to turn in fake papers at least once a week so the administration would think I was actually doing independent research. And I wasn't allowed to use a campus computer to do the work he gave me. I thought it was just Andreev being himself. You know, a little . . ." Sebastian twirls his finger next to his ear.

"Then the work he gave me started getting weirder," Sebastian says in a hushed voice. "He started giving me cryptograms to solve. I asked him what it had to do with his area of nuclear research, and he only said *Don't concern yourself with that*, in this bizarre voice."

My insides go cold.

"That was in October. I went to Isabella, asking if Andreev had her doing the same thing."

"What did she say?" I probe.

"She said I should quit right away," Sebastian whispers. "She said the cryptograms were only a test, to see if I was ready to try and crack a more complex code. When I asked her what was so wrong with that, she said she thought Andreev was having us do something illegal. Something he couldn't figure out how to do on his own."

Sebastian lowers his voice again, so I have to lean in until our foreheads are nearly touching to hear him. "Isabella said she looked into it, and she suspected the code was hiding some sort of military information. She told me she thought Andreev stole it from the lab where he used to work and wanted to sell the intelligence overseas."

I think of the fake passport and cash stored in Andreev's desk. The room seems to spin beneath me. "Sebastian, why didn't you go to the police after Isabella was killed?"

"Isn't it obvious?" Sebastian asks. "I was afraid I would wind up just like her."

This hangs in the air between us, as I think of what to say to him.

"You're a coward," is all I can manage.

"It's not that simple. Put yourself in my place!" Sebastian says as I motion to get up. "What would you do?"

I want to yell *Something! I would DO SOMETHING, unlike the rest of you*, but I can't. It's so easy for me to pretend I'm better than all of them, right? But if everything were on the line for me, my *life* even, would I throw it all away for a girl I barely knew?

Sebastian is right. It's not that simple. But I still can't look at him, so I hike my purse up my shoulder and stand up.

"Anne, wait," he pleads. "There's something else." He swallows and glances around the café. "Two days ago, I heard Andreev on the phone. The person on the other end was speaking another language . . . something I'd never heard before."

"That could mean anything," I tell him.

"Yes. But then Andreev marked something on his calendar."

Sebastian licks his lips. "He's meeting the guy next Tuesday at three thirty."

I know why he's telling me this: He knows I'm going to look into it. But I don't have time to overanalyze his motives. My phone tells me I have an e-mail from Molly.

And the subject line nearly makes me drop my phone.

CHAPTER
THIRTY-EIGHT

To: dowlinga@Wheatleyschool.edu
From: frankm@Wheatleyschool.edu
Subject: they're watching

Isabella's dead and Nothing can change That just stop
please and leave me alone i never thought he would hurt Her
Everything is Messed up And It's my fault Leave it alone i'm
not coming back

And then, at the bottom:

molly
268 21187

When I look up from reading the e-mail, Sebastian is gone.
"Son of a bitch," I mutter, rereading Molly's e-mail. My hands
are trembling, I realize. Molly's message is bizarre, and disori-
ented. With a wave of panic, I think of the scars on Molly's arms.
Could she have meant something else by "i'm not coming back"?

I immediately dial the phone number at the bottom of the e-mail, praying that Molly included it because she wants me to stop her from whatever she's planning to do. My brain can't even form the word. Can't process the possibility that I made whatever guilt Molly feels over Isabella's death worse when I confronted her and asked her if her scholarship was worth not going to the police.

"I'm sorry; your call cannot be completed as dialed."

I stare at the screen of my phone. Of course it can't. This phone number is eight numbers.

Which means it's not a phone number at all.

I claw at my scarf. It's about a thousand degrees in this café. Through the window, I see a cab idling at the corner of the street.

I hurry outside and tap on the window. The driver looks up from his newspaper and nods for me to get in the backseat. I can't help looking at the front page of his paper first.

There's a photograph of two men with microphones shoved in their faces. The younger man's mouth is open, as if he's in midsentence. And I've seen him before. He's Isabella's cousin—the one Anthony punched at her funeral.

Family of Slain Student Calls for Federal Investigation

Looks like mistrusting the Wheatley Police runs in Anthony's family.

The driver rolls down the window. "You getting in, sweetheart?"

"Yeah. Sorry."

He doesn't say anything when I ask him to drop me off at the Wheatley School. Good, because I'm not feeling particularly chatty.

I reread Molly's e-mail for what feels like the millionth time. *They're watching.* She must mean the school, obviously, since we're using their server. But what's with the bizarre capitalization and lack of punctuation? It's almost as if Molly's trying to tell me something she doesn't want whomever is watching to see.

I go back over the message, pulling out the capital letters. A small gasp escapes me.

They spell out IN THE MAIL.

This can't be a coincidence. Molly knows something. And apparently it's in the mail.

I checked my on-campus mailbox earlier this morning, though, and there was nothing from Molly inside. Then again, she could have mailed whatever it is today. The thought of waiting kills me a little.

Or maybe it's not in my mailbox at all. I count out the numbers at the bottom of Molly's e-mail. Eight. Three for the mailbox number, and five for the combination to open it.

"Can you let me off at the front entrance please?" I ask the cab driver.

I dig my nails into my knees as he pulls up to the student center. A security guard is stationed at the gate. It's almost laughable how the school thinks this will convince people that the campus is safe. I've lived here a few weeks, and I already know about a million other ways to get around the gate.

And under it.

"Stay safe, hon," the driver says to me as I slip him a ten. I slam the cab door behind me, flash my ID to the guard at the gate, and hurry to the student center. The mail room is in the basement.

I find box number 268 and try the combination 21-18-7. The lock clicks at the same moment it occurs to me I've possibly committed a federal offense. I tell myself it's probably not illegal to open a locked mailbox if the owner wanted you to open it.

My heart sinks. Molly's mailbox is empty, except for a slip of paper reminding everyone that there's a Student Government Association town-hall meeting at 7:00 P.M. this Wednesday in the student-center auditorium. This can't be what Molly wanted me to find. I got the same stupid reminder in my mailbox this afternoon.

I reach into the box for the note, even though I know it's about as useful to me as it was earlier this afternoon when I stuck my gum in it. As I'm placing the paper back in the tiny box, the top of my hand brushes against something.

I feel around the top of the box. There's a letter stuck there. No, *taped* there.

Well played, Molly, I think as I tug at the envelope, peeling it from the roof of the box. It's a standard white letter envelope, and it's pretty tightly packed. I don't know what's inside, but I'm not about to stick around and get caught finding out.

Once I get back to my room, I lock the door and tip the envelope and pull its contents onto my bed. I count six letters, all typed and printed on white computer paper.

Isabella, Arthur says you don't want to talk to me anymore. I don't understand what I did or why you're afraid of me. Please talk to me, or I don't know what I'll do.

My throat feels tight as I read the rest of the letters. Some sound more desperate than the others. One sounds almost angry.

Revulsion builds in me. These are obviously from Lee. I can't help feeling a little disgusted at Molly, too. How did she get her hands on these, and how could she not turn them in to the police?

Because these mean nothing, the rational part of my brain reminds me. To the police they'd mean nothing, at least. There's no proof Lee even wrote these: There's no signature or handwriting sample. To someone who doesn't know better, it looks like anyone could have been Isabella's stalker.

With shaking hands, I hide the letters under my mattress. I can't risk any more "lost" evidence, even if the evidence doesn't prove anything. For now. Molly wouldn't have bothered leading me to the letters if she thought they were totally useless, right?

I swallow away the anxious feeling rising in my throat. Lee's letters to Isabella prove what I've been afraid to face for a while now.

Lee. Andreev. Alexis. All of them wanted Isabella dead.

The only question left is: Who got to her first?

CHAPTER
THIRTY-NINE

I walk with Remy, Kelsey, and April to dinner. But I'm not really with them. My mind is in a million other places, so I barely hear Remy when she says my name.

"Huh?" I look over at her.

"I said you should come to Concord with me this weekend." Remy's eyes are hopeful. "I mean, almost everyone is going home, so you could come with me and we could hang out."

"Oh." This catches me off guard. I hadn't even thought about being on campus alone for President's Day weekend until Brent brought it up. "Um, that's really sweet of you, Rem, but I actually just bought an Amtrak ticket to go home."

Remy smiles, but there's the slightest trace of hurt on her face. "Awesome."

I want to say something more to her, but I don't know what. All Remy wants is to be my friend. Most girls here would probably kill for an invite to spend the weekend at Remy's house, and I'm the bitch who's planning on breaking in to her dorm room while she's away.

As we pass the boys' dorm, someone calls for us to wait up.

It's Cole, with Murali. Brent trails behind them, signaling for me to walk with him. The others share a knowing smile.

"Why did you take off on me earlier?" Brent asks.

I tell him how I followed Sebastian, and what he told me about Andreev. I'm getting to the part about Molly's e-mail and the letters from Lee when I notice Brent is frowning.

"What?" I ask.

Brent lets out a breath through his nose. "I don't know. This is all so crazy."

"Tell me about it," I say. "Once I figure out who this guy Andreev is meeting—"

"Are you out of your mind?" Brent asks. "You can't get involved in that."

"What do you mean?" I blink at him. "I'm kind of already involved."

Brent shakes his head and sighs. "I know. But if Sebastian is right, and Andreev is dealing in that stuff . . . you have to tell someone, Anne. This is too dangerous for you to mess with."

Anger flares in me. "I know it's dangerous, Brent. Someone breaking in to my dorm is also dangerous, and I didn't get much help with that."

"Obviously, I'm not saying go to Harrow or anything. But I think we need to go to the police with what we have."

"You really think they'd believe me? I don't have anything solid." I'm frustrated now, even though it's not his fault. I'm frustrated because I can tell I'm close to figuring out who killed Isabella, but there's still a missing piece I don't have.

"I still think you should tell them what you know," Brent says quietly. "You can't keep putting yourself in danger like this."

"I can't sit back and do nothing, either," I tell him.

"Anne." Brent stops me and grabs my hand. "Please just listen to me. You have to tell someone what Sebastian told you."

I study the lines of concern on his face. "Okay," I lie. "Just give me some time, all right?"

He sighs. His breath ruffles the front of his hair. "Okay."

"Okay," I repeat.

"You're not going to tell the police," he says flatly.

"Of course not."

Brent runs a hand through his hair, tugging at the ends. "If something happens to you . . ."

"It won't be your fault," I say.

"That's the last thing I'm worried about," he says as he squeezes my hand again. And this time, he doesn't let go.

Although I like having Brent around again, his newfound concern for my safety is really screwing with my plans. Ever since the other night, he's been conveniently showing up to accompany me to classes and meals.

Luckily, the SGA town-hall meeting is tonight, and being the president and everything, Brent has to be there. It's perfect: While everyone is at the meeting, I'll use the tunnels to sneak into the administration building and break in to Goddard's office.

Hopefully most of the security guards will be stationed around the student center for the town hall, because getting caught in the tunnels would seriously suck. Even worse is the thought that Isabella's killer could be watching me, waiting for me to go down there alone.

That's why I called Anthony and asked him to come with me.

I check the time on my cell phone. It's almost quarter to seven; everyone should be heading over to the student center soon. When Remy knocks on my door and asks if I'm coming, I fake a cough and say I'm going to bed early.

The sound of Remy chattering with Kelsey and April in the hall fades away. I stick my head out in the hall to make sure they're gone, then hurry into the bathroom, because there's nothing worse than having to pee in the middle of a stealth mission.

I lock myself in the stall, and moments later, the bathroom door creaks open.

"Liz, I'm borrowing your lip gloss," Alexis says.

I freeze as three sets of footsteps pause in front of the mirror. There's the sound of a makeup bag being unzipped. Someone runs the faucet.

"Brooke said she saw them holding hands," a husky voice says.

"Brent is totally gay, Jill," Lizzie replies. "She's probably a beard for him."

Someone snorts. Alexis. "And she's a *murderer*."

They're talking about me, I realize with a wave of horror.

"You really think she did it?" Jill says, her voice hushed.

"Of course she did it," Alexis snaps. "I mean, she has a record, right? And people are saying she's been fooling around with Isabella's brother. I'll bet they killed her together as some sort of sick game."

I want to throw up. Are people really saying those things about me and Anthony?

My nausea quickly turns into anger. I fling open the bathroom stall and meet Alexis's eyes in the mirror. They widen, her mouth frozen in an O, half covered with a horrendous shade of raisin lip gloss.

"Hey ladies," I say sweetly, even though my voice is threatening to shake. "You're going to be late for the town hall."

I flash them a huge smile. They're still silent, as the bathroom door slams behind me.

"Just so you know," I tell Anthony after I sneak him into the basement stairwell, "there are some rumors going around. About you and me."

Anthony's eyes move to my neckline, sending a flush up my body. "I might be able to live with that."

"I'm serious," I say. "If people see us together . . . they might think we were both involved in Isabella's murder. So I understand if you don't want to do this. With me, that is."

Anthony looks distracted, in a way that makes me wonder if he knows I'm still talking about breaking into Goddard's office.

"Let them talk," he says, reaching and tucking my hair behind my ear.

We enter the tunnel from the laundry room and follow the arrows to the administration building. The tunnels are quiet, except for the usual sound of water dripping on stone. Whispering, I tell Anthony about the letters in Molly's mailbox.

"This girl," Anthony says. "Do you know what happened to her?"

I shake my head. "My guess is the school thought she was going to talk, so they kicked her out."

After a beat, Anthony says what I've been too afraid to consider: "Or they found another way to shut her up."

The arrows lead us to a wooden staircase set within the stone wall. Anthony shines the flashlight over the first step. "Check this out. Someone carved something here."

> *The truth is that all men having power ought to be mistrusted.*
> —*James Madison*

"Sounds about right to me." I pull the sleeves of my sweater down over my hands, wishing I'd thought to bring a jacket. "Let's go."

The stairs dump us into a dark, cluttered room. I nearly trip over a mop bucket.

"Janitor's closet," Anthony says. "Looks like our lucky day."

He points the flashlight at the wall. No, at the key ring dangling from a hook on the wall. It's one of those big round ones with tons of keys on it.

"Oh," I say. "Guess we don't have to pick the lock to Goddard's office."

Anthony raises an eyebrow at me. "You sound disappointed."
I shrug and he laughs quietly. "You're really something, aren't
you?"

I push the closet door open and poke my head out to make
sure the coast is clear. We're on the first floor of the administration building. It's empty, dark, and completely terrifying. Those
hideous portraits stare at us as we inch up the staircase.

"I know this sounds weird," I whisper to Anthony as we approach Goddard's office, "but I can just *feel* that we're going to
find something in here."

"No. I kind of get that." Anthony tucks a stray lock of hair
behind his ear. "Here goes nothing."

A small, silver key opens Goddard's office door. I flinch, half
expecting an alarm to go off or something. But the only sound
inside is the gurgling from the radiator beneath the far window.

Goddard's office is three times the size of Bailey's. His desk
is an enormous semicircle. Behind it is a portrait of Edward P.
Sedgwick, the Wheatley School's founder. The engraving beneath the portrait is dated 1797.

"Where do we start?" Anthony asks.

It's a good question. "I don't know. Anywhere that looks like
a good place to hide something, I guess."

Surprisingly, most of Goddard's drawers aren't locked. I've
been sifting through the contents of them for what feels like
forever when Anthony says, "Anne. Check this out."

I look over to see him on his hands and knees, looking under
the desk. I join him. He points to a silver device that looks like
a small remote.

"What is that?" I ask. "And how'd you know to look there?"

"Seemed like somewhere a janitor wouldn't notice." Anthony
shrugs and reaches for the device, turning it over in his hands.
There are a bunch of buttons on it: stop, rewind, play. Almost
like a tape recorder.

"Oh my God," I say. "Someone bugged Goddard's office."

I take the recorder from Anthony and press play. Today's date flashes on the digital display. We listen to Goddard speaking, apparently on the phone, with someone about a meeting of the alumni board.

The sound clips are each seven minutes long. I rewind the tape to the beginning, fast forwarding through stretches of silence and one-sided conversations. Phone calls.

Anthony and I stretch out on the floor and let the tape play for what feels like forever before I hear a familiar female voice. I pause and rewind.

"Ah. Diana," Goddard's voice says. "Come in. I just brewed a lovely Ethiopian roast."

"Thank you, Benedict."

"Upton," I say aloud. Anthony looks at me. "My Latin teacher," I explain.

"What can I help you with today, my dear?" Goddard asks. He sounds like Santa Claus, asking a little girl what she wants for Christmas. Not a professional speaking to an employee.

"I was hoping to talk to you about Anne Dowling," Upton says. The hairs on the back of my neck prickle. Time seems to stand still as we wait for Goddard to respond.

"Ah. Our newest student." Goddard's voice is indifferent.

"Yes. She was also Isabella Fernandez's roommate," Upton says. "She walked out of my class today."

"That doesn't surprise me, given her track record," Goddard says. "But I doubt you've come here to ask my advice on a minor discipline issue, Diana."

Upton hesitates. "Benedict, she's noticed Molly Frank's absence. She seemed disturbed by it. I wonder how much she knows."

There's a clunking sound, almost as if Goddard has set a mug down on his desk. "Are you suggesting Molly talked to her?"

"I don't know." Upton lowers her voice. "I've been watching Anne in class. She's shown a sudden interest in Lee Andersen, which worries me."

"You say that as if you have a reason to be worried, Diana. I'm going to ask you what I asked you last spring: Did Lee Andersen ever lay a hand on Isabella Fernandez?"

"Not to my knowledge, no," Upton says. "But I'm wondering if we should have done more about his . . . obsessive behaviors."

"Diana, if he never touched that girl, this isn't even a conversation. A man can barely look at a woman without facing allegations of sexual harassment these days. I will not let that sort of liberal discourse dictate how I run my school." Goddard's voice is hard. "Lee Andersen is not violent. I know his father. And I won't let him hang for what I know was a silly schoolboy's crush."

Goddard's words hang in the air. My ears are ringing. Anthony is stone-faced beside me.

"You don't think we should be worried . . . if Molly Frank goes to the police?" Upton asks.

"Dr. Harrow has made a convincing argument that Molly is a danger to herself at the present moment," Goddard says. "I have no doubts the police will find the killer before Molly's stay in Providence is over."

Providence. As in Rhode Island? How did the administration pull off hiding Molly away there?

"And in the meantime, how should I deal with Anne Dowling?" Upton asks.

My insides go cold.

"Let me deal with Ms. Dowling," Goddard says.

Anthony's hand is on my shoulder. "We need to take this to the police. Now."

I find myself nodding. "Wait. Then they'll know we broke in to his office."

"Then we'll mail the tape to the department anonymously."

I slip the recording device into my bag, and we make our way back down to the tunnel. I move as if in a daze, nodding dumbly as Anthony suggests we exit out by the administration garage, where he parked his motorcycle.

Lee probably killed Isabella. Goddard is protecting him.

I'm in danger.

I'm so busy repeating these three facts in my head, I don't have time to react to the beam of light that lands on us as we come around the side of the parking garage.

CHAPTER
FORTY

"Don't move," the voice behind the light says. "Hands where we can see them."

Anthony and I freeze. A security guard and two police officers emerge from the shadows. One says something into his radio. The security guard surveys my Wheatley School uniform.

"You a student?" he asks. I nod. "IDs," he commands.

"I don't go to school here," Anthony says as the guard thrusts a hand at him.

"Then why are you on private property after hours?" the guard asks.

"He's my visitor," I say quickly.

"So if I call and check the visitor log, his name will be on it?"

I'm silent.

"Look, we got a call about a possible break-in on campus," one of the police officers intervenes. "You two wouldn't know anything about that, right?"

I shake my head. "Honest. We were just going for a walk."

The cop's radio blips, and the security guard frowns at Anthony. "You have any ID on you at all?"

Anthony sneers at the guard as he hands him his driver's license. When the cops aren't looking, I jab him in the side with my elbow as if to say *Don't make this harder on us.*

The security guard's paunchy forehead crinkles as he studies Anthony's license. "Stay here."

He joins the cops off to the side, and they talk in hushed voices. One of the cops says something into his radio. After a moment, a crackling voice responds with something that sounds like "Cuff him."

Panic wells in me as the cops approach Anthony. "What are you doing?" I ask.

"You're Anthony Fernandez?" the tall cop asks, ignoring me.

Anthony nods. "What's the problem?"

Something in my head screams *NO!* as the other officer slaps the handcuffs on Anthony. "You're under arrest for the murder of Isabella Fernandez."

CHAPTER
FORTY-ONE

Technically, I haven't done anything wrong, but since I freaked out when they took Anthony away, the security guard called Dr. Harrow. They let me have a nervous breakdown in the bathroom first, at least.

Now here I am, back in the administration building, in a cushy chair in Harrow's office. One of the police officers who found me and Anthony is in here, too. Harrow is wearing a long coat over flannel pants. The police must have gotten him out of bed for this, and I can't help thinking . . . *How ridiculous is it that he was ready to go to sleep at nine o'clock anyway?*

"Anthony didn't kill Isabella," I tell the police officer.

"You sound pretty sure of yourself, Anne," Dr. Harrow cuts in with a sigh. His eyes probe mine, and I tense in my chair.

"We have overwhelming evidence Anthony Fernandez killed his sister," the police officer says, and I'm not sure if he's talking to me or to Harrow. "A 7-Eleven clerk a block away from here recognized Anthony from the newspapers. We have him on tape visiting the store the night Isabella was killed, right when he told us he was with his girlfriend in Somerville."

Ex-girlfriend, I want to correct him, even though that's totally not the point right now. "How does that prove he killed her?"

Harrow gives me a sharp look, but the cop continues. "Someone withdrew a significant amount of money from Isabella's bank account two days before she was killed. We believe she found out it was her brother, and he killed her when she confronted him."

The floor is falling from beneath me. Any second, my chair will drop like I'm at the top of a thrill ride. Then I'll wake up from this, right?

"Anthony didn't need to steal from Isabella," is all I can choke out. "He has a job."

"We have him on a security feed using the ATM where her account was accessed," the cop says, almost gently. "He'll be arraigned in the morning."

"No." I shake my head. "I *know* he didn't do it."

The police officer watches me with pity in his eyes. "Mr. Fernandez—Anthony's father—used to hunt before he got sick. . . . One of the knives from his collection is missing."

I cry out. Harrow opens his mouth but closes it in favor of massaging the area between his eyes. Yes. I am a major headache. Got that. "Anne, I need to talk to Officer Deligatti alone."

Once it's clear I don't plan on moving, Harrow follows the cop out into the hall. I bury my face in my hands. I don't believe all of this. I don't *want* to believe it. I refuse to believe that after all I've found out, the police have decided Isabella was killed over something as stupid as money.

A few weeks ago, I would have believed it if someone told me Anthony killed Isabella. But the Anthony I've come to know is not a murderer. Maybe he didn't like his sister, and maybe he even stole from her, but he didn't lure her into the woods and cut her throat.

That's when it hits me: Anthony is going to be charged with Isabella's murder, and there's nothing I can do about it. Tears spring to my eyes and pressure builds in my chest. I let the sobs take over my body. The sound that comes out of me is small, barely louder than a distressed kitten.

I try to focus on something else. If I think of Anthony anymore, I'll fall apart, and I can't afford to do that here in Harrow's office. If I can't help Anthony right now, at least I can help myself by staying calm so Harrow doesn't call my parents.

I wipe my eyes; when I open them, all I see is Harrow's desk. There is a stack of opened mail positioned next to one of those inbox-outbox type plastic bins. The envelope on the top is stamped with FROM THE OFFICE OF SENATOR STEVEN WESTBROOK.

Only a seriously brain-damaged person would even consider snooping around after what I've been through tonight. With a police officer right outside the door, no less. But I just know Harrow is blackmailing Senator Westbrook, and if I can prove it, I can blackmail Harrow.

The more I think about it, that's a terrible plan, but I don't have much else to go on right now.

I strain my ears to check for the muffled voices in the hallway. Harrow is still talking to the police officer. I snatch the envelope from Senator Westbrook and glance inside. It's empty.

I turn my attention to the next envelope on the stack. It's from a bank, and there is a statement inside. I scan it quickly; someone deposited a check for five hundred thousand dollars into an account registered to the Wheatley School. There's also a form declaring the Wheatley School a 501(c).

I shove the bank statement back into the envelope. I have a strong hunch that the check was another "historic gift" from Senator Westbrook.

I remember something my economics teacher said at the beginning of the year at St. Bernadette's: All nonprofit institutions have to disclose publicly how they spend their money. That's what 501(c) status is about. St. Bernadette's is a registered nonprofit institution, so after my teacher told us the rules, we all had fun looking up how much money the teachers and Bailey made. (Hint: almost as much as the president of the United States.)

If the Wheatley School is a nonprofit institution, I should be able to access records detailing how Senator Westbrook's money is being spent. If Harrow did something like give himself a salary boost, it could prove he's blackmailing the senator, presumably over the video that could tie Alexis to Isabella's murder.

My head is swimming and my face is stiff with dried tears. But I have renewed energy. I can do this. I can prove someone other than Anthony killed Isabella.

The door clicks behind me, and I straighten in my seat, throwing a glance at the stack of envelopes to make sure I left them as I found them, even though there's nothing I can do now if I didn't. Harrow steps back into his office, alone.

"Where's Officer Deligatti?" I ask.

"Heading back to the police station. As you can imagine, there's a lot going on there at the moment." Harrow eyes me. "I hope you don't mind if I ask you a few questions of my own."

"Am I in trouble?" I ask.

"That depends." Harrow sits at his desk, and a ball of panic rises in my throat. I hope he doesn't catch me as I glance at the stack of envelopes again. "How long have you been involved with Anthony Fernandez?"

"Involved?" I blurt. "We met at Isabella's funeral. We're just friends."

Harrow holds up his hands and presses his fingertips together. "Is this the first you're hearing of him stealing from his sister?"

"Yes, of course. How would I know about that?"

"I'm trying to help you." Harrow's eyes are ice blue in the dim light of his office. "The only way that can happen is if you're honest."

Anger surges through me. I've heard this little speech from him before. Is he trying to help me the same way he's "helping"

Alexis Westbrook? Does "helping" at this school mean protecting guilty people from getting what they deserve?

"I don't need your help." I stand and pick up my bag. "I had nothing to do with Isabella's death, and neither did Anthony. So if you're done with me, I'd really like to go back to my room."

Something flashes in Harrow's eyes, but he gives me a small smile. "I admire your resolve. I only hope it doesn't get you into trouble."

I tighten my grip on my purse strap. I can't decide if there's a threat veiled by his words.

"Anne," Harrow says as I'm halfway out his door. "Security saw someone through a window in the administration building. You weren't there this evening, were you?"

"No, sir," I say, keeping my voice even.

"Good."

His frown is the last thing I see before the door closes between us.

CHAPTER
FORTY-TWO

By morning, everyone knows Anthony's name, thanks to a mass e-mail titled "A Message from your Headmaster."

> I applaud the work of the Wheatley Police Department in bringing Isabella Fernandez's killer to justice so that, as a school community, we may begin to move on and cherish her memory.

I click out of the e-mail. If I read any more, I'm going to punch something. The last e-mail I received before this one stares back at me from my inbox.

Molly. I hurry to type out a response.

> Molly,
> I got the letters. I'm not sure how they'll help just yet, but I found something better. Are you all right? I heard you're in Rhode Island. Please call me if you can.

I give her my phone number and click "send." Not even a second later, my inbox says I have a new message.

How could she have responded already? I scrunch up my forehead and open the message.

Delivery failed. <frankm@Wheatleyschool.edu> is not a valid recipient.

They've suspended Molly's e-mail account. I have no way of getting in touch with her. My chest constricts a little. I lift my mattress to make sure the letters from Lee are still there. I breathe a sigh of relief when I see them and decide I should probably hide the recording device there, too, until I decide what to do with it.

I feel around in my bag for the device. For a second, I think maybe I forgot to take it from Goddard's office. No, I definitely put it in my bag. I dump its contents on my bed, pushing aside tins of rosebud salve, hand sanitizer, and a mini tissue pack.

The recording device is gone.

My first reaction, especially after not being able to get in touch with Molly, is fear: Maybe I'm going crazy, or I hit my head after the fire at St. Bernadette's and I'm not really at prep school in Boston but at a rehab facility. Somehow I made Isabella and the murder up, and everyone is playing along like in that movie where Leonardo DiCaprio is a crazy person.

Panicked, I take a mental inventory of the last eight hours. The only time I left my bag alone was when I got up from Harrow's office to have my freak-out moment in the bathroom, while we were waiting for Officer Deligatti to arrive and explain what was happening with Anthony.

My heart stops. Dr. Harrow went through my stuff. There's no way the recording device fell out of my bag. But I was only in the bathroom for max five minutes. He couldn't have wasted any time deciding whether to look in my purse. It was almost like he knew what was in there.

Could Harrow be the one who bugged Goddard's office?

Maybe Harrow was watching Goddard's office the whole time and was the one who called the police to report a break-in. But if that's the case, and Harrow found the device in my bag . . . why hasn't he confronted me or expelled me?

My phone buzzes, and I nearly jump out of my skin. Remy is calling me, no doubt to wonder why I'm not at breakfast yet. I hit "ignore call" and drag myself back to my laptop. I might be late to my first class, but I can't wait anymore: Harrow is involved with Alexis and her father somehow. He may even be involved in Isabella's death. And now that he knows what I've found, I'm a sitting duck.

I hunt down Brent before classes start.

"Let's say I was in charge of a large amount of money and wanted to skim some off the top for myself," I tell him. "What would be the best way to do that without getting caught?"

Brent blinks at me. He's clean-shaven and smells like Dove soap. "You could put the money in a fake account. But you'd need to hide it among a bunch of real accounts so no one would notice."

"Got it. Thanks." I'm off to find a computer before he can ask questions.

It doesn't take me long to find a PDF of the Wheatley School's record of distributions of charitable contributions. I search until I find the most recent donation of five hundred thousand dollars, dated last November. There's a list of the million different organizations and areas within the school the money went to.

I pause with my mouse hovering over the words *Wheatley School Advancement Fund*. Whatever it is, seventy-five thousand dollars of the donation went there—nearly twice as much as the other areas received. I type "Wheatley School Advancement Fund" into my search browser. It doesn't turn up anything.

I thought I smelled bullshit.

My morning classes are unbearable. Listening to the rumors about Anthony's arrest, it's hard to separate fact from speculation. Most people seem to agree on two basic things, though: Isabella Fernandez was killed by her brother, and he will probably spend the better part of his life in jail for it.

By lunchtime, I have a killer headache. Plus, I want to call Anthony really badly. I can't even entertain the thought of the stories being true.

When I realize why I *really* don't want him to go to jail, my head pounds even harder.

Right before he got arrested, I was totally, completely falling for Anthony.

I mean, it never would have worked out: Aside from the fact that he lives in Massachusetts and I live in New York, we just don't *go* together. Kind of like sweatpants and heels. But I still really cared about him. I still do. Thinking about him going to prison for a crime I know he couldn't have committed makes me feel like my entire world is shrinking.

It's time for lunch, but I don't have the heart to go into the dining hall. I hover around the entrance for a bit, then find the number I entered in my phone this morning. I dial it, and someone picks up on the second ring.

"Wheatley Office of Alumni Affairs; Melissa speaking. How can I help you today?"

"Hi." I shift the phone to my other ear, lowering my voice. "I'd like to make a contribution. To the Wheatley School Advancement Fund."

There's the sound of clicking on the other end. "I'm sorry, but I don't believe we have a fund by that name. Did you mean the Wheatley School Association for Scholastic and Curricular Development?"

I hang up. It's just like I suspected: The Wheatley School Advancement Fund doesn't exist. The seventy-five thousand dollars that went to it definitely does, though. If Brent's theory is right, Harrow set up a fake account for a fake organization so no one would notice him skimming money off the top of Steven Westbrook's most recent donation.

And it's a smart idea: No one would notice a fake school organization buried in with all of the real ones, unless they were looking for one, like I was. It's not rock-solid proof Harrow is blackmailing the senator and pocketing the money, but it's enough to warrant an investigation. Especially if someone came forward with compelling evidence Harrow has something worth blackmailing Steven Westbrook over: the video Isabella made of Alexis.

I've got to get my hands on it. But first I need to convince everyone I'm actually going to New York this weekend. I have a strong suspicion that if Alexis finds out I'm staying here after all, she'll stay too, to keep an eye on me.

I convince myself to join my friends for lunch and act like nothing's wrong. The table gets quiet when I sit down, then Remy grabs me and hugs me. "I'm so happy this is all over," she says into my ear.

I hug her back, although she's so wrong. This is far from being over.

Cole meets my eyes over Remy's shoulder. When I realize he's looking at someone past me, I turn to see Alexis at the table next to us. She avoids my gaze and turns to Jill, who's sitting at the other side of her.

"I can't believe you're stuck with her this weekend," Murali says to Cole, who reddens.

"It was my mom's idea," he mumbles into his French fries.

"Cole's family is going skiing in New Hampshire with the Westbrooks," Remy whispers to me.

"I'm sorry," I mouth to Cole. This gets a smile out of him.

"What are you doing this weekend?" Murali nudges me with his elbow. "Want to come to *casa de* Thakur in Melrose?"

"She's going to New York this weekend," Remy says, a little possessively. "I already asked her if she wanted to come home with me."

Murali grins at me, like someone who knew the answer to his question before he asked it. I'm suddenly very aware of how close Alexis's table is to ours.

"Sorry, Murali," I say, loud enough for Alexis to hear. "Remy's right. I'm going to New York this weekend."

Everyone takes this as a cue to share their weekend plans. April is in the middle of telling us her parents will be in London, when I sense everyone around me stiffen. I turn around to meet Alexis's over-bleached, fake smile. "Hey, Cole. Ready to eat my dust on the Black Diamond this weekend?"

I can't help it: I let out a half snort/half laugh, 'cause really, the phrase *eat my dust* is so stupid it should be illegal. Alexis's head snaps to me. Something vicious flashes in her eyes.

"Oh, hi, Anne. Sorry your boyfriend got arrested."

The back of my neck heats, and I swear I can feel the whole dining hall fall silent. Everyone's eyes are on me, and their mouths are half open with shock. My mouth is dry, and all I want to do is slap the satisfied smirk off Alexis's face, until a voice sounds from behind her.

"Fuck off, Alexis. And move; you're blocking my seat."

Alexis gapes at Brent. He stands there holding his tray, with a small smile on his face. "Oh, I forgot my manners. *Please* move. You're blocking my seat."

Alexis looks from him to me, her face flooding with color. She spins on her heels and takes off. Brent slips into the empty chair next to me and asks, "Who got the orange chicken?"—like this is the most normal situation in the world.

Everyone sits for a minute, stunned, before following Brent's lead and engaging in pointless drivel until lunch is over. When it's time to go back to class, he pulls me aside.

I preempt whatever he was going to say. "You didn't have to do that."

"I know. I still wanted to." His eyes search my face. "You okay?"

"Great." I force a smile. "Never better. About what Alexis said—"

Brent holds up a hand. "It's none of my business."

Frustration floods me. "Anthony isn't my boyfriend."

"But you wanted him to be."

Pressure builds behind my eyes. "I don't know. Maybe. He didn't kill her."

Now Brent is the one forcing a smile. His voice cracks a little as he says, "Then you're going to need help proving it."

CHAPTER
FORTY-THREE

I hate myself for what I'm about to do.

"Are you sure you don't want to come to the station with me?" Remy asks, checking herself out in the mirror hanging on my closet door. She meets my eyes in it, and I nod.

"Nah, I'd be waiting, like, five hours for my train," I say.

"It sucks you couldn't get an earlier one." Remy pouts. "You're going to get to New York after midnight."

I shrug. "That was the only train available on short notice."

At the soft knock on my door, I feign exhaustion and yawn. "Can you get that, Rem?"

She nods and skips over to the door like an obedient puppy. When she sticks her head out the door, I reach into her purse and find my target in one fluid motion. Brent stalls outside the door until I hear Remy say, "Why are you here, anyway?"

I give Brent a thumbs-up, and he steps past Remy into my room. "I'm keeping Anne company until I need to accompany her to the station."

"That's sweet," Remy says, distracted. "I guess I'll go, then."

Remy gives me a hug good-bye. When the door clicks behind her, Brent sits next to me on the bed. "You got it?"

I reach under my pillow and pull out Remy's ID card/room key. "What if she notices it's gone before she gets to the station?"

"Remy's lost her key twice this year already," Brent says. "If she notices, she'll just get a new one when she gets back on Tuesday. But she might call to deactivate this card, so we shouldn't waste time. I saw Alexis leave an hour ago."

There're at least two feet of space between us, and I suddenly hate how formal his tone of voice is. "You don't have to help me. I mean, I'd understand if you didn't want to."

Brent sucks in a breath and studies Isabella's wall. His eyes move over her *Where's Waldo?* and *Star Trek* posters. "She was a really cool person. It's hard to believe so many people wanted her dead."

I tuck my feet beneath me. "Who do you think did it?"

"Not her brother." Brent sighs, as if he wishes he *did* think Anthony did it. "If he stole money from her, why would he risk getting in even more trouble by killing her? I think whoever did it figured they had no other option. Someone like Andreev." Brent looks over at me. "Who do you think did it?"

Anyone, I want to say. Instead, I do that trick where you empty your mind, close your eyes, and wait for the first thing that pops into your head.

"Lee," I say. Even though Isabella was clearly involved in so much more before her death, my gut tells me that Lee Andersen thought if he couldn't have Isabella, no one could.

I reach under my mattress and hand Brent the envelope holding Lee's letters. He reads one and sets the rest aside. "This is sick shit."

I explain how I found the letters, watching the shock spread across Brent's face. I also tell him about what I found in Goddard's office, and my suspicion that Harrow was the one spying on him. When I get to the part about Harrow blackmailing Senator Westbrook, Brent shakes his head.

"Dude, I can't even. Are you sure about all this?"

"I'm not sure how everything fits together, but if you're asking if I'm sure all this really happened, then, yes." I pause. "Is Isabella's video of Alexis really worth extortion and murder?"

Brent considers this, his teeth finding his lower lip. "Hopefully you can decide for yourself shortly."

The hall is empty. Even Darlene and Emma went home for the holiday weekend, so there's only one RA on duty. She's downstairs at the desk, reading *The New York Times*.

Brent keeps an eye on the elevator as I swipe Remy's key. I enter her pass code, exactly like I watched her do yesterday when we stopped by her room so she could get her French textbook. My stomach feels hollow and sick all at once. Remy will never forgive me for this if she finds out. I wouldn't blame her.

"We're in," I whisper as the light on the lock turns green. Brent follows me into the room and turns the light on.

"Leave it off," I say. "Everyone knows Alexis and Remy are gone."

"Okay." Brent flips the switch off. It's early enough in the evening that there's plenty of natural light in the room for us, anyway.

"How do we know Alexis didn't take the video with her to Concord?" Brent asks as we comb through her stuff. I've got her desk covered, and he's poking through her closet as if something might jump out at him.

"We don't. She may have even destroyed it by now," I say. "But I'm hoping we'll get lucky."

"How would this look on me?" Brent holds up a sweater with pearls for buttons. It's covered in horrendous silk daisies.

I stifle a laugh. "Salmon isn't your color. Can you focus, please?"

"Sure, sure."

We freeze as footsteps sound in the hallway. They disappear as quickly as they came. We share a look and begin to work more quickly.

"Hey. Check this out." I hold up one of the papers tucked away in Alexis's bottom drawer. "Little Miss Perfect got a C-minus on her latest Spanish essay."

"Now who needs to focus?" Brent says, but he snatches the paper away from me and scans it. "Hah. Looks like she got busted for using an online translator."

I turn my attention back to Alexis's drawer. The next paper on the pile is a B– paper from Matthews.

"You look deep in thought," Brent says.

"The rest of Alexis's schoolwork is in the first drawer," I tell him. "It's almost like this bottom drawer is stuff she wants to hide. She had that file folder covering the Spanish paper. . . ."

My eyes connect with Brent's briefly before I dig to the bottom of the drawer. When I feel a key, a triumphant feeling stirs in me. I hold it up for Brent to see.

It doesn't take us long to find the locked box in Alexis's closet. The key clicks and I open the top, revealing some cash, jewelry, and a CD. There's also a photo of two toddlers—a boy and a girl—sitting on a pretty blond woman's lap.

Alexis's real mother. I swallow, because I can't let myself be derailed by guilt when I'm so close to answers.

I hold up the CD for Brent. "How much do you want to bet this isn't the latest Taylor Swift album?"

He smiles with half his mouth. "That could be anything."

My gaze travels to Remy's desk. She has a desktop computer; it's on, her background a photo of her and her older brother on a beach somewhere. Cole's voice fills my head. *Remy is too nice.* Too trusting too, I think, with a wave of guilt.

I slip the CD into the drive. Brent and I stare at the computer as it makes grunting noises, reading the disc. Remy's media player pops up, and a still frame of Amherst's second-floor lounge fills the screen.

"This is it," Brent says.

I swallow and sit in Remy's chair as the video plays. The shot is at an awkward angle, but I can clearly make out Alexis's face and the back of Remy's head. The sound quality is terrible—so bad I'd have to blast the volume to hear what they're saying. Brent reaches into his pocket and hands me his iPod headphones. I plug them into the computer and turn the volume up.

"I can't believe you think I'm that pathetic," Alexis says to Remy.

"I didn't say that." Remy's voice is almost a whisper. She turns and looks right at the camera in a way that makes my heart jump, almost as if she's looking at me. "Lex . . ."

"She can't hear us." Alexis gestures to her ears, as if to say *Headphones, duh.*

I picture Isabella on the other side of the camera. Pretending to be in her own little Isabella world, when she was really spying on Alexis. Is this the moment that decided her fate—the decision that may have gotten her killed?

"I bet Brent is taking the posters down and trying to make it seem like I'm doing it." Alexis takes a sip from the Starbucks cup in front of her. "He's such a little thorn in my ass. It's exactly the type of thing he'd do."

I turn and raise an eyebrow at Brent. "This is what the big fuss is all about?"

Brent nods to the screen. "Keep watching."

I comply, watching Remy shift uncomfortably in her seat. It's almost as if she knows Isabella really *can* hear them.

"Peter Wu has a decent shot." Remy shrugs. "People like him."

"*Fuck* Peter Wu," Alexis announces. "No one wants the token Chink as their class president. He should be mopping the floor at Dynasty Buffet, not telling us what to do."

"Alexis," Remy hisses. "That's horrible."

"Come on, Remy." Alexis yawns. "Like you're not thinking it."

Remy rolls her eyes. "I wasn't, actually."

"This is all we saw at the assembly," Brent cuts in. "Someone stopped the video. But it looks like there's still a minute left." I shush him, even though Remy and Alexis are quiet.

"Anyway, who do you think paid for the new computers in the SGA office? My father gives too much money to this school for me to get screwed over by this election," Alexis continues. "I *need* to be president to get in to Penn. Since I'm not poor or a minority."

"You can't be talking about bribing Matthews to fix the election," Remy whispers.

"Why not?" Alexis shrugs. "Everyone does it."

That's when the video runs out. I don't even know what to say. So I remove the CD from the drive and study myself in its reflective surface.

"What are you going to do with that?" Brent asks uneasily, as if I'm holding a vial of smallpox.

"I'm going to hold it ransom," I say.

Brent raises an eyebrow. "For what?"

Isabella's fingerprints are probably on this disc. And I'm sure the police have the technology to prove Isabella made the video on her computer. It's convincing evidence connecting Alexis to Isabella. I don't have to think about it for long. "Answers."

CHAPTER
FORTY-FOUR

"Now what?" Brent asks after I get my purse from my room and hide the video at the bottom. I'm not letting this thing out of my sight, especially after what happened with Harrow and the recording device.

"Beats me." I know Brent is really asking *What are we going to do for the rest of the night?* We're finally alone together. My answer should be easy. Except it's not, because I can't stop thinking about Anthony and whether he's made bail.

Brent sighs, as if he can read my thoughts. We settle on getting frozen yogurt from the dining hall and watching some Judd Apatow movie I'll probably think is gross.

On the way back to Brent's dorm, I check to see if I have any messages. Brent glances at the picture of Abby on my phone's wallpaper.

"You have a dachshund," he says.

"Nice observation."

Brent holds his phone in front of me. His wallpaper is also a dog. It's darker and hairier than Abby, but it's clearly a dachshund.

"Mine's cuter," I conclude.

"Bet mine has a cuter name," Brent says. "Stitch."

"Like the Disney character?"

"Yup."

We walk in silence until Brent says, "It sounds lame, but my dog is the thing I miss the most about home."

I look at him and feel a surge of warmth, because I feel the same way about Abby, and also because right here, with him, is the first time I've felt happy all week. "It's not lame."

We grow progressively quieter the closer we get to his dorm. We're probably thinking the same thing: We're going to be alone in Brent's dorm. Will we watch the movie in his suite's living room or his bedroom?

It's as if something zaps the thoughts from my brain when I see a tall figure leaving the dorm. Lee Andersen. I feel all the blood drain from my head as he walks past us, his eyes on the ground.

"I wonder why he's still here," Brent says. "He usually goes home every weekend."

I don't want to think about why Lee is hanging around campus when everyone else is gone. For my own sanity, I make a vow to myself to not care, either. Not tonight. I need a break from Isabella's murder. I need tonight to be normal.

"So," Brent says as he unlocks the door and we step inside his dorm room.

"So." I look into his eyes, and notice some of the color has drained from his face. I take his hand and squeeze it. "Thanks for staying here with me this weekend."

"There was no way I was going home if you were here." He gives me a weak smile. "I'm gonna use the bathroom quick."

I sit on the couch while he's gone, trying to fight off memories of the party. Was I sitting on this couch the very moment Isabella died?

"Anne." Brent is back after what seems like an eternity. I

know something is wrong as soon as I hear his voice. His face is white and covered in sweat. I jump to my feet.

"Help," is all he manages to say before collapsing in my arms.

I sit in the infirmary waiting area. A woman in jeans and a scrub top comes out and gestures to me. "He's asking for you."

"I'm going to go," says Brent's RA, Kyle, who's sitting beside me. He helped me get Brent here. "He's probably going to have to spend the night here."

I nod and follow the doctor-nurse-infirmary-person through a door and past a white curtain. On the other side, Brent lies on a cot, his face still empty of color. But he's conscious now, so I guess that's an improvement. He smiles when he sees me.

"What the hell are you trying to do to me?" I sit in the plastic chair next to him and grab his hand. With the other, he traces the outline of the silver Tiffany heart pendant around my neck.

"You were wearing this the day we met," he says. His voice is hoarse. "I was afraid it meant you had a boyfriend."

I pull his hand closer to my face and kiss it. Brent closes his eyes. "So this is what I had to do to get you to kiss me."

"Stop it. Please tell me what's going on."

Brent opens his eyes and fixes them on a point on the ceiling. "Type-one diabetes. Only Cole and Remy know. And now you, I guess."

"Why didn't you tell anyone?"

"No offense, Anne, but . . ." He nods to my hand in his. "Everyone feels like they have to take care of me. My mother, sisters, Remy. It's too much sometimes, especially when Remy babies me in front of people who don't know."

He traces the area between my thumb and index finger. I think of the way Remy is always asking Brent if he's okay. The way she pushed a bowl of strawberries at him when he was late to dinner that night. "You could have told me," I say.

"I almost did, once." Brent pauses. "I didn't have an SGA meeting when I bailed on you the day you broke into Andreev's office. I forgot I had to see the doctor."

"Are you going to be okay?" I ask.

"Mm-hmm. In the excitement of the evening it seems I forgot my insulin injection." Brent winces. "You seem to have that effect on me. It's kind of why I tried so hard to keep this from you. . . . I was afraid you'd stop being so . . . *you* around me."

"I'm like this with everyone. Don't consider yourself special." I give him a smile. A real one, because even though we won't get to watch that movie after all, I wouldn't trade this moment for anything. I'm finally seeing the real Brent Conroy, and although it kind of sucks he's in a hospital bed, I feel like I belong to an exclusive club or something.

The nurse-doctor-infirmary-person pops her head around the curtain again. "Brent needs to get rest now. You can come see him in the morning."

Disappointment floods me. I can't stay here. Brent squeezes my hand as I get up. "It's probably dark by now. Have Kyle walk you to Amherst, okay?"

"Um. About that. He left," I say. "I'll be fine though. It's a five-minute walk."

Brent's face is skeptical. I give him a swift kiss on the forehead. "Really. Don't worry."

"Text me when you get back," he says. And this time Kelsey's not here, so he has to give me his phone number.

I'm still beaming when I get outside. There's something kind of liberating about smiling in a moment where the thought of smiling seems completely inappropriate. I'm grinning so hard I barely notice the shadow that passes over mine on the ground.

I whip around, the street lamp beside me illuminating a tall figure running around the side of the infirmary. My heart slams against my lungs as I set off toward Amherst. Goddard's voice fills my head: *Let me deal with Ms. Dowling.*

I want to call out to whomever is following me. *Come try to kill me. Do it right here, in the middle of campus so someone can see you.* But instead, I pick up my pace and cut through the woodsy path leading from the infirmary to the quad.

The sound of leaves crunching behind me confirms that the person is still following me. I can feel him closing in on me. I scream as loud as I can, then I turn around and hit him square in the face.

I gasp as Lee Andersen stumbles backward, pressing a hand to his nose. I look down and see blood smeared across my knuckles.

"Why are you following me?"

Lee takes a step toward me and I hold my purse in front of me like a shield. "Come any closer and I'll kick you in the balls."

"I just wanted to talk to you." It comes out of him like a whimper. It's the longest sentence I've heard from him, so it nearly knocks me backward.

"What?"

"You think I killed Isabella," Lee says, his tongue poking out and licking blood off his upper lip. "I wanted to tell you it's not true. I loved Isabella."

"You had a great way of showing it," I snarl at him. "Creepy letters, drawing her without her knowing."

"I never hurt her," he says.

"You hurt her every time you gave her attention she didn't want," I spit at him. "You scared her. She felt like she had to change her schedule to get away from you, and you still found a way to scare her!"

Lee takes off his glasses and makes a horrible choking sound. For a moment, I think he's going to throw up, until I see the tears spilling from his eyes and mixing with the blood leaking from his nose. "I didn't know. I didn't know I was scaring her."

"You did know. You just didn't care." I stare Lee squarely in the eye for the first time. I refuse to feel any pity for this pathetic guy who made Isabella's life hell because he wasn't used to hearing *no*.

"Please." Lee steps toward me, and I raise my hand, making it clear I have no problem hitting him again. "Please believe me."

I watch fear take over his face. I look at my hand, poised and ready to strike. I'm shocked at how badly I want to hurt Lee, to hit him over and over even though it'll never match the pain he caused Isabella by making her live in fear.

I lower my hand. This isn't me. I didn't decide to find Isabella's killer so I could hurt him or her. And worst of all, something in Lee's expression almost makes me believe him that he didn't murder Isabella.

I take off running and don't stop until I get back to Amherst. I lock myself in my room and stumble over to the window overlooking the quad.

There's no sign of Lee.

CHAPTER
FORTY-FIVE

Things Brent and I do over the weekend: Go ice-skating in the Boston Common, visit the Museum of Science, have a competition to see who can yell inappropriate words on the T louder without getting embarrassed.

Things I don't do: Get into trouble or gather any more information related to Isabella's murder.

It was a difficult decision, deciding to lay low for the rest of the weekend, but my confrontation with Lee seriously rattled me. I mean, he could have easily killed me. If he wanted to. The fact that he didn't makes me believe he may not have had anything to do with Isabella's death after all.

All of the signs are leading back to Alexis, Senator Westbrook, Dr. Harrow, and the video. The senator is clearly paying Harrow off . . . probably to keep quiet about Alexis's involvement with Isabella. Maybe they even know that Alexis killed Isabella and want to cover it up. But before I make any sort of drastic move with the video, I still have to consider the possibility Andreev had Isabella killed, too. So when the long weekend ends and Tuesday afternoon rolls around, I put on my sunglasses, tuck my hair into a knit cap, and wait across the street from the science building.

Andreev leaves through the side entrance at exactly 3:16. My phone chimes from within my bag, and it doesn't stop. I scramble to turn it off after seeing Remy is calling me.

Andreev crosses the street while the light is still red. A taxi driver leans on his horn, and Andreev shouts something at him in Russian. I stay on the opposite side of the street, following him and keeping my eyes glued to the back of Andreev's wool coat.

Something hard smacks into my shoulder. An older man in jeans and a ski jacket apologizes to me. "You should watch where you're going, honey."

I ignore him and start moving. Andreev is turning the corner onto Massachusetts Avenue. When the light turns green, I cross the street. The guy who bumped into me is behind me, yapping away on his cell phone. And he said *I* should watch where I'm going.

Andreev stops outside a post office and looks over his shoulder. I'm about fifty feet behind him, but I still turn so he can't see my face. I pretend to read the menu hanging in the window of the café I'm standing outside of.

That's when I notice the guy who bumped into me is doing the same thing.

I search his face for some sign I know him. He gives me an odd look and breaks eye contact.

Andreev starts walking again. I follow him, forgetting about the weird guy. The wind picks up, and I wrap my scarf so it's protecting the lower part of my face. Andreev stops again, this time outside a deli. We're in Harvard Square.

Andreev paces outside of the deli. He checks his watch and pulls something out of his jacket. A manila envelope. My breath catches in my throat as a voice behind me says, "Waiting for someone?"

I spin around to face the weird guy who bumped into me. "That's none of your business," I say.

The guy slips his phone into his pocket and buys a newspaper from the same guy I bought mine from. I really want to get away from this creep, but I can't risk losing Andreev. I walk around to the opposite side of the newsstand, where I can still see Andreev.

The next thirty seconds happen as if in slow motion. A car backfires at the curb. Andreev looks up to see the source of the noise.

His eyes land on me and they squint. Recognition floods his face. My heart leaps into my throat as he takes off around the corner as if he never saw me.

I have about .025 seconds to decide whether to give up and act like seeing him was a coincidence or to take off after him. I run across the street just as Andreev disappears into the crowd gathered outside a store.

"Hey," a male voice behind me yells. I look over my shoulder to see the creepy guy pursuing me. I run faster.

"*Stop*," he commands, and something about his tone of voice tells me I should. I turn to face him, and when he flashes a badge at me that says FBI, I'm left with one thought.

It's all over.

CHAPTER
FORTY-SIX

The FBI agent and Dr. Harrow are talking outside the administrator's conference room, and all I catch of their conversation is *following the suspect of a federal investigation.* I sit across from Dean Tierney at an empty table inside the room. She gives me a small smile. It's not a friendly smile. It's more of a *You're absolutely fucked and there's nothing you can do about it* smile.

The door to the conference room opens, and Harrow steps inside, trailed by the FBI agent. "Well, Anne," he says, "you can't seem to get enough of me lately, can you?"

My mouth twitches with the ghost of a laugh, but the death glare Tierney shoots in my direction shuts me up. The FBI agent sits across from me and pulls out a notepad. "So tell me, exactly, how you knew we were investigating Eugene Andreev."

"I didn't," I say. Tierney twitches a little in a way that lets me know this is news to her and Dr. Harrow as well.

Harrow and the FBI agent watch me expectantly. I have to tell the truth, I realize. Or at least parts of it. I settle on a modified version of the real story: I tell the FBI agent that Isabella told me what Andreev was doing.

"I thought maybe he had something to do with her death," I say. "I know it was really stupid of me, but I decided to follow him."

Harrow's eyes dig into me as if he can tell I'm lying and Isabella never told me anything about Andreev. I grip the table in front of me and focus on the FBI agent.

"Eugene Andreev has been on our radar since he left the national research lab four years ago," he says. "We believe he stole weapons intelligence that's heavily encrypted. You're saying Andreev used *students* to try to access it?"

"Yeah, pretty much."

The FBI agent rubs the stubble on his chin. Tierney's eyes are practically crossing. Probably thinking what a PR nightmare this is all going to be.

"Andreev didn't murder Isabella Fernandez," the FBI agent says finally. "We looked into him when we discovered she was working for him. One of our operatives was watching Andreev the night Isabella was killed."

"Oh," is all I manage to say. Andreev didn't kill Isabella. I repeat that in my head, dissecting each word until I decide it makes sense. I should probably feel relieved. One of the puzzle pieces has been removed; it should be easier for me to put the rest together now. But I feel nothing.

The FBI agent says something to Tierney and Harrow that I don't catch. Then he's gone, and suddenly I feel everything all at once. Fear. Paranoia. Some other nameless, unique brand of emotion that comes along with being in a room alone with these two.

"I'll have to call Benedict," Snaggletooth announces, before exiting without looking at me.

"The headmaster's coming?" I turn to Harrow.

He cracks his knuckles. "Dr. Goddard is away. Fortunately for you."

I'm not sure what, exactly, is fortunate about this situation. I'm about to ask, when Harrow slides into the chair across from me. "I think it's time you and I had a heart-to-heart, Anne."

I flinch. The Old Anne would smile at Dr. Harrow and ask where the scones and tea are if we're going to have a heart-to-heart. But there is absolutely nothing I can do, short of curing cancer, to get my parents to forgive me if I get kicked out of two prep schools in two months, so I meet his eyes and say, "Okay."

"We have quite a mess here, as you can imagine." Dr. Harrow leans back in his chair and crosses one leg over the other.

"What's going to happen to Professor Andreev?" I ask.

"Obviously we can't have a suspected criminal teaching our students," Harrow says. "But letting him go now may tip him off and compromise the investigation even further."

Even further. Meaning, I compromised it when I followed Andreev this afternoon. "I didn't mean to screw everything up."

Harrow nods, his eyes on a point on the wall behind me. "Anne, I need to know the truth. Did Isabella really tell you what she suspected Andreev was doing?"

I swallow. "Yes."

Harrow keeps on nodding. He traces an invisible line on the table in front of him. "That just seems like something she would have told me, that's all."

I know he doesn't believe me. But there's something else in his voice that disturbs me: the way he said *She would have told me.* My tongue sticks to the roof of my mouth.

I need to get out of here.

"Anne, if you know something about Isabella's death you're not telling me—"

"How would I?" I force myself to smile. Play the rich little airhead he probably thinks I am. "I only knew Isabella, like, a week."

Harrow stands up, leans across the table until his nose is inches from mine. My heart catches in my throat; he smells like coffee and aftershave. It looks like he's going to yell in my face, but a small laugh escapes his nose instead. "Can I trust that we won't be seeing each other again this week, Anne?"

I grip the sides of my chair, my heart crashing against the walls of my chest. That's a promise I can't keep. Not now when I'm certain of one thing: Harrow knows who killed Isabella. But I nod, and smile again.

"Of course you can, Dr. Harrow."

CHAPTER
FORTY-SEVEN

Remy is waiting for me in the first-floor lounge. "Anne, where have you been?"

I check the screen of my cell phone. Class has been over for more than three hours, and I have five missed calls from Remy. "What's going on?"

"I can't find my ID," Remy tells me. "Student Services wants to charge me fifty dollars for a new one since I've already lost two cards this year."

My throat constricts. "Oh. That sucks. Is that what you called me about?"

A giggle sounds from the corner of the lounge. I look up to see Alexis and Lizzie hanging posters titled RESIDENT COUNCIL PRESENTS: SPRING FLING ICE CREAM SOCIAL! Lizzie appears completely absorbed in telling Alexis a story, but I can tell Alexis has one ear on us.

"Well, I know I had my ID before I stopped by your room Friday night," Remy says. "Could I check to see if I dropped it there or something?"

Across the room, Alexis freezes. She picks her head up and

locks eyes with me. I look away and back to Remy. "Sure, Rem. Wanna come up now?"

"Yeah, that works." Remy smiles with relief. "Thanks, Anne. I'm sure it's in there somewhere."

I can't tell Remy her ID is currently making its way through the school's waste disposal system. My ears ring and my breathing becomes shallow as we leave the lounge. Alexis watches me the whole time, smacking the stapler in her hand against her opposite palm.

I know what you did, her expression says. *I know what you did, and you're dead.*

It's only a matter of time before Alexis goes through her stuff to see if anything's missing. I have to decide what I'm going to do with the video. Now.

I call Brent as soon as Remy leaves my room, distraught and muttering, "I just don't understand how I lost it *again.*"

"We have a problem," I say to Brent.

"You said 'we.' I kind of like the sound of that."

"Brent, I'm serious." I shoot a glance at my door. "Harrow knows what I've been up to. And I think he knows Alexis killed Isabella."

"Wait, wait, slow down. Why would he cover for Alexis?"

"So he can extort the shit out of the Westbrooks," I say. "I've got to do something."

"By 'something,' I hope you mean go to the police."

"I will. After I confront Alexis."

"Are you high?" Brent's voice slides up an octave.

"No. It's the only way I'll get answers out of her. I'll have my phone in my pocket, recording what she says."

"Alexis isn't dumb. And if you really think she killed Isabella, what's gonna stop her from hurting you?"

"I'll be ready. That's the difference between me and Isabella.

And it'll be hard enough to get Alexis to talk without you there. Please, Brent."

"Anne, I—"

He's interrupted by a beep telling me I have another incoming call. I nearly drop my phone.

Anthony.

"Brent, I have to call you back."

My heart is beating so fast, I'm seeing black spots. Where is Anthony, that he's able to call me?

"Hi."

"Hey." His voice is panicked. "I thought you might not pick up."

"Of course. I mean, I could never . . . what they say you did." I can barely get the words out, I'm so happy to hear his voice. "Where are you?"

"My uncle's house. He posted my bail." Anthony's voice is broken down. "My parents are at the hospital. My dad . . . this hasn't been good for him."

"I'm so sorry." The corners of my eyes are getting moist. *Keep it together, Anne.*

"I can't talk for long." Anthony pauses. "A detective came to my uncle's house this morning and asked about you."

My stomach plummets. "What do you mean, asked about me?"

"He asked if I thought you might have found something in Isabella's room you weren't telling me about," Anthony says. "I told him no, but he wouldn't leave. Like he thought I was lying."

I immediately think of the security box beneath my bed. "Anthony, wait. I did find something I never told you about. I thought it was just something really personal she wanted to stay hidden—"

"What *is* it, Anne?"

"A security box. An electronic one, with a code. Do you know about it?"

"No." Anthony is quiet for a moment. "Did you open it?"

"I couldn't. You think this could be what the detective was looking for?"

"Maybe. Depends what's inside. Try one-two-seven. That's Isabella's birthday. Our birthday."

"Hold on." I flatten myself onto the floor and reach for the security box. I type in Isabella's birthday, but the red light flashes red still.

"Anthony, what else could it be?"

"I don't know. Maybe one of our parents' birthdays. She couldn't remember shit, so it's gotta be something obvious."

Of course. I picture Isabella the day I first met her, with her dimples and sheepish smile as she unlocked our door: 4-3-2-1, because of her awful memory.

With trembling hands, I type 1-2-3-4 into the keypad. Something inside the box whirs, and the light turns green. "I'm in."

Anthony is silent as I open the box. A photograph of Steven Westbrook stares back at me. He's at a street corner with a blond woman.

I bring the photo closer to my face. It's not just any blond woman: It's Mrs. Redmond.

There are two more photos in the box. One of Steven Westbrook entering a hotel, alone. Then Mrs. Redmond entering it, also alone. All the photos are time stamped. March 14, last year.

Cole's mother and Alexis's father. Are they having an affair?

"Anne, are you there?" Anthony asks.

We had an agreement.

Elaine Redmond.

You dragged Lanie into this.

"Shit," I say. "Anthony, are you sure the guy who came to your house was a detective?"

"He had a badge." Anthony is quiet. "But I guess I didn't look close at it."

"What did he look like?" The room is shrinking around me.

"Tall. Probably midthirties. Dark brown hair, blue eyes, I think. Had an accent like he's definitely not from Boston."

"Anthony, I have to go."

"Why?"

"That guy's not a cop." I swallow. "He's my vice-principal."

CHAPTER
FORTY-EIGHT

To: westbrooka@Wheatleyschool.edu
From: dowlinga@Wheatleyschool.edu
Subject: (none)

It's time for a chat, just us girls. I have something you need, but luckily you have something I need, too. Let's meet up tonight and we'll discuss . . . or I'm taking the video to the cops.

To: dowlinga@Wheatleyschool.edu
From: westbrooka@Wheatleyschool.edu
Subject: Re: (none)

8 P.M., in the forest across from the parking garage. Come alone or I won't talk.

I go to the bathroom and throw up. When I get back to my room, Brent is calling.

"Sorry," I whisper, then hit ignore. Then I program 911 into my speed dial and send Brent a text.

If you don't hear from me by 9:30, call the police. And open the security box under my bed. Code is 1-2-3-4. Room's unlocked for you.

I check my bag to make sure the video is still in there, since I'll need it as leverage. I leave the photographs of Senator Westbrook and Mrs. Redmond in the box for Brent to find in case the unthinkable happens.

But it won't. I have a pepper-spray key chain and a possibly overinflated sense of confidence that I could take Alexis down if it came to it.

I sit on the edge of my bed. *Breathe in through the nose, out through the mouth.* I'm really doing this. Doing what might easily become the stupidest thing I've ever done. Even stupider than lighting that report on fire and getting kicked out of St. Bernadette's.

But this is different. This is the type of stupid that matters. The type of stupid that could actually change something.

I have no other option. The police won't believe me: It's my word against a senator's daughter's and the vice-principal of the most prestigious prep school in New England. I could run away, back to New York, but everything will catch up with me eventually. I know too much.

I owe Isabella too much.

Brent keeps calling. I silence the call and send him one last text message.

I really wish I had just kissed you the night of the party.

I don't wait for his response. I know he's probably outside Amherst, waiting to stop me, so at 7:50, I move the bookcase in the laundry room and descend into the tunnel.

After I emerge in the parking garage, I move deep enough into the forest so I can't be seen, but still leave a clear path of escape. In my pocket, my phone is ready for me to hit *record sound.* In my other hand, I clutch the pepper spray.

Then I wait. A pair of yellow eyes glows at me from the tree overhead, sending a chill down my spine. Spastic fluttering sounds behind me, as if something has frightened the birds.

"You shouldn't have come here, Anne."

The voice behind me isn't Alexis's. I turn, feeling cold metal press against my temple. Then hear the click of the gun.

"Don't scream," Dr. Harrow says into my ear. "Then maybe I'll consider leaving you a vegetable instead of killing you flat out."

CHAPTER
FORTY-NINE

I collapse into the leaves beneath me. I should be trying to use my pepper spray, but my limbs won't work. I am a puddle on the cold forest floor. I am going to die here, just like Isabella did.

They say your entire life is supposed to flash before your eyes. My head is empty, though. I can't form the words to plead, beg. All I can do is whimper.

"Shh, shh," Harrow says. His voice is comforting, which is a million types of fucked up, considering he's pointing a gun at me.

"You killed her," I choke out.

Harrow actually looks surprised. "But you knew that already, didn't you? She must have told you about us."

About us. Suddenly, everything makes sense. The way Zach said Isabella had a boyfriend but wouldn't tell anyone who. The way Dr. Harrow was surprised Isabella didn't tell him about Andreev.

"You . . . and her?" I squeak.

"Before you judge me, you should know your roommate wasn't as innocent as she pretended to be. She had me rough

Andersen up. She wanted it. She wanted *me*." Harrow's eyes are manic. "I was the one who tried to break it off. She threatened to go public with the photos if I did. She was going to tell everyone I was blackmailing the senator."

A choked, high-pitched sound escapes my throat. "You didn't have to kill her."

"I didn't mean to." The hand Harrow holds the gun in shakes a little. "She's the one who brought that knife along whenever we met here. She said it made her feel safe. I never wanted to kill her."

Harrow's voice is pleading, almost as if he's trying to convince me. It might just be a way for me to buy more time.

"How could you *accidentally* cut her throat?" I ask. My hands press into the cold earth behind me. My elbows ache, and I want to sit up, but I'm afraid he'll shoot.

"She thought I was blackmailing Senator Westbrook over her video," Harrow says. "She confronted me because she was afraid she'd get expelled if something went wrong and people found out she made it. That's why I told her about the photos." Harrow licks his lips. "After I tried to end things with her, she stole the photos. That night . . . she said she needed to see me. She said she had the photos and was going to Goddard with them. I grabbed her. She got scared. When she pulled out the knife, something snapped in me. I didn't even realize what I was doing."

I'm crying, and Harrow is telling me to be quiet, but I can't. "Where's Alexis? She's supposed to meet me here."

"Alexis was smart and came to me when you e-mailed her. You, Anne, were *not* smart."

My chest heaves, as if I'm going to be sick. I roll over and gag. That's when I get the words out: "Please don't kill me."

"You should never have gotten involved, Anne," Harrow says, his voice mournful. "I didn't want her to die. I don't want you to die, either."

"I don't want to die," I say, loudly and hysterically, hoping there's someone out here who will hear.

"You should have kept your mouth shut then, like everyone else," Harrow growls, taking a step toward me. I crawl backward, wincing as my palm presses down on something hard.

A rock.

"I'm sorry, Anne." Harrow's face is contorted as he points the barrel of the gun at me. Something clicks into place. "But you know too much."

Harrow is raising the gun as a blistering holler sounds outside the woods. His head jerks to the source of the noise, and I grab the rock. In the split second it takes him to turn his attention back to me, I lob it at his face.

The rock hits Harrow in the jaw. He stumbles backward, dropping the gun—but not before it goes off. I dive forward and reach the gun before Harrow does. I point it squarely at his chest.

His hands immediately fly up. Blood drips from the corner of his mouth, which is twisted in a half smile. "Going to kill me, Anne? I wouldn't count on a self-defense plea with your record."

My hands are trembling around the handle of the gun. I've never even held a gun before. Harrow is smirking at me as if he can tell what I'm thinking. *I can't do this; I can't do this.*

A voice splits the silence. "ANNE!"

Rustling sounds through the trees, and Brent emerges, breathless. "Holy shit." He bends over, holding his chest. "I heard a gun go off. I thought you—"

"It's okay." I try to keep my voice even. I look over at Brent, trying to give him a reassuring smile. "It's all going to be okay."

I look away from Brent just in time to see Harrow pulling the knife from his pocket.

Lunging at Brent.

White light explodes in front of my eyes as I scream and pull the trigger.

CHAPTER
FIFTY

Harrow lies on his back unconscious, blood seeping through the leg of his pants. His temple is leaking blood, too, from hitting a rock on his fall to the ground. He's breathing, though.

Brent lies on the ground, too, holding his chest. I rush over to him, feeling relief flood me when I don't see red staining his shirt. I don't even want to think about what would have happened if I had missed Harrow. I bend down next to him, and he grabs me, pressing me to him.

"When I heard the first gunshot . . ." His voice trails off. His mouth is at my ear, then on my lips. His are soft, and they fit mine perfectly. I kiss him back, warmth flooding every inch of my body. He holds my face, kissing me harder as if to make up for all those times we could have kissed but didn't. Everything disappears, and it's just him and me, and I finally realize how much I wanted this to happen all along.

The sirens are what finally interrupt us.

"I hope you don't mind I made a phone call or two," he says as we pull away. "I finally found someone to let me into your building, and Alexis was there. When you didn't come back, I figured you'd met someone else here."

"It's okay." I hold on to Brent's arms still, almost as if I'll never get him back if I let him go now. "Dr. Harrow needs a real doctor."

We look over at our vice-principal. He's still unconscious, but the blood stain on his pants is growing larger. "I better not have hit his femoral artery," I say. "I *so* do not feel like dealing with my dad if he dies."

Luckily, Harrow doesn't die. He does open his eyes, though. Brent holds the gun on him as I move to the edge of the forest, waving my flashlight so the emergency vehicles can find us.

"Hey." Brent grabs me before I motion to leave him. He kisses me again. "Sorry. Had to."

Detective Phelan pushes a cup of coffee at me. "Drink, before you get hypothermia."

I shake my head from under the blanket one of the paramedics gave me. "I'm okay. Really."

"You're in shock," Detective Phelan says.

I want to tell Detective Phelan that since I started at this school, I've discovered my roommate was sleeping with the vice-principal, the vice-principal was extorting a senator, the headmaster covered up a sexual-harassment case, and a science teacher could be the reason we all get blown to smithereens one day. Oh, and I shot a guy.

Honestly, nothing really shocks me anymore.

Still, I let the paramedics strap an oxygen mask over my face. It's kind of nice to breathe, for once. I don't have the energy to look for Tierney or Goddard in the mass of police officers and detectives swarming the scene outside the forest.

My heart hammers against my chest as a stretcher holding Harrow rolls by. He's handcuffed to it, and luckily there's too much gauze and other crap around his face for him to see me.

"He can't hurt you now," Detective Phelan reassures me.

I look up at him. "You had no idea it was him, did you?"

The detective's lack of a response is all the answer I need. We sit in silence, watching the media-police-EMT frenzy unfolding around us. A news copter flies overhead, but I'm hidden in the back of an ambulance. For now.

"We overlooked Harrow," Detective Phelan finally says. "He was helpful, charming. Powerful. Those are the people who find ways to slip through the cracks in the system. Should be one hell of a trial, that's for sure."

I shake my head. I don't want to think about a trial now. A trial means I'll have to relive everything that happened. I'll have to admit to breaking the law to get the answers I needed. I'll have to watch my friends get hurt—and sit by and do nothing as Cole realizes I'm the reason people will find out about his mother's affair with Senator Westbrook.

"That's bullshit," I tell Detective Phelan. "If they slip through cracks in the system, it's only because the system isn't good enough."

I think of the tape in Goddard's office. God only knows what Harrow did with it. I think of Isabella, and how scared she must have felt when Lee got off with a slap on the wrist. I think of Molly, who probably for the rest of her life will be afraid to do the right thing because of what standing up for Isabella cost her.

I squeeze my eyes shut, fighting off hot tears. Sure, Harrow may go to jail, but none of this is right.

"Young man, you can't cross that tape!" a voice barks.

I look up, and my heart flip-flops. Anthony is pushing his way toward the ambulance, ignoring the police officer trailing behind him.

I drop the blanket and rush into his arms. His hair tickles my ears as he pulls me in tight. "I can't believe you did this. You're insane. You're stupid. You're amazing."

I break away from him. Once the shock fades that he's really here, in front of me, and not in jail or anywhere else, it feels as if there's a wall between us. It would be easy to blame it on me kissing Brent, but the first brick in the wall was laid the second I found out he stole from Isabella.

"Did you really . . . ?" My throat is dry and tight. Anthony's eyes darken.

"Would it matter to you?"

"Of course it matters, Anthony. I want to trust you. . . ."

"That's the thing. I still don't think you'd trust me again if it wasn't true." His face is angry and sad and something else I can't quite place. "Glad you're okay. Enjoy your fifteen minutes of fame."

"Anthony." I shout for him to wait, but he's already letting the police officer escort him to the other side of the tape again.

"He doesn't know what he's missing."

I turn to see Brent, smiling this completely devastating smile. "He's—"

"He's something to you." Brent steps toward me and kisses my forehead. "I'll wait for you to figure out what."

"You're . . . something to me, too," I say stupidly. And then it hits me: This is how it is. I'm not dealing with two awesome pairs of shoes here. I can't have both of them. Even if I choose one, we'll all be thinking about the other.

No matter what I do or don't do, everybody gets hurt.

CHAPTER
FIFTY-ONE

My parents take the next flight out of JFK and arrive at the Wheatley School in the morning. So do everyone else's parents, though. There are no classes this week—just constant meetings and assemblies, where I assume Goddard and Tierney and the rest of the trustees will try to convince parents this whole ordeal has not traumatized their children.

Senator Westbrook and the Redmonds are conspicuously missing. I catch up with Cole at breakfast the next morning. He gives me a rueful smile before I can say anything.

"You did what you had to do," he says. "Everyone would have found out anyway if Isabella went forward."

I don't like the bitter tone to his voice. "I'm sure she didn't know what she was doing, Cole. She obviously was crazy over Harrow and—"

"Don't you get it, Anne?" Cole says. "None of what she did was an accident. Isabella hated all of us, and she screwed with everyone just because she could. I know you think she was your friend . . . but if she had stayed alive long enough, she would have screwed you over, too."

He walks back to the table without me. As I watch him move farther from me, the weight of what I've done hits me. I've seriously screwed up the power structure around here. That's why no one would talk after Isabella was killed: They all think it's better to exist within a corrupt hierarchy instead of being outside it, trying to fight it.

But I'm not one of them. I'm going to keep fighting it, even if they expel me. Which, let's face it, is looking extremely likely.

Darlene finds me in the dining hall and says Goddard wants to see me. I knew this was coming, so I didn't even get breakfast. I stand up straight, throw on some rosebud salve, and make my way outside. Everyone I pass watches me with quiet reverence and wide eyes. I don't blame them; I'm not just the girl who burned down part of St. Bernadette's now. I'm the girl who shot the vice-principal.

Goddard's secretary leads me to his office. I take a seat across from him, taking a sort of pleasure in the fact that he doesn't know I've been in here before.

"Well, Ms. Dowling," he says. "You've had quite a year, and it's not even March."

I stare into his watery old-man eyes. "I suppose."

"In light of recent events, the future of the Wheatley School is uncertain at best." Goddard folds his hands and levels with me. "But nonetheless, I'd like to discuss *your* future here."

"Yeah, about that. I pretty much assumed I didn't have one."

A small smile plays at the corner of Goddard's mouth. "You know what they say about assuming."

My jaw nearly drops. "You're . . . not expelling me? How could you still want me here? What makes you think I *want* to be here?"

Goddard shifts in his seat. I can tell no student has ever talked to him like this before. "Ms. Dowling, you brought Isabella Fernandez's killer to justice. You may have bent a few rules in the process, but imagine how it would look if we decided to expel a student the media is calling a hero."

So that's what this is about. They won't expel me because of how it will *look*. I should have known better. Goddard doesn't think I'm a hero. Judging by his ironic smile, Goddard thinks I'm a gigantic pain in the ass, and he only wants me here because the best way to deal with a problem is to contain it.

I want to tell the wrinkly old bastard to fuck off, that there's no way I'm staying in Massachusetts or at his stupid school.

Then I think of gummy worms.

It sounds ridiculous, I know. It's such a simple thought, but the fact that Isabella loved them so much and will never get to eat them again fills me with sadness. Then anger. Because even if Lee Andersen didn't kill Isabella, and Goddard isn't responsible for Isabella's death, he could have been.

And everyone deserves to know that.

Guess I'll be sticking around, after all. Someone needs to testify at Harrow's trial, and the tape from Goddard's office is still out there. I still have a chance to get Isabella the justice she really deserves.

"Thank you, Headmaster," I say. "It's very generous of you to let me stay."

Before exiting his office, I give him a smile. His face falls just a little, almost as if he detects the message behind it.

Get ready. Because I'm going to take you down.

CHAPTER
FIFTY-TWO

My father stands beside me, stone-faced, as I identify James Harrow as the man who held a gun to my head and confessed to killing Isabella. I try to keep my gaze on the wall behind them as the men in the line-up shuffle away, but Harrow still manages to look right at me. He's on crutches, and his face is covered in patchy stubble. I know he can't see me, but I still want to throw up all over the police-station floor.

He can't see me. But he still smiles at the two-way mirror. The smile spreads from his lips to his eyes. The same crystal-blue ones that find me in my sleep.

Dad's grip on my shoulder tightens protectively. "I want that bastard remanded without bail," he tells Detective Phelan.

"He's not going anywhere," the detective says. He shakes his head, his gray eyes haunted. "Men like him . . . All I can say is sometimes I wish we still had the death penalty here."

"Yeah, well," I say, "I'm sure his fellow inmates will have fun with the pretty new guy."

"Really, Anne, do you have to talk like that?" my father says, but Detective Phelan winks at me. His smile fades a bit as he stops me on our way out.

"We searched Harrow's house for the recording device you told me about," he says. I stiffen. When he doesn't say anything else, I know they haven't found it. Or maybe he doesn't believe it even exists.

"Thanks for trying," I tell him wryly. I look up at the television over the detective's station. It's broadcasting CNN, and while there's no volume, there's a caption below the newscaster. It reads:

Senator Westbrook expected to resign at 1:00 P.M. today.

"You'd better get going." Detective Phelan nods to the TV. "You don't want to miss a good show."

My father leaves me outside of Amherst. I knew he'd have to go back to New York eventually, and even though he's still pissed at me for getting involved in this mess, I don't want him to go.

I hold on a little tighter when he hugs me this time.

"We could find a school in New York for you to finish out the year," he says, for the millionth time since he got here. I shake my head.

"I can't start over again this late in the semester."

He tells me he loves me and he'll see me for spring break. Then he's gone, and there's a hollow feeling inside of my chest, because I can't go with him. I have too much I need to set right here. I need Cole and Remy and everyone to understand why I did the things I did. Why I lied to them and hurt them.

They're nothing like my friends at home, but I don't want to lose them now that I have them.

Darlene comes out of the stairwell as I'm showing my ID to the RA on duty.

"There you are," she says. "Isabella's brother was just here. He left something for you."

My stomach sinks. Anthony was here, and he didn't call me or try to see me or anything?

Darlene emerges from behind the desk with a cardboard box. "It's some old textbooks of Isabella's. He figured maybe you might need some of these for next year. Whatever you don't want, I'll bring back to the bookstore."

I nod mechanically. Next year. Will I even be here next year? I can't think that far right now—I can't think past the fact that Anthony was here and he didn't want to see me. The thought of that still feels like a slap across the face.

This is how it's going to be. I probably won't see Anthony again until Harrow's trial, if he even shows up.

I drag the box of books into the lounge. I don't plan on keeping any of them, but I want to know what other classes she took here. I want to know more about the girl I never got to know—the girl who changed everything for me, even if she'll never know it.

Beneath an older version of the same biology textbook I have in my room is a familiar-looking book with gold lettering.

A History of the Wheatley School.

The library book Isabella never returned.

I swallow and flip through the pages, stopping at a chapter that's flagged with a Post-it note. The heading reads: "Closing of the Tunnels, 1960."

So that's how Isabella found out about them.

I've been reading the book for nearly an hour, I realize, by the time I get to the chapter about Wheatley athletics. My heart catches in my throat when I see a sepia-tone photo captioned *Nationally Ranked Wheatley Crew Team.*

I recognize Matthew Weaver from the newspaper article I read. But I also recognize the broad-shouldered blond guy standing next to him.

Steven Westbrook.

I swallow away the dryness in my throat, and I read about the crew team's victory at the Harvard Invitational. There's no mention of Matthew Weaver specifically, or of his disappearance.

I turn the page. A photograph is sticking between the pages. It's identical to the one in the book, but it has a glossy finish and the quality is slightly better.

I turn it over, and a chill runs through me. Someone has written something on the back.

THEY KILLED HIM.

Turn the page for a head start on
Anne Dowling's newest investigation

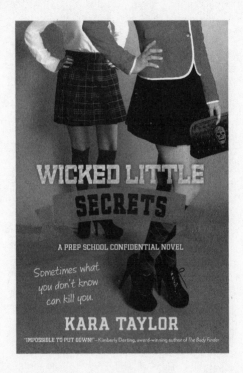

AVAILABLE IN 2014

CHAPTER
ONE

Revenge, at first though sweet,
Better ere long, back on itself recoils
—Paradise Lost, Book IX

They say only the good die young. At least, that's what they *used* to say about Isabella Fernandez.

Now, no one talks about Isabella at all—even though she was murdered two months ago, and our vice-principal is the one who killed her.

I guess that's the type of thing the Wheatley School—ranked #2 on *U.S. News and World Report*'s list of best prep schools— would like to pretend never happened. Or maybe everyone sleeps a little better at night now that they know Isabella was screwing Dr. James Harrow before he cut her throat in the middle of the woods. Almost as if they believe she deserved what happened to her, or at least brought it on herself.

A little known fact: Almost 80 percent of people who get murdered know their killers. My dad used to remind me of this when I was ten and going through a phase where I couldn't sleep because I thought I'd get stolen from my bed in the middle of the night. He actually told me that as if it would make me feel *better*. But then again, my dad also brushes his teeth in the shower to save time and explained the scientific impossibility of Santa Claus to me when I was four.

Isabella was my roommate, so my parents are making me see a therapist in Boston every few weeks. His name is Dr. Rosenblum, and he always tries to get me to play Uno with him. He likes to use phrases like "Our goal here." *Our goal here is to help you accept that the ordeal of Isabella's murder is over, and that James Harrow is no longer a danger to you.*

He says I need to make peace with Isabella's death, because even though I only knew her for a week, we were friends. Isabella didn't care that I got expelled from my old school for burning part of it down. She said that being an arsonist officially made me the coolest person she'd ever met. (Which is totally false, by the way. It's only arson if you set something on fire on purpose. I Googled it.)

The fire I set at St. Bernadette's Preparatory School on the Upper East Side of Manhattan was an accident. And, for the record, it wasn't my idea. It was Martin Payne's idea, and I was only hooking up with him because I was bored. I know having the nerve to be bored in the greatest city in the world makes me seem like a spoiled brat. I told Dr. Rosenblum I felt this way, and he suggested that maybe all of my acting out and getting into trouble back home was my way of trying to get my father to notice me. Like, from a young age I knew I could never live up to his impossible expectations, so I tried to subvert them by mouthing off in class and filling up Jake Crane's gym locker with tampons. Or whatever.

Anyway, I don't know if Dr. R. is right about all that, but he was right when he said that Isabella's murder turned my world upside down. I thought seeing her killer get arrested would flip it right side up again, but I'm learning that things are never that simple. The dead leave lots of things behind. Like messes you can't see. Or sometimes, actual things.

Like the photograph I found in an old library book Isabella checked out before her death—the one of Matthew Weaver, a student who disappeared almost thirty years ago, standing with the Wheatley crew team.

The one with *THEY KILLED HIM* written on the back.

For a while, I wondered if there was more to Isabella's death than Dr. Harrow blackmailing Senator Westbrook over his affair. Did Isabella know about the photo? Did she figure out what happened to Matt Weaver before she died?

Dr. Rosenblum is the only person I've told about the photograph. He says the Matthew Weaver story is something of an urban legend burned into the collective consciousness of Wheatley. The appeal of the story is that people are drawn to the unknown. Dr. Rosenblum said a student was probably playing a prank when they wrote *THEY KILLED HIM* on the back of the photo.

He also asked me if I found myself bored in the weeks after Dr. Harrow's arrest. I'm not an idiot: He thinks I want there to be more to the mystery. Sort of like I'm having mystery withdrawals.

But part of me thinks he has a point.

Either way, I have too many questions and no way to get answers. When I told Dr. R. I felt this way, he agreed.

"Sometimes, it's best for our sanity to let sleeping dogs lie," he said.

I hope he's right.

I sit on the sun-warmed steps outside the dining hall. Its proper designation is the William J. Brown Refectory, because if it didn't have an unnecessarily pretentious name, this wouldn't be the Wheatley School. Brent said he would meet me here after crew practice.

A few minutes after I sit down, strong arms wrap around my middle and a thin layer of stubble grazes my neck. "You're warm."

"And you're wet." Still, I turn and run my hand through Brent's damp curls. He hasn't had time to get a haircut now that training for crew season has begun, and while I'm a clean-shaven-guy type of girl, Brent manages to pull off the extra scruff.

Brent leans into me and closes his eyes, as if he'd be happy if I kept playing with his hair all day. A sharp cough sounds from behind us.

Murali Thakur is looking at us as if we might as well be hard-core making out all over the steps. He raises a thick black eyebrow. "Hello to you too, Anne."

I shrug and grin at him, although an anxious feeling settles at the bottom of my stomach. If Murali is here, Cole Redmond must be nearby.

"Where's Cole?" Brent asks, his hand moving to my lower back as if he can feel me tensing up.

"Showering." Murali squirts water into his mouth from his bottle.

Cole's mother, Elaine, was having an affair with Senator Westbrook when Dr. Harrow tried to blackmail him with incriminating photos. Since the district attorney put a gag order on anyone involved with the extortion until Dr. Harrow's trial is over, no one knows Cole's mother is the reason Senator Westbrook resigned. But his father moved out a couple of weeks ago, and even though Cole swears he doesn't hate me, every time I see him, I wonder if we'll still be friends in a year or so when the media is allowed to talk about the affair and I ruin the Redmonds' lives all over again.

And here's the other awkward thing: Cole and Brent are best friends. And not just typical teenage guy, "Hey dude, wanna go to the gym?" best friends. Cole is the only guy at school who knows about Brent's diabetes. They actually argue about things like what nature noise they're going to set their sleep sounds machine to before they go to bed every night. Brent likes the whale calls, while Cole prefers the musical waterfall.

I'm totally interrupting their bromance by dating Brent.

Brent and I say good-bye to Murali. When he turns the corner to the boys' dorm, Brent grabs my face and kisses me. I let myself get lost in the feeling of his stubble grazing my upper lip, his thumb in the crook behind my ear. I still can't believe I get to do this with him, whenever I want.

"Hi." He breaks away and leans his forehead against mine.

"Hi back. Where are we going today?"

I was taken aback when Brent told me he had a surprise for me today, since my seventeenth birthday was last weekend. We went out for my favorite food, sushi, and he snuck me into his dorm so we could stay up late watching a hidden camera show where these comedians make strangers completely uncomfortable. I didn't even remember telling Brent that I love the cookie crumble on ice cream cakes, but he hid a small one in his freezer and we polished it off together.

"You'll see," Brent says. "But we have to leave now if we want to catch the train."

The walk to the station takes almost fifteen minutes. Even though it's only early April, I have to take off my cardigan. There are no clouds in the sky, and what seems like the entirety of the Wheatley School's population is crowded on the campus quad sunbathing.

Brent and I pass the time on the train by playing Would You Rather? I've just asked him if he'd rather get his nipples pierced or show up to class in his underwear every day for a month when the automatic voice on the T announces we're at Fenway Park.

Brent motions for me to get up, and I barely stifle a groan.

"Oh, come on," he says, laughing as we step off the T. "They're playing the Yankees. I thought I'd bring a piece of New York to you."

"I'm not dressed for a baseball game." I gesture to my strapless Free People dress.

"Good thing I'm so prepared." He pulls two balled-up Red Sox caps out of his pocket and unrumples them. Unable to figure out the mechanics of fitting a baseball cap around my ponytail, he slides the elastic off and onto his wrist. My hair falls around my bare shoulders.

"Shouldn't this be a Yankees cap if you're bringing New York to me?"

Brent's eyes gleam. "Trust me, this is for your safety. Red Sox fans won't care how pretty you are. They'll throw beer on you."

I grab the neck of his T-shirt and pull him toward me. "You think I'm pretty."

He kisses my forehead, then my nose, and finally lands on my lips. The world seems to dissolve around us until he tugs my hand.

I was eleven the last time my father took me to a game at Yankee Stadium, but my memory is good enough that I realize Fenway Park is smaller and louder. I follow Brent to the row of seats behind home plate.

A leggy blonde in a Sox T-shirt holds up her hand, and I think she's waving at someone behind us until Brent waves back. My brain automatically demands, *Who is this pretty bitch?*

"Forgot to mention my sisters were coming," he says to me with a devious glint in his eyes.

"Oh."

My heartbeat picks up and we wriggle our way to the seats. It's not that I'm nervous, or anything. It's just that usually I like to have advance warning about meeting a guy's family.

"Anne, this is Claire," Brent says. Claire smiles at me, and my nerves dissolve. Her smile is perfect, unlike Brent's, but they have the same pointy nose and warm brown eyes. Claire tells me she's a senior at Brown and says she heard I was from New York. I nod, thankful she leaves it at that and there's no mention of me shooting anyone.

"Where's Holly?" Brent nods to the empty seat next to Claire. She gnaws her bottom lip.

"Don't be pissed. She's only home for a few days and wanted to see her friends." Claire's eyes move to the aisle, to a man talking into a cell phone and making his way toward us. Brent's cheery expression clouds over.

"You let *him* come?"

From the way Claire hisses, "They're *his* season tickets, Brent," I conclude that *him* is their father.

Things I know about Brent's father:

1. He owns the biggest newspaper in Boston.
2. Brent doesn't see him much.

"Sorry in advance." Brent squeezes my hand as his father makes his way toward us.

"Does he know who I am?" I blurt. "I mean, like, what I did?"

"I don't know. But Steve Westbrook has sued his paper three times in the past year, so you're good."

I look over at Brent, unsure if he's serious. He gives me a lazy grin that makes my toes curl in my sandals.

Brent's father ends his phone call when he gets back to the seats. He's Brent's height—which is short for a guy—with wavy gray hair. He and Brent do an odd little standoff type thing before he extends a hand to his son. It's all really bizarre to me, seeing someone give his kid a handshake. My father always hugs me.

Brent's father turns to me. "Pierce Conroy," he says. "And you must be . . ."

"Anne Dowling," I say, even though it's obvious this is the first time he's hearing my name. His handshake is dismissive, as if he can't wait for this day to be over. I study his face. It seems very familiar to me. Probably because it's so much like Brent's: strong jaw. Asymmetrical smile.

We all shut up for the national anthem and then sit down. I sit between Claire and Brent, who gives clipped answers to his father's questions about the crew season. Claire says she loves my dress. We wind up talking about Newbury Street and I don't even notice that Brent's seat is empty until he comes back holding a cardboard tray. He picks a fully loaded hot dog from the top and passes the tray down to Claire and me.

Claire tears a soft pretzel in half and hands a piece to me. Brent inhales the hot dog in two bites and takes a pull from his extra large soda. Mr. Conroy watches from the corner of his eye the whole time. It doesn't take me long to figure out why: Brent is diabetic.

"Are you sure you should be—" Mr. Conroy starts, but Brent freezes him with a look and tears open a box of Cracker Jacks. Beside me, Claire sighs, as if this pissing contest is a frequent scene in the Conroy household.

Mr. Conroy's BlackBerry rings, and he excuses himself. When he's gone, Claire mutters, "Real mature, Brent."

"I am the *epitome* of mature."

I snigger to myself. Just last night, Brent donned a ski mask and mooned the security cam outside the boys' dorm because Murali dared him to.

Brent tosses a Cracker Jack at Claire and puts a hand on my knee. He doesn't move it for the rest of the game, except to stand up and shout whenever the Sox score a run. I feel like I should at least cheer my team on, but the Yankees wind up winning and I don't want to get followed and shanked on the way back to the train.

Claire hugs Brent good-bye, then me. "You're the first girl from school he's ever even talked about," she whispers in my ear. "Keep an eye out for him, okay?"

"You enjoy the game, Dad?" Brent asks Mr. Conroy, whose mouth forms a line. He spent about six of the nine innings on his phone. I can sort of see why Brent doesn't like his dad. The only thing Mr. Conroy seemed to care about was Brent's crew season. He barely even acknowledged the "new girlfriend" thing.

Claire flicks Brent's ear and tells him to bring me home for dinner sometime.

"Where is home for you anyway?" I ask around a yawn as we catch a train back to school.

"Bedford." We plop into two empty seats and he plants a kiss on the top of my head.

"Bedford," I repeat. "I have no idea where that is."

"I'll show you sometime."

"Good." And I mean it. I want to know everything there is to know about Brent Conroy. I know his favorite song is "Bohemian Rhapsody" by Queen and his favorite class is British literature, but I want to know the important stuff, too. That's why I can't help but say, "What's the deal with you and your dad?"

Brent stiffens. "It's stupid family stuff."

"You can tell me, you know," I say.

He hesitates. "My dad lived away from us for two thirds of my life."

"Your parents were separated?" I wonder if anyone at school knows this.

"Not technically. But they may as well have been. We have a condo in Boston, near my dad's office. He stayed there more than he stayed at home with us."

I contemplate this. My mom has totally accused my dad of being a workaholic before, but when I was little, he'd still come into my room no matter how late he got home to tuck me in and talk to me with my Lamb Chop puppet.

"Anyway, every time he's home for long stretches of time, he acts like we're not practically strangers or anything," Brent goes on. "He tries to tell me what to do, when my mom and grandparents are the ones who raised me. And he's never afraid to tell me what a disappointment I am, as if I give a shit what he thinks."

I think of how Brent baited Mr. Conroy into saying something about eating all that crap at the baseball game. I picture the shell-shocked look on Mr. Conroy's face. A funny feeling comes over me. Brent has already changed the subject, and I nod at what he's saying even though I can't really hear him over the ringing in my ears.

Because I know where I've seen Mr. Conroy before.

He's the boy standing next to Matt Weaver in the crew team photo.